REY SIRAKAVIT

Start Praying

Book 1

By Rey Sirakavit

Chapter 1

I stared at the man-child across from me, his face scrunched up in anger. I shouldn't have been surprised at his temper tantrum. I raised my chin, ever so slightly, but just enough for him to know who was in charge. I didn't want him to think I was being aggressive, but I was tired of his bad boy behavior. And he needed to be taught a lesson, a lesson that his mother should already have taught him: no hitting.

I held my hand out for the toy he had just used on my knee. The two-year old pouted once more, then finally allowed me to take the plastic shovel from him. I set the shovel in the toy box, along with all the other seemingly innocent toys that could easily serve as make-shift swords.

I sighed, pulling my sweater dress down over my knees. Just thirty minutes earlier, I'd been attempting to skulk by the nursery, hoping that the carpet would mask the sound of my heeled boots. Even though I had been late, as usual, I had hoped to at least catch the end of worship.

But Monique, the nursery director, must have had bat-like hearing.

"Sierra!" she called as I tip-toed by, her head popping over the half door. I paused. Was she going to call me out for not responding to her emails or voice messages to serve in the nursery? Was I going to have a good enough excuse for ignoring them?

"Can you give me a hand?" She bounced a little girl on her hip. The little girl had a thousand beads, and every time Monique bounced her, they clicked rhythmically. "My assistant teacher never showed up and there are a ton of kids in here!"

I looked around the brightly painted room. An assortment of toddlers crawled around the Noah's Ark rug, gurgling, giggling, bopping toys and making noise. My heart pulled. And that is how I found myself in the wrong clothes, with the wrong shoes, in the middle of the floor, rubbing at a bruise on my knee.

But as quickly as the boy's temper tantrum had erupted, it was gone. And the little boy- Jaylen? Jayden?- ran off to find another toy to bang. Before I could stand, another child pulled at one of my locs, his hands covered in something sticky.

"Cookie!" He shouted as if I were all the way in the sanctuary instead of only inches away. He held his hands out for me to unwrap the package. I complied with a smile, then stood awkwardly to my feet. Even as I smoothed my hands over my sweater dress, I looked around the room, ready to help prevent any other crises that might arise. I had entered the chaos and I loved it.

Sure, the kids were loud. And sticky. And loud. Definitely loud. But from the moment I entered, I forgot all about the program I was writing for work that had some kind of error in it. And about being single on Valentine's Day. Again. No, the nursery was its own little world, where for 90 minutes, I didn't have time to think about my problems because I was too busy wiping noses, kissing owies, changing diapers, and drying tears.

But everything I loved about the nursery was also exactly why I had been avoiding it. At the end of the service, you had to give the babies back to their parents. I shook my head, hoping to dislodge the negative feelings.

Enjoy it while it lasts, I told myself.

Monique, who was smartly wearing jeans and a sweatshirt with the children's ministry logo, smiled at me over the head of the little one I held, then reached out her arms out for him.

"Sierra, you're a lifesaver, but you can take off now."

"Is the service over already?" I glanced down at my watch.

Monique shook her head. "No, we're releasing the children early to join their parents in the sanctuary. They're having a baby dedication today."

Baby dedication?

I felt my face do something, and I hoped it was a smile, but it may have been an eye roll. From the look on Monique's face, it must have been the eye roll.

Get it together, Sierra, I chastised myself, grabbing my wool coat off the hook. *Maybe it won't be so bad.*

"I don't particularly care for baby dedications," I said, hoping that Monique would understand. She was a single woman, too. I secretly hoped that parents would linger or "forget" to pick up their children, but within minutes, the nursery was empty and Monique was shooing me out.

I found a seat in the back of the sanctuary, listening as the pastor read the passage of how Hannah, a once-barren woman, gave birth to a child then dedicated him to the Lord. I should have been inspired by the story, but I wasn't. Instead, all the positive feelings I'd felt from the nursery oozed out of me. I sat stiff in the pew, willing my face to not match my mood.

The parents stood on stage next to the pastor, leaning over the child with wet eyes and clasped hands. One of the singers from the

7

choir, fittingly wearing all black, approached the microphone. She opened her mouth and began to sing about hope and new life. While everyone else dabbed their eyes, I narrowed mine. The old woman on the pew beside me leaned over and squeezed my hand, smelling of eucalyptus and peppermint.

"Don't worry, it'll be your turn soon," she said.

Was that supposed to be a consolation? Did I wear the number of my decreasing childbearing years like a scarlet letter emblazoned on my chest? But more importantly, would it be wrong to slip out the back door?

Even as I smiled politely and said, "Thank you Sister Johnson," inside, I wrestled with my conscience. I didn't want to be one of those people that came to church late and left early, choosing the parts of the worship service like dishes at a buffet. But as grandparents, aunts and uncles, nephews, nieces and neighbors, cousins, second cousins, and play cousins streamed onto the stage beside the pastor and parents, I could feel the corner of my mouth start to twitch, purse, and lower. That was my cue. I was done. I didn't come to church to get an attitude, even if their baby was so adorable in his tiny purple suit and purple tie.

Why didn't they have completely separate services for baby dedications, like they did for weddings? They didn't stuff weddings down your throat. And at least at a wedding, there was the chance that you might meet somebody. At a baby dedication, I wasn't going to get any extra eggs. I stood up. Baby dedications were just a meaningless ritual that screamed, *Look at me! I'm so special because I got knocked up.* I hoped no one could see me rolling my eyes. I didn't know if my bad attitude was the result of my so-called biological clock or exhaustion from serving in the nursery. Either way, I was out.

The last time I had to leave early, I raised a small finger, pulled my purse and Bible close to my body, and tiptoed out, hugging the wall of the church, just like my grandma taught me. That wouldn't be necessary today. Today, nobody was paying any attention to me. I walked tall and straight down the center aisle and out the back door. Before my heeled boot even hit the pavement, I was already thinking about my to-do list and the wasted hour and a half. The parking lot was covered in a thin layer of snow, and one of the parking attendants offered me a hand down the stairs. A wide gold band circled his fourth finger. I declined the hand, and just lifted my chin in silent thanks and headed to my car.

Because I'd been almost forty minutes late that morning, I had the worst spot in the lot, my usual spot, all the way in the furthest corner from the modern church building, near the intersection with a rundown covered bus stop. It wasn't surprising that no one was at the stop at this time of day on a Sunday and in this kind of weather, but the empty enclosure looked sad and lonely with its graffiti-covered walls. I imagined that the stylized letters were modern messages from lovesick teenagers who wanted the world to know the strength of their emotions. I envied these brave Romeos, risking fines and tickets for vandalism, all in the name of love.

The sky was dark, but it didn't look like it was going to snow anymore, so I pulled out of the parking lot and towards the closest shopping plaza to run errands. In addition to green tea, grits, and eggs, I threw in a tub of pecan praline ice cream and whipped topping into my cart. It was just one week before Valentine's Day, one long, bitter week, filled with glowing stories of romantic gestures from excited co-workers whose significant others couldn't wait until Friday, and a little extra ice cream would go a long way to easing my loneliness.

From the grocery store, I headed to the home improvement emporium, where you could get anything from plywood to cotton socks. I should have gone home and changed out of my Sunday best, feeling awkward walking around the huge store in heels and a dress, but I was tired of using the refrigerator light to help me see around the kitchen at night. I quickly grabbed the cheapest multi-pack of 60-watt light bulbs then stalled in front of the display of replacement shower heads. My current shower head was covered in lime and rust, and if I ever got a date, I'd be too embarrassed for him to see it peaking above the shower curtain. I stared at the shiny chrome dual shower head with twelve spray settings, including pulse and massage. That sounded nice after a long day at work. But even in my mind's eye, all I could see was one body where there should have been two. I settled on the single sprayer, for the single woman.

Most days, I didn't dwell so much on being single, but most days weren't a week before the sixth year in a row of being single on Valentine's Day. While I had dated off and on over the years, it had been a long time since I had been seeing someone *on* Valentine's Day. And, frankly, I was tired of it. The Lord had had all these years to bring a good man into my life, and for whatever reason, he hadn't. Maybe it was time to do things my way. I scanned the aisles before me. There was a white man in front of me with oversized jeans that drooped down a little too far, scuffed up work boots, and holes in his flannel shirt. I immediately dismissed him, and was turning my head to see what other options there were, but was startled to see a trim African American woman approach him and loop her arm around his. They smiled, shared a joke that only they could hear, and pushed their cart forward. I slid into line behind them, wondering how it was that even Mr. Droopy Drawers had found love, but I couldn't.

The young brother at the register smiled as I handed him the bulbs and shower head, then my credit card. "Did you find everything you needed, Mrs. Harris?" he asked, reading my name from my card. I returned his smile, gently tossing my locs over one shoulder.

"It's just Sierra," I replied, meeting his gaze.

"So, there's no Mr. Harris?" he asked, his eyebrows lifting. He was bold, I had to give him that. And he was cute, with flawless skin and teeth, but he was at least ten years younger than me. I wondered if I had enough courage to be a cougar. I did not. I thanked the young man and took my bag, letting his question hang in the air. Pulling my cell phone from my purse, I sent a quick text to my best friend, Carmen. Carmen and I met years ago at church. She was one of the few married friends I had.

TO CARMEN EVANS:

A young cutie at the store is flirting with me!

I need to get out of here! 😣

FROM CARMEN EVANS:

Not surprised. You're beautiful, smart, successful. You're a catch.

Call me when you get home. I have something for you.

I stared at the gift emoji, wondering what it could be. Five minutes later, I pulled up to my ranch-style house that I had bought the year before, proud that I had finally taken the plunge and not waited any longer for a man before buying a house. Everybody thought I was crazy when I bought the three-bedroom house, encouraging me to wait: "You still might find somebody." I rolled my eyes in recollection.

I pushed the garage door opener and let myself in, kicking off my shoes and dropping my bag onto the kitchen counter beside me.

Changing into sweats and a comfy tee shirt, I cranked up the heat on the thermostat, wanting the house to warm up before I got to work. I opened the freezer, bypassed the salmon and all the other healthy options, and grabbed the bag of hot wings. I threw them in the microwave, then sat on the couch, eating alone in front of the TV. I stopped flicking the remote at one of my favorite episodes of *Living Single*, but my laughs seemed to echo off the walls and ceiling, reminding me of my aloneness. I flipped the channel to a courtroom drama instead. After lunch, I got to work changing the light bulb, and then the shower head. The shower head directions were easy to follow, and I felt good that I had been able to do it on my own, but hated that I had no one to call.

It was one of the many things I had done alone, fixed alone, and tried alone. And it wouldn't be the last. Al Green's song, "Tired of Being Alone" came to mind, and I started singing it, for once glad that I was alone and no one could hear the cracks in my voice and flailing falsetto. It wasn't a song that you shouted, but moaned. And so, I did. I moaned, I moped. And when I got tired of that, I flipped through my playlist, playing every sad love song I could find. I reminisced with myself about old boyfriends, ones that could've been, should've been, or would've been, but for one reason or another had come and gone. My mind flitted from one old boyfriend to the next, inevitably wrapping itself around my last boyfriend, Drisk.

I could still see Drisk's smiling eyes, feel his large arms wrapped tight around me. I could almost smell the woodsy cologne he wore. I inhaled deeply, letting the memories flood back. We met at the printing shop he owned, and after an hour of chatting and flirting while he completed my printing job, I knew what church he went to, that he had never married, had no kids, and was a Cowboys fan. When I told him that I was celibate, and wasn't going to have sex before I got married, he just smiled. Seven months later, when I still hadn't changed my mind, things seemed to just fizzle out with no explanation. That was almost a year ago. My heart had almost broken, and I was tempted to give in, but I knew it wasn't right. I'd been celibate a lot longer than I'd known him, and he wasn't offering marriage, just sex. So, I walked away. When I was 23, young with lots of options, I wasn't worried. But at 32, walking away from a good thing, with no promise of anything else, it had been frightening. Yet, I did it. And here I was, a year later. Still alone. No closer to being a wife or mother. I walked over to the phone resting on the end of the kitchen counter and called Carmen.

"Hey!" I couldn't tell if she was yelling at me or at one of her two boys who always seemed to be up to something. "I was just thinking about you. I didn't see you at church today."

I grimaced, slightly embarrassed, not wanting to admit I had left early.

"You left during the baby dedication, didn't you?" she asked, a smile in her voice.

I laughed. "Guilty."

"Yeah, it was a little much. I thought the stage was going to collapse-"

"Right! They had so many people, it was crazy! And everybody had to say something."

"Honestly, I don't even blame you for getting out of there. But enough about that. You know the church is having a singles event," Carmen paused. Was she waiting for me to say something?

"Well, I bought you a ticket!"

13

I didn't know if I should be pleased or offended.

"Girl, I'm not interested in going to some tired church singles event. And I can get my own date, Carmen, thank you very much." A small smile curved the edges of my lips as I thought back to the young clerk at the home improvement store.

"Sierra, please. You better take this ticket. They're having some big online dating guru as a special speaker, and they're doing some different mixers. It's more than just throwing a bunch of sad, lonely singles in a room and hoping somebody makes a love connection. I don't know. It sounded fun. But I already bought the ticket, so you're going."

"Well, what if I already have plans?"

Carmen laughed before I was even done with my sentence. "You would have blown up my cell phone before the man even finished talking!" She was right. But I still wasn't excited about going to a singles event at church. That is not how I wanted to spend my Valentine's Day. So, I made up an excuse about having to do chores and being too busy to come pick up the ticket that afternoon, but I promised to call before Friday. Carmen knew me too well, but she didn't argue.

I hung up the phone, trying not to envy my best friend's life, even with the loud kids and sometimes snarky husband. I knew I was supposed to be happy being single. As a "strong black woman", I was supposed to be invincible, able to break diamonds between my thighs. As a Christian, I was supposed to see singleness as a gift from the Lord. And most years I did. Most years, I volunteered in the church nursery on Valentine's Day to give parents a night out. One year, I gathered all my female friends together for a *Gal*-entine's Spa Day. Regardless of my relationship status, February 14 had never made me feel so bleak or hollow. Why was it different this year?

I dropped the phone onto the nightstand, then pulled a framed picture of Drisk and me from under my mattress, where I still kept it. I climbed into bed, pulling the covers up to my chin, stroking the picture of Drisk as a plan began to form in my mind and I eventually fell asleep.

REY SIRAKAVIT

Chapter 2

Somewhere, there must be a list of laws about calling exes. Common sense best practices to protect you and them from embarrassment. Like: *Do not call an ex when you're lonely. Do not call an ex two days before Valentine's Day. Do not call an ex from work.* But as I sat in my workstation with a legal pad and black pen between my fingers, jotting my list of pros and cons, none of those laws came to mind. Of course, I should have been working. As a Software Developer for a healthcare company, I should have been writing the code that would one day turn into a program or website. But today, that would have to wait.

Two cubicles to my left, John from Accounting drank from his Denver Broncos stainless steel mug. Normally, I wouldn't have even noticed such a banal act, his thumb absentmindedly scratching at the peeling *B*. But Drisk had also been a big Broncos fan. Maybe it was a sign. A confirmation of the idea that had begun brewing the night before. Call Drisk. That was the only way to really find out why things ended.

What would it hurt? I traced and re-traced the question mark at the top of the sheet, then wrote *Pros*.

<u>*Pros*</u>:

To finally know the truth.

To get closure.

To reconnect with an old friend.

To satisfy my curiosity.

The most important reason, the reason that I did not write down was, *Maybe he's still single and open to reconnecting...*

On the other side of the paper, I started my list of cons.

Cons:

It might be embarrassing.

I re-read my list, then drew a line through "It might be embarrassing". On the pro side I wrote, *Drisk is a good guy. He won't embarrass you.*

I told myself that even if he didn't feel the same way about me, at least I would get my questions answered. And so I lifted the phone from its cradle, convinced that I really just wanted to know why. Why did our relationship end?

I pulled the cord, untangling it and punched in Drisk's cell phone number from memory. It felt so easy, so right, as if I had been practicing the numbers for months. I hesitated briefly, for a moment questioning the wisdom of the decision, but I was driven by a need to know. There had been no fight, no big blow up, just a gradual parting of the ways. "Let's take a break," he'd said. And that break had turned into a few weeks, a month, then a year.

Drisk answered on the third ring, and I could tell he was surprised to hear from me. I quickly commenced with the pleasantries, asking about his business, sisters, nieces and nephews.

"You sound good," I said, meaning it. His voice sounded strong, and I could imagine his broad shoulders bulging underneath his tee shirt. "Are you busy?" If there were customers coming in and out of his shop, I didn't want to disturb him.

"Nah, I'm good. It's kinda quiet in here right now. What's up?"

Taking a deep breath, I pushed forward. Maybe I should have called him that night, but I really didn't want to wait. "I have a random question to ask you," I began, forcing the words out. "Why did we break up?"

"I don't know if it's such a good idea to go down that road," he said hesitantly.

"Why not? If you're seeing someone, believe me I'm not trying to interfere."

"No, it's nothing like that." So, he was still single, or single again. I wondered whether I should ask, but decided against it.

"I'm a big girl, I think I can handle the truth."

He chuckled, and I could feel myself relaxing. He'd always been so easy to talk to, honest and a straight shooter. I leaned back in my office chair, stretching my legs out in front of me. Waiting to hear his response.

"We were good together, and it was fun, but..."

"Was it the abstinence thing?" I'd always known that my commitment to abstinence was a deal-breaker for a lot of men, but I hadn't thought Drisk was like that. He was a committed believer, too.

"No, it wasn't that. Not really. I mean, you take your faith seriously, which is a good thing." I waited, not wanting to interrupt him. "You know, some people hide behind their faith, but in reality, they're not really that interested in sex. When we were together, I didn't really feel the passion. It just made me worry that there wasn't enough of a spark between us."

"Spark?"

"Yeah, you know chemistry."

I had to break the one-word responses, but I was at a loss as to what to say. Drisk was a handsome man, with strong broad shoulders.

How I had loved staring at him. Even last night, I had spent hours just staring at his picture. Staring at the picture of a man who thought we had no chemistry. I rolled my eyes, squared my own shoulders and pursed my lips. Some people just couldn't handle a righteous woman. Well, I was not sorry for my decision.

"You know, Drisk, I really thought you were a much stronger Christian than that. Well, I'm sorry if I wasn't willing to compromise my faith." I could hear the iciness of my tone, but I was tired of so-called Christian men pressuring women to have sex.

"'Compromise your faith'? You weren't so much faithful, as frigid. Kissing you was like kissing a cold fish." *Frigid? Cold fish?* I could hear him shift on the other end of the line, like he was tapping his pencil against the counter, waiting for me to respond, but any words I had were stuck in my throat. The sudden harshness in his tone surprised me. My skin felt clammy and hot and itchy and all I wanted to do was hang up, but I had no idea how to end that horrible conversation. Should I just click the red button? Or should I thank him for his honesty? My gut wanted to shout a few choice expletives at him, but that wasn't me. My head and heart were spinning and his words looped as if on auto-repeat: *like kissing a cold fish.* A cold fish. As opposed to a warm or hot fish? What did that mean? Was I a sloppy kisser? Did I turn him off? If we had made love, would that have proved to him that I was not a cold fish, and that my feelings were as hot as anyone's?

"I'm sorry, I shouldn't have said anything."

"No, thanks for being honest with me. A year later. But since you're still single, Drisk, have you considered that the problem might not have been me, but you?" With that, I hung up the phone, proud of the dignified way I'd handled myself, yet still shaken. I wanted to laugh his words off, to pretend I was not bothered. I ripped off the top sheet of the legal pad, balled it up, and tossed it in the wastepaper basket under my desk, all while silently chastising myself for making the phone call while at work.

Of course, John from Accounting took that moment to stand up with mug in hand. He stretched his arms completely over his back as if he were doing some yoga pose. John the Broncos fan, with his stupid Broncos mug. Ugh.

Suddenly, I felt a nudge on my shoulder.

"Hey, what's wrong? Did John kill your dog?" I looked up, startled to see Mikaela standing beside my cubicle. Mikaela, with her cheery singsong voice, perky smile, and Mary Poppins optimism. Her smiling cheerfulness only exacerbated my own cheerlessness. I longed for an earlier time. Even the hours I had spent on my couch crying were better than the seconds I'd lived since knowing the truth about Drisk's feelings, and the complete lack of privacy to respond as I truly wanted, with gut-wrenching, bone-shattering sobs. Alas, working in an office of 40 cubicles was not exactly conducive to pouring out one's tortured emotions. I had to pull myself together.

"What? Oh no. I was just thinking about something else," I muttered.

Mikaela smiled, raising her eyebrows. "There are donuts in the break room. Want me to get you something?"

I shook my head no. "I'm good, thanks. I need to get back to work." I jiggled the computer mouse, bringing the screen back to life, and let Mikaela's smiling face fade into the background.

I am destined to be alone and single, I thought. *And that's just fine.* Not everyone is meant to get married and have kids. I thought about the ticket to the Single's event Carmen had bought for me. I didn't want to waste her money, but I also didn't want to feel the pressure and unrealistic hope of making a love connection, either. It was decided. I would not go. I would not subject myself to the torture of meeting, mingling, or mixing. I would go home and watch a movie. Or work on my taxes. Or give myself a pedicure. As a single, independent woman, I could do anything I wanted, and that was exactly fine with me.

Drisk, who was my last chance at love, had turned out to be no chance at all. I wondered why God would even have allowed me to care so much for someone who didn't feel the same way about me. It obviously wasn't meant to be. In fact, it had been so obviously not meant to be for a long time, but I had been holding onto a glimmer of a hope that maybe someday we'd get back together. If he'd said, "You're too critical." Or, "You're too demanding," I would have been able to look at my life, talk to friends, figure out if he was right. Figure out how to change myself to be what he wanted.

But being a cold, wet kisser?

How was I supposed to know if he was right or not? It wasn't like I could ask Carmen or one of my co-workers. For the first time in days, a small smile scratched the edges of my lips as I pictured myself setting up a kiosk outside my cubicle with all the men from work lined up, golf pencils and scorecards in hand. Would a 4-point or 10-point scale be more accurate? I smiled even more at the absurdity of the thought. For an instant, I felt the urge to contact every single last boyfriend, everyone whose lips had ever touched mine, and get their feedback. But that would be crazy….Yeah, that would be crazy.

REY SIRAKAVIT

Chapter 3

Drisk's hurtful words continued to swirl through my mind, and I pictured him trying not to gag as he was kissing me. By six pm, I was still working on my list of exes and compiling phone numbers. By seven, I decided I had had enough. I texted Carmen.

TO CARMEN EVANS:
Where are you? I'll pick up the tix.

The next two days at work were brutal with deliveries every 30 minutes. Roses. Lilies. Bears. Chocolates. It seemed like every woman on my floor had received a delivery, and half the men. It was disgusting.

I couldn't walk to the restroom without being accosted by the sight of bright pink and red ribbons and bows, gushing cube mates, and tender hugs. Ugh. I couldn't wait for Valentine's Day to be over. I wanted life to continue without the incessant reminders of being an unhappy single lady.

On Friday, I wore my sexiest winter church dress: a green slim sweater dress with a scoop neck. The event was in the church gym. The hospitality team had obviously put hours into making this the event to remember. The wooden floor and plain walls had been transformed into an underwater reef. It glittered and glowed. It was breathtaking. It was just the right atmosphere to meet someone and fall in love. The romantic in me swelled up, hoping for my own happily ever after. The realist in me grabbed a plate and took my place in the buffet line.

In front of me stood a tall man who was also holding a plate. He had long locs, longer than mine, and a wild beard. No ring, of course. He served himself a roll and salad, no dressing. Probably a vegan. I, on the other hand, grabbed a couple turkey meatballs, a scoop of macaroni and cheese, skipped the salad, and grabbed a cookie. I giggled, thinking how very different our plates were. He looked over his shoulder at me, his eyebrows knit in a question. I silently shook my head, then ventured, "Your plate's very healthy." I raised my own, a stark contrast with his.

"Your body is a vessel. Don't pollute it with junk."

Immediately, my smile disappeared. "Thank you for those wise words." I rolled my eyes. Some brothers were so "woke", you couldn't even have a normal conversation with them. I shook my head, silently saying a prayer for the woman who would one day become Mrs. Vegan.

Scanning the room for an empty seat, I found one in a corner. Several men were huddled up, their metal chairs pushed away from the table, their shoulders leaned forward. One had shoulder length locs, and the other two had short cuts. They seemed professional, dressed casually. But no women were at the table. I hesitated for a second, scanning the room once again. There was a group of women seated a few tables away. I decided to head for the men.

As I walked to the table, I could feel someone brush by me. Mr. Vegan. Headed straight for the same table as I was. I paused for just a second. He seemed to know I was headed to the same table, because he set his plate in front of a chair, and then pulled out the one to his right, as if knowing that I was right behind him.

The men nodded at Mr. Vegan as he sat down, the one closest to him pulling him in for a back-clapping man-hug. I scanned the faces and, instinctively, the hands of each man at the table. No rings, not even as an accessory. They continued with their conversation, politics, the movement, justice. They sounded like they were in a lecture hall instead of a singles event. I was beginning to understand why there were no women at the table. They weren't looking for female partners as much as co-speakers for a Black Lives Matter rally. Well, since Valentine's Day was smack dab in the middle of Black History month, I guessed it was fitting. Again, a small giggle escaped before I could suppress it. After days- weeks, really- of being in a funk, I finally found a reason to smile, and it was at the most inopportune times. Mr. Vegan paused, put his arm on the back of my chair, and leaned toward me.

"So you think the unlawful detainment of an African-American youth is funny?"

At that, I almost choked. "Of course not. It's just…" I looked at each of the men. "Well, what are we all here for? I think the struggle can survive without you all for one night. Try to have a little fun. You never know- you just might meet your very own Winnie." I popped one of the meatballs in my mouth with a confidence that I did not feel, but I could tell that I had sold it. All eyes were on me. Mr. Vegan brushed his hand on my shoulder and said something. I have no idea what because as soon as he touched my shoulder, he shocked me. Like when you drag your feet on carpet and build up too much static electricity in your body. Our eyes locked, and for a second, I thought

27

he was going to say something more, but then I guess he thought better of it. And before I knew it, they were all talking again.

After the appetizers and socializing, the associate pastor walked to the front of the room. The speaker spoke. The servers served. And the singles, well they were singles.

How many Sundays have I gone to church, been touched by the sermon, said "Pastor really preached today!" then gotten into my car, turned on the radio, been cut off, started thinking about my to-do list, and never thought again about that sermon? That was how it normally happened, and that's what I would have expected from anything a Valentine's Day speaker at a singles event would deliver, but that Friday night was different.

I expected him to talk about common struggles for singles on Valentine's Day, how to combat loneliness, and how to be strong and wait for the Lord to send you that special someone. That's the message I was expecting and thought I needed. Instead, this young and handsome associate pastor, who probably had more than his fair share of women throwing themselves at him, gave a very short, very different message.

"I won't be before you long," he said to the laughter of the audience, "I won't be before you long," he repeated. "But the title for my message is, 'What is Love?' We know what romance is. We know what lust is. But what is love? The Bible tells us that the greatest command is to love God, and to love others as we love ourselves.

"So, we ought to know what love is. We set aside this day every year to celebrate love. So, we must be experts at it. You've all been to weddings and heard First Corinthians chapter thirteen quoted. But what is love?

"In our culture, we've got it all mixed up. Love is not finding that special someone who will be patient with you. The Bible says that love

IS patient. Love isn't finding someone who will be kind to *you*. *You* be kind. *You* don't envy. *You* stop boasting. *You* don't be proud. *You* don't dishonor others. *You* don't look out for your own needs first. *You* don't get angry too quick. *You* forgive and let the past go.... See, when we think about love we think about receiving. We think about being on the receiving end of forgiveness, kindness, patience. Instead, we need to think about how we will *give* love. *Show* love. *Be* love.

"See, a baker doesn't just bake for someone he's in a relationship with. He bakes because that's who he is. He'll bake for his neighbors, he'll bake for God, he'll bake for strangers, he bakes for himself. You don't need a special title to receive baked goods from a baker. You don't have to 'put a ring on it' to get the baker to bake you a cake. A baker bakes because that is who he is on the inside. Give him some flour, water, and sugar, and he's gonna give you bread.

"If you call yourself a Christian, you ought to love. Not because you're in a relationship, or want to be in a relationship, not because you want to look good, but because that is who we are called to be— people of love. The greatest command is to love God and to love your neighbor.

"We live in a hurting world. I challenge you to stop navel-gazing and to start giving out the love of God. Stop worrying about your biological clock and share the love of God. Stop worrying about when it's going to be your turn to walk down the aisle, and when somebody's going to love you, and start loving others. Be love!"

I waited for the pastor to make a joke about bakers not giving away their cookies for free, but he didn't go there. His message was simple and heartfelt: Be love.

Pastor was right. It was time for me to show love to someone other than myself. I knew it wasn't wrong of me to be sad about being single, but I had completely crossed over from sadness into self-pity.

Well, that was over. For the first time in over a week, my mood actually matched the happy face I had been wearing for the world. Instead of focusing on myself and how I didn't have anyone to spend Valentine's Day with, I could have "been love" to my best friend and offered to babysit her boys while she went out for a romantic evening with her husband. I clapped with everyone else as the pastor took his seat, grateful for the encouragement, the renewed perspective, and atypical Valentine's Day message.

By the time my feet hit the parking lot, I felt like a weight had been lifted from my shoulders, even if it hadn't led to a love connection. But before I could file the message away under "Great Messages that Made Me Feel Better", and that I didn't have to act on, my eyes were drawn to the bus stop across the street from the church. From the dark red beanie that was pulled low over her ears to the thin tee shirt that was stretched across her midsection, my eyes tracked her even as I headed to my car on the other side of the church parking lot. Why wasn't she wearing a coat? It wasn't a warm February night, and she must have been freezing. As if in response to my question, she shivered. I sat behind the wheel of my car with my fur-lined wool coat buttoned securely up to my neck. Before I knew it, I was driving over to the bus stop, offering her a ride.

She was sitting under the same bus enclosure with the same graffiti-covered walls, but this time I didn't see the stylized letters as romantic gestures. It just looked sad, abandoned, and lonely.

"I don't usually accept rides from strangers," she said as she got into the passenger seat. "But this bus is like an hour late."

"I don't usually offer rides to strangers," I replied, heading towards the cross streets she named. "I'm Sierra."

"Like the mountains or the singer?" I laughed. I hadn't heard that comparison before. Especially living in Colorado near the Rocky

Mountains, few people thought about the Sierra Nevada Mountains in California.

"Like the mountains."

"Well, my name's Crystal. And before you say anything, yes I am pregnant and I know I shouldn't be out here at this time of night. These dang ol' busses, though. Whenever there's even a little bit of snow, they take forever."

I thought back to my days in college when I was either hoofing it or relying on public transportation, too. I smiled commiserating.

"How old are you?"

"Sixteen. But I'll be 17 in a few months. I'm gonna have my baby shower and my birthday party together." I don't know if she said it was going to be "lit" or "on fire", but either way, the irony of a child having a birthday party and baby shower all rolled in one was not lost on me.

I knew that giving someone a ride a few miles out of your way did not entitle you to get all in their business. So, I bit my lip and shoved the questions I was dying to ask down deep. Luckily, Miss Crystal was chatty.

"Everybody was saying how I should just give my baby up for adoption, but ain't nobody gonna love my baby like me. Nah. I'm keeping my baby." Crystal wrapped her arms around her protruding belly as if to protect him- or her- from an invisible intruder.

I didn't want to infect her with my fear, but I couldn't help but ask. "Aren't you afraid? I mean, it's a lot of work and so expensive to have a baby."

"My mom is helping me. Nobody will hire me right now because I'm so big, but once I have the baby, I'm gonna get a job. And my mom can watch the baby while I work, so I won't have to pay for daycare."

I wanted to ask what kind of job she thought she could get at 16- or 17- without a high school diploma and no training, but it wasn't my place. Besides giving her a ride, I wanted to do more for her, for her baby, the innocent life she was so cavalierly bringing into the world. I wanted to help her. I wanted to shake some sense into her. But what could I say? The deed was already done. Could I tell her to use protection? To wait for the right man to come along? To wait until she was a middle-aged woman like me with a career and steady income, but wrinkled eggs and an empty home? The baby was already formed inside her.

"I'm gonna be so happy when I have this baby. It's gonna be me and him." She was facing the street, but I could see the smile on her face, the look of love and peace. It was the same look many brides wore at the altar. She was in love with her baby and there was nothing anybody could say to help her be more realistic. And what was the point? There would be enough time for reality once she was up all night with a hungry, crying baby. The pastor's words came back to me. *Be love.*

I pulled up to the curb of the apartment she pointed out and put the car in park.

"I don't know what your background is, but could I pray for you?" When she nodded, I closed my eyes, unsure what I wanted to say, feeling rusty and unpracticed. When was the last time I had prayed for someone other than myself? When was the last time I had prayed aloud?

My words were clunky and sounded shallow and trite even to me, but I didn't know what else to do. So, I prayed. I gripped the steering wheel with one hand and placed the other tentatively on Crystal's shoulder. I asked for favor and wisdom, a healthy baby and a safe birth. I prayed that Crystal would be the mother that her child needed, and that God would be a father to them both.

After I said "Amen", I contemplated giving her money, but that didn't feel right. So, I just gave her my number and told her she could always call me if she needed a ride or anything.

As I pulled away from the curb, my mind raced with doubts and fears for Crystal and her baby. I turned the radio to my favorite gospel station, hoping to find some peace. Normally, I would sing along, having my own little praise party in the front seat of my car. But as I drove back towards my neighborhood, the songs all blurred together. From "You Brought the Sunshine" to "Every Praise", I only caught a word here and there. The confident assurance of the psalmists chafed against the mood that had descended upon the car since Crystal's exit and I reached out to turn the radio off. But the singing was replaced with a voice, and my hand stilled.

"James 1:27 declares that 'religion that our Father accepts as pure and faultless is this: to look after orphans and widows in their distress.' At Alpha and Omega Adoption Agency, we invite you to learn more about answering God's call for adoption. Couples *and* singles may apply. Visit our website for more information."

For some reason, the idea of adopting a child suddenly seemed offensive to me. Even though I had just been ready to encourage Crystal to give her baby up for adoption, I didn't see it as an option for myself. Maybe what Crystal said was true, maybe nobody could love a child like their birth mother. But didn't we encourage girls like Crystal every day to choose adoption over abortion? Or maybe I just didn't want to consider adoption for myself because that would mean that I had given up on my dream of getting married and having babies of my own. At the thought, hot angry tears burst through my eyes. What could I offer a child or baby? Broken dreams? Was I just a reject, a husbandless woman that apparently no man wanted? What was so wrong with me? If I wasn't good enough to be a wife, was I good enough to be a mother? And was I a bad person because I didn't want to be saddled with someone's...mistake? I was too angry to feel ashamed. But the more I thought about adopting, the more and harder I cried. I wanted a family, with a husband. I wanted to be loved. *I want to be loved!* I shouted. As if in response, I heard the pastor respond, *Be love.* My sobs didn't immediately subside, but it was as if someone had turned the volume down, way down. I wiped my face with the back of my hand, then reached for the tissue box under the passenger seat. From out of nowhere, a car slid into my lane in front of me, with only inches between me and their rear bumper. I slammed hard on the brakes, forgetting all about the box of tissues and the reason for them.

"Thank you, Jesus," I muttered in anger at the car who'd cut me off in order to get in the far right lane to make a quick right turn. Grateful that I hadn't hit them, but heart still pounding with adrenaline at what could have been. I huffily watched their right turn light blink on and off, on and off, as if trying to appease me and lull me into a state of tranquility. I glared at their back bumper, imagining myself inching up just close enough to give them a little push, knowing I would never do it, but fantasizing about it nonetheless. The metal of my front bumper would hit there's, just hard enough to give them the same fright I had just had. That bumper that read- what? *I 'heart' adoption.* Really? Really? Even the jerk's bumper was sending me not-so-subtle messages.

It was nothing clever, nothing written in the stars, but I could feel the prodding of the Spirit and for some reason, it just made me mad.

Chapter 4

When I woke up the next morning, I felt like I had a hang-over even though I hadn't had a drop of alcohol. I had a splitting headache, my head was foggy, my mouth was dry, and I couldn't remember much of what had happened the day before. I lay in bed wondering if it was a workday, Saturday, or church day. I pulled my cell phone off the nightstand. It was Saturday. Thank God. I rolled over, burrowing my face into my pillow, trying to recall the singles event. As expected, I hadn't met anyone. Actually, that wasn't true. I'd met Crystal, the 16 year-old pregnant girl who thought she could be a mother. She didn't *think* she could be a mother; she was *going to be* a mother.

The girl had no husband or boyfriend, just a "baby daddy". No job, no place to live, no family, no transportation, no money at all. But, she was just courageous- or foolish- enough to believe that everything would work out. I shook my head. On the one hand, I pitied her *and* her child. What did she have to offer a child except a life of poverty and struggle? On the other hand, I respected her decision to keep her baby. She wasn't letting fear of the unknown prevent her from looking forward to the future. But what kind of life could she offer the child? In my heart, I knew that life was more than about financial security, but love and good intentions weren't enough to feed her belly.

Again, I shook my head and pulled myself out of bed. I muddled through my breakfast of dry wheat toast and tea. I could hear the wind, and looking out the window, could see only about an inch of snow, so there was no reason to stay inside all day feeling sad and lonely. I could call Carmen, but she was probably on a post-Valentine's Day high. Travis wasn't generally into grand gestures, but he always surprised her with something sweet and romantic that had her gushing for days. I could go to the movies, but I wasn't in the mood to go alone. I sat at the kitchen table, considering my options, from binge watching a favorite show to ordering take out to walking around the mall. I sighed, not wanting to spend my day in the house all by myself. Maybe a bit of retail therapy would do me good.

* * *

A few hours later, I was walking around the mall, happy to be out of the house, but questioning the logic of my decision. Most stores still had their Valentine's Day décor up and were aggressively marking down Valentine's-specific items. Every jewelry store had huge banners reading "50% OFF" and "6 MONTHS NO INTEREST". Every jewelry store was packed. How many couples had gotten engaged the night before and were now at the mall to seal the deal? It's like the department stores had sprinkled fairy dust over the mall, inducing everyone into a shopping frenzy.

Who was I to resist? I cut across the mall pavilion and as soon as I stepped into the jewelry store, immediately regretted my decision. Everything was bright and shiny and sparkly and beautiful. Was I just a glutton for misery? I stared down at the matching his/hers wedding bands. Yellow gold. White gold. Titanium. Platinum. Emerald cut. Pear cut. Princess cut. I willed my feet to keep moving. Why had I even come into this store?

"Is there something I can show you?" I shook my head, and the saleswoman walked toward an exhausted-looking customer on the other side of the counter. I saw man after man standing by while the women at their side held up their ring fingers. Another couple was trying on matching bands. One woman was trying to convince her boyfriend -and herself- that she didn't need a larger size ring. "It fits. I'll take this one." And then I saw it: a watch so cheesy and gaudy that only a clueless man in love would buy.

The watch had a pink face with pink hearts in the background and diamonds at each quarter hour. The band was pink-gold plated. It shouted, "I love you!" and was so over-the-top. I didn't need it, I didn't even like it, but it made me smile.

Was wanting the watch the inevitable result of marketers' well-executed campaign to entice lovers to spend obscene amounts of money to prove their love for each other? Had I been lulled into a state of "gotta-have-it" with their glittering hearts hanging from the ceiling and love songs playing on loop in the background? Or, was buying the watch a declaration: "I don't need a man to buy me ridiculous, over-priced, shiny baubles"? Before I could talk myself out of it, I pulled my credit card from my wallet and told the clerk to ring it up. Before the ink had even dried on the receipt, the watch was out of the box and on my wrist.

Walking around the mall with the garish watch on my wrist, I felt a little lighter. Every other minute I lifted my hand and flicked my wrist to see the time, much like newly engaged women who are constantly flashing their ring finger. I loved the way the watch sparkled and caught the light just so. I counted the hearts. Thirty-one. Only two less than my age. I don't know why that made me smile, but it did. Whereas I had been regretting coming to the mall earlier, now I bopped from store to store, lingering over marked-down displays of chocolates, bears, and balloons. Something had broken inside of me, but instead of feeling destroyed, I felt free. New. Whole. I wanted to buy everything pink and red I saw.

I bought a large white bear with an embroidered red heart on his belly that was 50% off. I bought three boxes of chocolates (red boxes, of course) that were already 75% off. Everywhere I turned, there seemed to be another deal waiting for me. I filled my arms with trinkets and treats. I even bought a onesie that read "Mommy's Little Valentine" with a picture of a skunk on the front. Its tail was raised and sprouted out and had the texture of soft doll hair. I didn't particularly care for skunks, but it was cute, so I bought it.

I thought about Crystal and her upcoming birthday party/bridal shower. Would her family and friends come through for her and make sure she had all the things a newborn needed? Or, was she in for the rude awakening I feared?

By the time I made it to my car, my arms were filled with bags. I felt a little guilty, but a lot happy. At home, I pulled each of my purchases out, just as excited as if I was receiving them from a special someone. I put the bear on my nightstand. I put the chocolates in the fridge. Everything found a home. But what to do with the onesie? It was too small to hang up in my closet. It would just get lost among the clothes in there, and for some reason I wanted to look at it and not have it hidden away. I stepped across the hall to the guest room. It was decorated in blues and greens, colors that would be welcoming for a female or male guest. There was a full-size bed with half a dozen pillows all neatly arranged just so. Above the bed was a floating shelf with a few frames of art. There was a small print of three African women, one wearing a blue dress, one wearing green, and one wearing gold. I held the onesie up beside it, then crinkled my nose.

On the nightstand sat a colorful handmade basket from Kenya, filled with toiletries and incidentals. From face wash and toothpaste to nail clippers and tweezers, I tried to include everything an out-of-town visitor might have forgotten or been forced to toss by TSA. Beside the basket, there was a roll of fluffy bath towels and washcloths. Another basket on the floor in the corner of the room held extra blankets for those occasional sub-zero, Colorado-cold nights. And, of course, everything was either blue or green and complemented each other perfectly. I wasn't an interior designer, but I had taken the time to create a beautiful space that even impressed me. I didn't get overnight guests very often, but when I did, I wanted them to feel pampered and special.

I draped the red onesie over the bed, and immediately picked it back up, cradling it. I held it up to the far wall, beside the window, next to the closet, and above the bed. It only screamed, "I don't belong here!" The adorable red onesie with the black and white skunk just didn't fit. Looking around the room one last time, I walked out and closed the door behind me.

Next, I headed to my home office. Unlike the guest room, which was a haven of peace, my home office was…a work in progress. There was a beat-up, black metal two-drawer filing cabinet. A tall mahogany bookshelf filled with books and a plastic globe on top. An unfinished cheap plywood desk and a red velour desk chair completed the room. There was no wall art. No pretty, exotic baskets. No matching anything. It was functional. I went in there once a month to use the laptop to pay bills online, an extra time in April to file my taxes, and that was about it. Unlike the guest room, this room was oppressive. Nothing matched and it was just plain ol' ugly. Except for the red velour chair. The chair was beautiful and comfortable and completely out of place. I ran my hand along the back of the chair. The chair was pushed into the desk, and the space on the wall above the desk was empty. Like all the walls in this thrown-together room. I lifted the onesie and smiled. Grabbing a hammer and a nail from the closet (which also kept my random assortment of tools), I hammered the nail into the wall, and hooked the tiny hanger over it. It was beautiful. It was… adorable. I replaced the hammer, sat down at the desk, pulled out a legal pad, and began making a list.

1. *Look up Alpha & Omega Adoption Agency*
2. *Open an adoption savings account*
3. *Get old baby furniture from Carmen*
4. *Get a book of baby names*
5. *Learn some nursery rhymes*
6. *Take chocolates to office- put in break room*
7. *Be love*

But after spending the rest of the weekend researching adoption agencies, the small seed of hope that had just been planted was uprooted, crushed, ground into a fine powder. And the only thing I knew for certain was that I would not be adopting through Alpha & Omega.

REY SIRAKAVIT

Chapter 5

I stared at the number on the website, my eyes bulging at the sticker price. $35,000. At a minimum.

I scanned the screen to make sure I had not misread the figure. Unfortunately, I hadn't.

Their adoption fee included a home study for $2,500, agency fees of $17,000, legal fees of $4,000, birth mother expenses around $3,000. And $8,500 in "other fees". All I knew was that $35,000 was almost half my yearly salary, and even after paying all those fees, the agency could not guarantee that a birth mother would actually choose me. I looked at about a dozen other private adoption agencies in Colorado, Nevada, and California. Unfortunately, the final costs were about the same. And even though they each said that singles could apply, they were all in agreement that birth moms were more likely to choose happily married couples. They also typically had shorter wait times, 18-24 months as compared to 30-36 months.

My dream of being a wife or mother was being sidelined once again.

I slid my chair back from the desk and stared up at the adorable red skunk onesie. I could picture a small baby smiling up at me, me tickling their belly, changing their little diaper. Ha! It finally hit me why the skunk was funny. I couldn't believe it had taken me so long to figure out that the designer was comparing babies to skunks. Or, at least, their stinky diapers.

I knew that I wanted to be a mother. I also knew that I couldn't afford to pay $35,000 for *maybe*. I pulled out my legal pad, flipped to the next blank page and started a new list: *How to Become a Mom*

1. *Get married, get pregnant ... too old?*
2. *Adopt (too expensive)*

I hesitated. What other options were there?

3. *IVF- what is this?*
4. *Artificial insemination*
5. *Overseas adoption?*

There were more questions than solutions on my list, but I felt better knowing that I had some options. I glanced down at my gaudy pink watch, with the 31 hearts, my V-Day watch, the one that signaled my victory over fear of singleness and being alone. It was past midnight and even though I was no closer to an answer than I had been the night before, I still felt peace. Unlike dating and marriage, becoming a mother felt like something that was in my control. I didn't have to wait to meet somebody, go through the whole dating process. I could just move forward. I closed my laptop, set the notepad down, and went to bed.

* * *

The next weekend, the weekend after the Lord began to turn my life upside down, Carmen and I sat in a crowded coffee shop. It was one of those trendy spots that spring up with overpriced coffee, exotic options, and plenty of atmosphere. It could have been a nightclub in a former life, with the low lights and small stage. Carmen and I sat at a round table in the corner beside the empty stage and a wall of bookshelves that you could peruse while drinking your favorite brew. My back was to the rest of the crowded shop, and every once in a while, I felt the pressure of someone brushing by. I scooted my chair in as much as was comfortable, trying not to slosh my chai. After telling Carmen all about my Valentine's Day, I was impatient to hear her reaction.

"This is a huge decision. You really don't think you'll get married?"

"Of course that's the goal, but you know the statistics are not in my favor. About sixty percent of Black women never get married."

"You could be one of the 40!" Carmen smiled, trying to sound optimistic.

"Well, the Lord has had ten years to make it happen. I don't want to sit around waiting another ten. If I want to be a mom, I can make that happen, with or without a husband."

"That's not exactly what I was hoping you'd get out of the singles' event, but praise God. You're going to make a great mom." Carmen looked genuinely happy for me. Tucking a curl behind her ear, she leaned forward, excitement etched on her face.

"Well, let's not celebrate yet. I'm still not sure what path to pursue. Adoption and IVF are so expensive, but artificial insemination...the price is right, but the success rate isn't very high."

"What is it?"

"Only a 10-20% chance of success with each treatment."

"I had no idea. That can't be right."

"That's what Mr. Internet says."

"Wow." Silently, Carmen took my weathered *How to Become a Mom* list from my hands. She scrunched her face up like she was trying to see something far away. I knew that look, though.

"What's wrong?" I asked.

"I don't know. I just feel like the conviction you had was about focusing on how to love others…"

I scooted my chair closer to the table, letting another customer inch by me. On the one hand, I felt awkward having such a private conversation in such a popular coffee shop. You could be assured that you would bump into someone you knew pretty much whenever you left the house. That's one of the things I loved about living in Denver, but it also made having private conversations in public places pretty difficult. I lowered my voice. "Yes, like loving a baby, even if I didn't give birth to it myself."

"I don't know. Obviously, I wasn't there and don't know what the Lord put on your heart, but the way you described it to me, I was just thinking about adoption."

I sighed. "It's so expensive."

"How many agencies did you look at?"

"At least a dozen. There are tax breaks and incentives, but that doesn't help with upfront costs."

"You know, one of my co-workers had an adoption fundraiser. I think they did one of those sites where people set a goal and invite their friends and family to contribute online. I can reach out and ask how much they were able to raise. If you want." I could tell that Carmen could tell by the look on my face that I was not interested. "Or, you could just put it on your credit card," she said with a grin.

"Mommy," I said using my best little kid voice, "how come we live in a car?" I switched back to my voice, but with the tone that childcare workers always seem to use when speaking to a child. "Oh, that's because Mommy put $40,000 on her credit card to adopt you and at 20% interest, she'll be in debt until *you* retire." Carmen and I both laughed, then sighed. "Honestly, I don't know how people do it. And the crazy part is that there are no guarantees that an expecting mom will choose you." I sipped my tea, wishing that somehow the answer would magically appear, but it didn't.

"What about overseas adoption? There are so many orphans that need families."

I rolled my eyes. "Don't even get me started. International adoption is just as expensive, if not more so, because you have additional costs like traveling to the child's home country. I mean, I have a good job, but as a single woman, it's just out of my reach. That's why I was thinking about doing the artificial insemination. I really felt like God was saying that I didn't need a husband to become a mom and to not be afraid."

"I agree. You don't need a husband to be a mom. I just don't want you to miss what God is telling *you*."

I could feel my heart start to race, and I forced myself to calm down. "Carmen, you weren't even there. Why are you so insistent on this whole adoption thing? I've already said I can't afford it, unless you and Travis are giving out scholarships to single, would-be-moms." I tried to bring some levity back to the conversation, but I was still annoyed.

"I'm sorry, Sierra." She covered my hand with hers and squeezed. "You know how I get. But what about..." Carmen paused, then held her hand up, as if preemptively protecting herself from my response. "Before you get an attitude, have you considered adopting a foster child?"

"A *foster* child?"

"Yes, surely you've heard of them. I'd have to look into it, but I don't think it costs very much."

I hesitated. Of course, I knew that you could adopt a foster child, but I honestly didn't know much else about it. "I don't know. Some of these kids are born addicted to drugs and I don't know if that's my calling."

It was universally accepted, if never outright acknowledged, that a Christian could get out of just about anything by saying something wasn't their "calling".

Can you help in the nursery? Serve in the kitchen? Go on this mission trip?

Sorry, that's not my calling.

It was like a super-spiritual "get-out-of-jail-free" card that no one could argue with. Unfortunately, Carmen wasn't buying it.

"Are you serious? You know that's not true, right? Kids wind up in foster care for lots of different reasons. Parents die, neglect, abuse, accidents, illnesses, natural disasters…"

"Drugs." I cut in.

"Yes, but not all mothers were using when they were pregnant. I don't know. I think you should look into it." *Look into it?* Who did she think I was? Who did she think *she* was? The audacity.

"Carmen, you have two beautiful, healthy sons and a husband who loves you. But I'm supposed to adopt a possible drug baby- *by myself?*" I didn't know why I was trying to pick a fight with my best friend, but I couldn't seem to help myself. "How about you? Are you going to adopt a child from foster care?" I raised my eyebrows, knowing I might incur her wrath, but confident that I had backed Carmen into the proverbial corner. Checkmate. However, I was shocked at her response. Not only was she not angry, it looked like her eyes were filling with tears. I prayed that I hadn't unknowingly hit a raw nerve.

"Actually, we have considered it," she began. "Travis's parents were foster parents for a while when he was a kid and it's something we've talked about off and on."

"Really? I didn't know that." I leaned forward, waiting, knowing that a full story was forthcoming. Carmen looked over my shoulder with a far-off look on her face.

"Yeah, he actually had a little foster sister. She was three or four when she lived with him and his family. The girl's mom was messed up. She was addicted to crack and never completed a rehab program. But somehow, she was able to convince the judge that she was clean and sober and she regained custody of her daughter. Within a month, the little girl was dead. I guess she found some of her mom's drugs or the mom gave them to her. They never figured out exactly what happened. However it happened, the girl had a reaction and died." Carmen paused, dabbing at her eyes with the back of her index finger. My own eyes watered up, too. I pictured a little girl innocently leaning over a coffee table, picking up a pipe, mom passed out on the couch. My heart ached at the vision, but also made me angry. Hearing stories like that brought out the mama bear in me.

"She was only a part of their family for a few months, but ever since then, Travis has always wanted to adopt."

"And how do you feel about it?"

"I don't know. I mean, I guess I was kind of like you. Turned off by everything I saw and heard on the news."

"Like children of the corn."

Carmen rolled her eyes, but smiled. "Yep. Just like that. But most of these kids are in the system through no fault of their own. My boys are really young right now, so I don't know if the timing is right, but when will it ever be? Maybe this is just the push I needed, too." Carmen's tears really started to fall then. "I'm sorry if it feels like I'm pushing you. I must sound like a total hypocrite."

I grabbed her hand. "No, you're not. It's just that this- all of this- is so new. I mean, a week ago, I was just hoping to meet a nice guy, go on a few dates, get married one day. Now I'm talking about adopting a child by myself. I feel empowered and excited, but it's also kind of overwhelming."

"*Be love.* Isn't that what you said?"

"No, that's what the pastor said." This time *I* rolled *my* eyes.

"Well, just give it some thought. I know you're gonna go home and do a ton of research, but maybe you should start praying about it."

Although I never would have admitted it, I had to confess that as much as I had been thinking, planning, making lists, and talking to Carmen, I hadn't actually stopped and taken time to pray.

I shook my head. How ridiculous to hear a word from the Lord and not go back to the Lord to process it.

"Finally, you're right about something," I laughed. "I do need to start praying."

But, honestly, what was the point? God had obviously stopped listening or caring or both. My prayers didn't even make it to the ceiling. I didn't want to think of my relationship with God like a job that you couldn't quit because you had already put in too many years and were close to retirement, although that was how I felt. I could not "turn back now" as the old song went. But neither could I pretend that I believed – truly believed- that God was listening and cared and would actually do something based upon my prayer…not because my life had been too hard, because God had been too silent.

Chapter 6

As much as I hated to admit it, Carmen was right. About everything. She was right about focusing on adoption as opposed to fertility treatment. She was right about looking into foster care. She was right about needing to pray. For some reason, though, I couldn't pull myself away from the computer screen. First there was Shalia. Shalia was 14, had two younger siblings and a messy bun that looked dry and frizzy. I imagined myself washing her hair at the kitchen sink, running my fingers over her scalp with some sweet-smelling conditioner and hair oils, just like Debra had done for me so many years ago.

I could still see Debra standing there with her faded blue apron on, the same apron she wore whether she was cooking or doing hair. I wrapped a loc around my finger, lost in the memory, transported back to the faded kitchen with brown patterned wallpaper, brown cabinets, and brown appliances. We had stood in the middle of that kitchen every week for years, for our "girl time", as she called it, and I remember wanting her to rescue more than just my hair. But she didn't. Wasn't a mother supposed to protect you? But Debra hadn't. Instead, it was like she had pressed her hand across my mouth forcing me to stay silent and ashamed. Swiping at the invisible hand, I shook myself, bringing myself back to the present and the picture of Shalia with the messy bun.

Then there was Loveyouforever. The child's name was Loveyouforever. I shook my head. It seemed like some people were trying to get the award for most creative name, instead of thinking about how a child would have to introduce themselves someday. As I read through the profiles, though, I was struck by how superficial and irrelevant the names were.

Loveyouforever's name was more than ironic. Her profile said that she suffered from post-traumatic stress disorder and depression from being abandoned at a drug house and would need ongoing therapy. "Prospective adoptive parents would need to be willing to maintain her relationship with her current therapist." There was no picture available for Loveyouforever, just an age: 9 years old. My heart broke for the girl whose mother made her a promise that she could not fulfill, whose story probably involved more than just abandonment. I bit my lower lip. What made me think that I, of all people, could be a good mother to a child who was going through trauma? I had more than enough of my own issues. But for some reason, I could not pull myself away from the screen. Over the next few days and weeks, in every moment of my free time, I felt drawn back to the county website, running the same search, hoping to not see the same children, praying that in the hours that had passed, that they had been adopted and removed from the site. Soon, though, I could name all the available African American children in my county. So, I moved on to other websites, regional and even national photo-listings that gave just enough information to make you think you knew the children, but still not enough to satisfy the urge. I ran the same queries, read and reread the same profiles, looked at the same pictures. Most were older, 10-18 years old. Most were part of sibling groups. The largest I saw was six. Six children, brothers and sisters, whose birth parents had lost all parental rights and who were hoping to be adopted together. One of the children was medically fragile, in a wheelchair with a feeding tube. In the online pictures, all the children were smiling, clean and neat. As I clicked through the photos, I felt less and less afraid of what might be "wrong" with the children, but also more and more inadequate. Who was I to even think about taking in six children? I had no husband, no family to help. Just a heart that was breaking at the thought that countless children were going to wallow in foster care and might never know the love of a safe and healthy family. I wanted to do something, but I knew I couldn't. I couldn't.

And that is when I finally started to pray.

These were not the super-spiritual prayers of the saints. No, these were short throwaway prayers that pinged off the walls of my office, windows, and computer screen. Prayers so small that God would have to strain his neck to hear. Prayers so brief that if he blinked, he would miss them.

Lord, Jesus.

That poor baby.

Father, why?

Hmmmm.

These prayers bubbled up inside of me, like condensation on the outside of a cup. My prayers were like those tiny droplets, a minor inconvenience, easily wiped away and forgotten. But there were just so many children and it didn't seem like they were going anywhere. I could not reach through the screen and pluck them from their circumstances, from the bad hands they had been dealt. I could do nothing for these children. I could not even adopt them.

So, I really started praying.

Neither were these the super-spiritual prayers of the saints who could tear down strongholds and pray you into the presence of God.

These were more like the prayers of a newborn who wants to be fed, but doesn't have the words to say to get her mother's attention, so she wails.

Lord, Jesus!

That poor baby!

Father, why?!?

Hmm-hmm!

After thirty years of going to church and calling myself a Christian, I realized I had no idea how to pray, no idea how to pray for something beyond blessing my food, no idea how to pray for something with faith that I wasn't sure God would grant, no idea how to pray for something that I couldn't just buy myself.

Because after years of praying in faith for a husband, there I was, still single. Either I was doing something wrong, or God didn't love me as much as I thought.

My knees were scuffed from the hours I spent praying at my bedside like my grandmother used to do.

I had a dusty closet with unanswered prayers taped to the sides of the walls like I'd seen in a movie.

And I had a drawer full of prayer journals that were destined for the recycling bin.

Things that seemed to work for everybody else, but not for me.

God supposedly loved me so much that there was no good thing he would withhold from me. But was that really true? Did he really care about me?

And if God didn't care about me, maybe he didn't really care about these children, either.

And if God didn't care about me, and didn't care about children who have been beat and abandoned, then what was the point in being a Christian? Was that the God that I supposedly served?

I was stuck.

On the surface, nothing changed. I kept going to work every day. I kept going to church every Sunday. I found time to meet with Carmen for brunch. But inside, I was having a crisis of faith. Did God truly love me? Did he love everyone? Did we have a right to think that God would intervene in our lives and answer our prayers? I thought back to one of the girls whose profiles I had read: Loveyouforever. Maybe that wasn't just a mother's promise to her daughter, maybe that was also a reminder of the Father's love for us. That regardless of what happens and where we go, he promises he will love us forever.

I started praying more.

I clicked back to the county's website and pulled up Loveyouforever's profile. Weeks had passed since I had first come across her profile, and there was still no picture.

Her profile was simple. Part petition, part testimony.

African-American. Female. 9 years old. Loveyouforever is a sweet, quiet girl who has been in foster care for three years. She enjoys playing with dolls and playing dress up. Loveyouforever suffers from post-traumatic stress disorder and depression from being abandoned at a drug house and will need ongoing therapy. Loveyouforever needs an adoptive family who is patient and consistent. Prospective adoptive parents will need to be willing to maintain her relationship with her current therapist.

I could not imagine what being abandoned at a drug house encompassed, and frankly I did not want to. Suddenly, seeing this little girl be adopted seemed so much more important and urgent to me than any prayer of mine about getting married.

Lord, my faith is so weak. I've been praying for years for a mate, someone to share my life with, and for whatever reason you've said no. I have tried to be faithful. Tried to be obedient... I swatted at my eyes. *I don't know why you've said no, why you've been silent, but I have to believe.*

I pulled a couple tissues from the box and rubbed them under my nose.

I have to believe that you are real. I need to experience you, Lord, like I never have before. I'm tired of just going to church and going through the motions. Your word says that you will love us forever.

My eyes went back to the screen.

Your word says that nothing can separate us from your love. So, Lord, I'm asking you for a miracle for Loveyouforever. Lord, I pray that you would heal this young girl of the scars of being abandoned. Help her to know that you will never leave nor forsake her.

My eyes rested on the word "abandoned" in her profile.

Lord, I don't know why this young girl has already had to deal with so much pain in her short life, but you say that you can turn mourning into dancing. I pray for adoptive parents for this girl. I pray for a family who will love her. I pray that she would experience your love.

I trailed off. I had not prayed so much for something or someone since...I couldn't remember when. But it felt good. After I blew my nose one final time, I clicked print and listened to the whir of the printer come to life. Pulling the warm paper from the output tray, I tore off a piece of tape and used it to affix the printout to my office door.

REY SIRAKAVIT

Chapter 7

For the hundredth time, I looked at Loveyouforever's profile. No picture had magically appeared, but every time I looked at the profile taped to my office door, I stopped and touched the paper and prayed. Sometimes, I prayed short prayers.

Keep her safe, Lord.

Lord, I pray that she knows your love today.

Lord, protect her from the evil one.

Other times, I prayed long, audacious prayers for healing and reconciliation and a ministry that would be born out of her pain that would be used to bring healing to others. I imagined her like a young Juanita Bynum, preaching and teaching young women about how to lean on God for strength and hope.

At the bottom of the profile, was the social worker's phone number and email address. After a week of praying for Loveyouforever, I decided to call the social worker.

"I was just wondering if I could get a little more information about one of the children on your website. Her name is Loveyouforever."

"Have you already completed your home study?"

"No..."

"Who's your case manager?"

"I don't have one."

"Have you completed your application and taken the foster-to-adopt classes?" My silence must have spoken volumes. "I'm sorry, until you complete your home study, I can't talk to you about any specific children." She gave me a list of dates of upcoming informational sessions and hung up. I didn't know if I was meant to adopt Loveyouforever, but I had been praying for her so much, I felt more connected to her than anyone else in my life. So, I decided to go to the next available informational session. There had to be a reason I felt such a strong urge to pray for her. Maybe I was meant to be the answer to my own prayers for her.

* * *

Two weeks later, the county's informational session for prospective adoptive parents was held in the basement of an office building. The walls were drab and gray, the carpet stained. There was a mishmash of furniture. Some high-backed wooden chairs with stained and torn blue upholstery were mixed in with off-white plastic chairs. There were about a dozen of us in the room, including three other African American women. I chose a plastic chair next to who had a shoulder length bob and looked around my age. Her name-tag read Yvette. She smiled as I sat down, scooting her chair over a bit, making room for me at the table. For the next ninety minutes, we listened to the presenter, a social worker and adoptive mother, describe the process for adopting in Denver County.

"The kids that are available are kids from hard places. Their parents' rights have been terminated. They've suffered abuse and neglect. Reunification hasn't worked. So, we're looking for stable families that can give these kids the love and structure they need to thrive. If you're looking for a baby, you're in the wrong place. We rarely have infants whose parental rights have been terminated. If you're struggling with infertility, I don't mean to be insensitive but, again, you're in the wrong place. We need people who want to parent children who come from trauma and probably have a lot of baggage."

After that very discouraging spiel, she passed out a fifty-page packet and went over each page. Each. Page. In addition to the informational session, there were 32 hours of parenting classes each person had to take. Once the classes were complete, it would take another 3-4 months to complete the home study, which included meeting with a social worker one-on-one and having a home inspection. I thought about my semi-unfurnished office, and my heart filled with dread. She talked about some of the kids who were available, describing their backgrounds and special circumstances. I raised my hand.

"On your website, there was one little girl whose profile really touched me. Her name is…" Before I could finish, the social worker cut me off.

"I'm sorry. I can't discuss specific children until your home study is complete and has been approved." She sounded just like the woman from the phone.

Another prospective parent raised his hand. "Does that mean some parents aren't approved?" All eyes turned nervously back to the social worker.

"Well, the home study is an in-depth report. The home study worker will talk to you about your philosophy of child-rearing and discipline. She will learn about your background, your finances. We want to be sure that every family we place a child with is prepared mentally, emotionally, and physically, and that we're not putting them in another potentially abusive situation. So, yes, there are times when a couple or individual's home study is not approved." I looked around the room. *God, I pray for every person in this room. I pray that every person who is called to adopt would feel your perfect peace surround them.*

A few others asked questions, and that was the end. Going to the informational session had been incredibly helpful, but it also made the whole thing so much more real. Talking to Carmen about adopting, searching through photo-listings, even praying for a girl whom I might never meet, were easy and safe. But holding the application in my hand was real. Introducing myself to a room full of other hopeful parents was real.

As I drove home, the magnitude of the decision hit me anew. My heart began to race. Was I ready for this? Did I know how to parent a girl who had been abandoned at a drug house? Did a girl who had been abandoned at a drug house even *want* a parent, or was she too jaded? As I sat at my desk, staring up at the red skunk onesie, it felt like someone reached inside my heart and squeezed. Each breath became a labor.

What if I was rejected and Loveyouforever wallowed in the foster care system for years, waiting but never being adopted? I grabbed the side of my desk, willing my heart to slow down, but the only thing I could see was a girl with a messy bun towering over me. In my mind's eye, she looked like Crystal, the pregnant girl I had met weeks before, but without the pregnant belly. Her face was contorted into an angry scowl and she seemed at least 7-feet tall. She was standing over me, pointing down at me, yelling. As hard as I tried, I could not force the image away. *God, I know you are bigger than my fears, bigger than a home study, bigger than any problem. I pray that your will would be done.* My breathing began to slow and I repeated the words over and over. *You are bigger. You are bigger. You are bigger.* As my heart and breathing slowed to normal, I opened the packet and began flipping through it.

The one positive was the cost. Carmen had been right: adopting a foster child through the county was practically free. Taking a deep breath, I pulled out the application and began filling out my information.

The first couple of sections were easy. Name. Address. Social security number. The basics. Except for "Marital Status". For some reason, checking "single" felt like an admission of guilt, like confessing to some crime I had committed. And what was my crime? According to society (and my biological clock), being 33 and single with no kids. According to Drisk, being a bad kisser. Or, more precisely, he had accused me of being a cold dispassionate kisser who was hiding behind my faith. Surely that would not be reason to reject my application to adopt. I moved on.

Income. The social worker from the informational session had assured us that as long as we could prove that we were financially stable, we didn't have to be rich. I looked around my house. It was no mansion, but I wondered if Loveyouforever would like it. Which room would be hers? Would I need to move?

I thought about turning the blue and green guest room into a true bedroom for a little girl. There was already a full-size bed, but I knew I'd have to get rid of all the pillows, baskets, and most of the African décor. It didn't really scream "little girl", but the transformation would be easy. Should I wait, though? What if something happened and I wasn't able to adopt Loveyouforever after all? I dismissed the thought. *You are in control, Lord.* The Lord works all things together for our good. What was more, I had no idea what she liked. She could love unicorns and mermaids or be totally into sports. I would have to wait. I turned my attention back to the application. One page down, 27 more to go.

After the basics, there were questions about childhood, romantic relationships, personality quizzes. I didn't know if I was applying to adopt a child or to join the CIA. As midnight approached, I finally slid the application aside. I wished I had someone to go over my answers with, especially the questions about childhood. The questions had started to raise some feelings inside me that I had long ago buried away. They started innocently enough, like "Describe your family." But they quickly devolved to, "Have you ever been abused?" And they didn't just want to know if you'd been physically abused, but mentally abused, sexually abused. Those were questions I didn't want to think about, and answers I didn't have. I skipped the section, forcing thoughts and memories away, just as I had done for years. But this time, they assaulted me, playing on auto-loop, tugging at the edges of my mind. Searing pain ran up and down my spine. It had taken me years to put that all behind me, and I couldn't afford to let all those memories and all that pain rise to the surface again. I didn't know if I could survive it.

So, I did what I had done a thousand times before. I swiped at the imaginary hand covering my face. I took a deep breath. I opened my eyes. I found something in the room to focus on- the red skunk onesie. I reminded myself of what the onesie meant and how funny it was. I knew, though, that if I tried to go to bed right away, I would be up all night, replaying the past.

I changed into a grungy tee shirt and a pair of old sweats. I pulled out a bucket, filled it with water and pine sol and started scrubbing. In the background, I put on an old Destiny's Child CD, "Survivor". I dunked a giant microfiber rag into the bucket and started scrubbing the walls and light fixtures, then worked my way down to the ground. On my hands and knees, I scrubbed every inch of tile, every slat of wood, every baseboard in the house. By the time I was done, it was almost 4 a.m., my sweats were soaked, and my hands felt raw. But I was once again in control. I had mapped out the next few months, envisioned how I would redecorate the guest room, make the announcement at work, walk into church with Loveyouforever, and introduce her as my daughter. I was even used to her name now, and it rolled off my tongue as easily as if I was the one who had made the promise to love her forever. And I didn't just scrub, I prayed. I prayed for her as if my life depended on it. I prayed for peace. I prayed for comfort. I prayed for healing. I prayed for anointing. And the more I prayed, the more I felt our lives coming together, as a family. By the time I finally fell in bed, I had prayed and scrubbed until my arm was about to fall off, all while ignoring the gray cloud that continued to hover over me.

REY SIRAKAVIT

Chapter 8

For weeks, my life entered a new pattern. Work all day, work on bits of the application at night, attend training all day Saturday, church on Sunday, and pray, pray, pray.

The more I prayed, the more assured I felt that the Lord was calling me to adopt Loveyouforever.

The more training I received, the less certain I felt.

I was on an emotional roller coaster and couldn't anticipate the next bend, turn, or drop.

At the first adoption training, we all had to go around the room and introduce ourselves and share our reason for adopting. We were all seated at a large circular table. There was a couple who already had five kids and felt called to open their home to children in need. They couldn't stop smiling, like they had won the lottery. There were two childless couples. They didn't use the word infertility, but the longing was written all over their faces. There was a lesbian couple who kept holding each other's hands and seemed on the verge of tears.

Then, there were the unattached women. There was a woman, Jessica, whose husband was "unable to attend today". She kept nervously looking all around, like she was in the witness protection program.

Yvette, who I had already met at the informational session, was on my right. She was a Denver native, a veritable rarity, and had married her high school sweetheart. After a few years, he cheated and they got divorced. She had never remarried. Never had kids. "At this phase in my life and career, I'm not interested in having an infant. But I still want to be a mom, so I thought I would look into foster care adoption."

As Yvette sat down, all eyes turned towards me. I was conscious of not wanting to look like the Lucky Number winner, but also not like I was being dragged into this, even if I was. I smiled, but not too big.

"I'm Sierra. Like the mountains. The other mountains." A couple people smiled. "I moved here from southern California for a job in IT, so you can blame me for Denver's inflated housing market." More chuckles. "Like all of you, I'm here today because I have room in my heart and home for a child. So, I'm excited to learn and grow together." I sat down, pleased with the smiles and chuckles I had received.

For four consecutive Saturdays, we crowded around the same table, watching videos about adoption, listening to adoptive parents share their stories, learning about "trauma-informed" parenting techniques. We had to agree to no spanking, no yelling, no time outs, all strategies that our parents may have used on us, but that would be sure to trigger an already traumatized child. At first, I wanted to dismiss the strategies as New Age, psychobabble. Hadn't we been taught since the beginning, "Spare the rod, spoil the child"? But as the presenters shared more and more stories about the situations that many of the children were coming from, I began to agree that these kids had had enough of "the rod" to last a lifetime.

The presenters also went into detail on the various kinds of coping skills that children invariably used to protect themselves physically and emotionally. Could I parent a child whose defense mechanism was to push everyone and everything away? To make you pay for all the pain and misery that had been poured out on them? That did not match my dream of motherhood. I backed away from the table, mentally closing the door on adoption through foster care. The class wasn't over, but I was done. Unless someone left a baby on my doorstep, I'd just have to save and save and save until I had enough to afford a private adoption. I could do it, just like I had saved enough for the down payment on my house. I started doing the math in my head. If I could save $5,000 a year, it'd only take me the next 5-7 years to be able to afford the agency fees. My shoulders sagged. I'd be almost 40 before I was able to bring a child home!

As much as I tried, I was stuck on the emotional tracks of this roller coaster, and the ride was far from over. We broke around noon for lunch, and the presenters encouraged us to get out of the building for our 30-minute break. Jessica, whose husband still hadn't found time to attend the class, joined us.

Across the street, there was a burrito bar. With our scarves pulled tight around our necks to brace against the cold mountain air, we headed out. Yvette, Jessica, and me, eating our $9 burritos.

"I can't believe the time has passed by so quickly! We're almost done."

"Every week we're one step closer to bringing our little blessings home," Yvette said with a smile. Of the three of us, Yvette was the most committed and optimistic. She knew exactly what she wanted and was all in. In the four weeks I'd known her, I had not heard her waver once. On the other hand, Jessica and I were all over the place. Jessica teared up. It didn't take much for her. She had been hoping that her husband, Jack, would get on board once she started the classes, but so far, he hadn't. And if he refused to take the classes, they wouldn't be able to move forward with the home study or get their foster care license.

As if reading my thoughts, Yvette said, "Next step, home study." She was the only one of us who smiled, as if she couldn't wait to have her home and mind inspected by a stranger.

"I don't even know what to expect," I sighed. "When I'm stressed, I clean, so I'm not really worried about that part, but the interview... I don't know."

"They said it takes 4 or 5 sessions," Jessica offered.

"But what kind of questions are they going to ask?" There were some topics that were just off-limits and I wanted to keep it that way.

"Right! It's kind of like therapy, but if you're too honest, 'No kid for you!'" Yvette wagged her finger at us as if she were the soup Nazi from Seinfeld, rejecting our adoption applications as cavalierly as one rejected a soup order. So, maybe she had some insecurities, too.

"Exactly. But if you sound too perfect, that's also gotta be a red flag," Jessica chimed in.

"So, we have to be just messed up enough, but not too messed up," I said and they both laughed. As the conversation lulled, I turned to Jessica. "Do you think Jack is ever going to come around?" I couldn't hold the question back.

"I don't know. I'm praying for him, but it doesn't seem to be doing much good." Jessica's chin began to quiver, and Yvette and I simultaneously reached out to put our hands on hers.

"Can I pray for you?" I asked hesitantly. This was starting to become normal instead of an after-thought.

Jessica nodded and we all bowed our heads. With orders being called out in the background and people shuffling around the tiny burrito joint, I asked God to intercede and bring unity to Jessica and Jack's marriage. *Lord, I pray that your will be done. Every good deed doesn't need to be done today or in this season. Give Jessica patience to wait on you and your timing. Amen.*

"You know what, we should exchange contact info. No matter what happens, we should continue to pray for each other." Yvette started a group text and after saving each other's contact info, we hurried back to class.

If I had known what the topic of the next session was going to be, if I had flipped through my packet in advance or had paid better attention to the agenda, I still don't know that I would have done anything differently. The final session was called Trigger Alert. As usual, the presenters introduced the topic and everyone turned to the correct page to complete the fill-in-the-blank handout. This time, though, one of the presenters said something about feeling free to excuse yourself at any point if you needed to. I looked around the room, and seven minutes into the presentation, a woman stood and walked out. Her head was down, but the room was dark, so I couldn't tell if she was crying or not. Maybe she was just going to the restroom. Maybe *I* should just "go to the restroom". But I didn't. I didn't want to move. No, I couldn't move. My feet were frozen to the floor; my hips like magnets stuck to the chair. I couldn't lift my head. The only thing moving was my heart. It was racing so fast I felt like it would explode. The pounding in my ear drowned out most of the video, but not all of it. A father who supposedly loved his daughter. A mother who forgave her husband. A daughter who was scarred for life. At least, that last part is what I assumed. The narrator in the documentary didn't say, but I knew without even looking at the girl that she would be scarred for life, that she would hate herself for what she did, and hate her mother for knowing about it but not protecting her. And she would not think about her father, or would try not to, because if she did she might crumble apart and would never be able to put herself together again. So, I sat there. Not moving. Not listening. Barely breathing. Completely exposed in the dark. Waiting for it all to be over. And, finally, it was.

The presenter flipped on the light and there was not a dry eye in the room. A tissue box was passed around the table and my tears mixed with everyone else's. The woman who had "gone to the restroom" earlier returned, face wet and red. It was a somber end to a class that had started off with laughter and smiles. As the roller coaster train pulled back into the station, I was filled with dread and doubt. But what could I do? I envied the couples around me who had each other to lean on. Who could literally lean into someone else's strength and say, "My feet won't move. Help me. I can't breathe. Help me." I had no one to dry my eyes, pat my back, or hold my hand. I had no one. And as much as I wanted to be that "someone" for someone, I dreaded what it might cost me. I doubted that I would be able to fulfill that promise. Eventually, the class was over. Certificates of completion were handed out. I smiled perfunctorily as I received mine, moving for the first time since the beginning of the Trigger Alert. I slid the certificate into the folder with the handout, noticing for the first time that the blanks on my handout were all filled in with heavy, dark slash marks. Loops had been drawn around each word, then filled in, then filled in some more, until the entire page was completely covered in ink and tiny rips. I quickly closed the folder. I had to get out of there. All I wanted to do was go home. I pictured the inside of my oven. If I left right away, I'd still have time to drop by the store and buy new cleaning gloves. But first, I had to move my feet.

,

Chapter 9

Rolling over in bed the next morning, I considered sleeping in and staying home from church. My back was aching from all the scrubbing I had done the day before. In addition to cleaning the oven, I had cleaned the fridge and all of the cabinets. I pulled out every plate, every bowl, every pot, and every pan. There was not a crumb or scratch in sight. Unfortunately, I still hadn't been able to sleep. Nightmares- or memories- consumed me all night. I laid my head back on my pillow, still damp from tears and sweat. After twenty-five years, I still wasn't free. I was still the same eight-year-old girl, praying that someone would rescue me. But for all the pain, it was only memories. I knew that I was stronger than my pain, stronger than the memories. So, I rolled myself over until my feet touched the floor and pushed myself up. I massaged my face, temples, cheeks, and chin hoping to relieve at least some of the tension that had taken up residence in my face. I considered lying back down for another twenty minutes, but then I would definitely miss worship, and I really needed to hear a good song that would lift the oppressive spirit that had seemed to follow me since that awful class the day before.

So, I pulled myself up and out of bed and into the shower. The warm water felt good on my face, back, and neck, but I wished that I hadn't talked myself out of buying the deluxe shower head weeks earlier. I dragged through my morning, but an hour later, I was finally ready to go. Considering how my Saturday night had ended and my day had begun, I was proud that I was only a few minutes late, and was even able to park in the second row of the church parking lot. Every step, though, felt forced. My heart felt heavy and full, and even though I had forced myself to come, I wasn't convinced that it would do any good or make any difference. I found my usual seat toward the back and fell into the plush pew.

As I sat down, there was polite clapping. I had missed the opening song, but it obviously wasn't one of those songs that brought the entire congregation to its feet. I followed along in the program the usher had handed me on entering. I didn't recognize the woman reading the announcements from the pulpit, but there was nothing special going on this week. The church would NOT be cancelling mid-week Bible Study regardless of the predicted snowstorm. April in Colorado could be beautiful and sunny. But it was just as likely to have a blizzard. You could never know for sure, and as much as weather forecasters tried, they were just as often wrong as they were right. One inch might easily turn into four, or it might just blow over altogether and bypass the city while dumping a few feet in the ski towns. The reader also encouraged everyone to come out to Friday night prayer service. I smiled to myself. What a night to have prayer! I wondered how many of the three hundred person congregation actually came out on a Friday night to *pray*. I could not imagine it was a packed crowd.

After the woman sat down, the choir stood up again and the soloist took the microphone. At the first bars of the song, all of the emotion that I had been trying to contain and repress all weekend boiled over.

"I never would have made it. Never *could* have made it…without you." The soloist belted out the words of the Marvin Sapp modern gospel classic while I immediately- and involuntarily- bowed my head and bawled. It's as if someone had turned up the water pressure to full power and then opened the valve. I didn't just cry, I sobbed, tears and goo spewing out from my face like a sprinkler, especially when the singer sang, "I would have lost my mind a long time ago." It was hard to believe that God was with me, that eight year old girl who was afraid to say yes, and afraid to say no. It was hard to believe that God was with me when I was called a liar. And, yet, if God hadn't been with me, I surely would have lost my mind a long time ago. I never would have been able to walk out of that room. I never would have been able to finish school, move away from my family, go to college, and start a new life in Colorado. I never would have been able to have a romantic relationship or deep friendships. All those years ago, and even in the years since, I could have curled up and died. I could have given in to the guilt and shame and ended my life. I could have turned to drugs or promiscuity. But somehow, someway, God had seen fit to preserve my life. I never would have made it without God. My body shook with long-repressed sobs that refused to be held in. I had survived by the grace of God. *Thank you, God,* I shouted with arms lifted high. The spirit was obviously at work in the room, as my shout rose to the rafters of the church with a dozen others. Oddly, I felt comforted knowing that I wasn't the only one who had experienced some profound pain and yet had lived to tell about it. And although I had no intention of telling anybody about my experience, not even at church, I knew I wasn't alone.

The soloist repeated the lines "I made it" maybe a hundred times, and each time I felt myself getting stronger. But I also felt something breaking in me. *I made it!* My story could have had a different ending, but I made it. Those three little words were my meditation, my prayer, and my worship. From my core, I could sing "I made it"- not because of something special about me, but because of the power of God.

As the song eventually began to wind down, so did my sobs. I took the handful of tissues that the usher kindly pressed into my hand and collapsed into my seat when the soloist took hers. I felt like I had just run a marathon. I was exhausted and spent. Even as I dried my face, my heart felt lighter and I finally felt like I could breathe again. This time when I pushed the memories down, they obeyed, and I was able to turn my attention fully to the pastor who stood to speak. I did not envy him having to come after that amazing solo, though. However, he rose to the challenge. I did not know if he adapted his message to build off the response of the song, or if the song had been chosen knowing the pastor's topic. Whatever the case, the pastor's message was a powerful follow-up.

As if the pastor had read my thoughts, he exhorted the congregants to not miss the presence of God while in the midst of trial. I thought about how hard it was for me to recognize God's presence in my trials and in my darkest hours. But I had made it, I reminded myself. I had survived everything the enemy had thrown at me and I was still standing.

"Has the answer to your prayers already come, but it's packaged in a way you do not prefer?" I thought about my prayers to have a family and to be a mother. It seemed like God was indeed answering my prayer through adoption. It wasn't the way I wanted, the way I hoped, but I promised myself I would not be one to pray for harvest, and yet curse the rain. I thought about the upcoming home study that I had yet to schedule and resolved to make an appointment the next day. I did not want to miss my opportunity, my answer to prayer, because of a few interviews and home visits. If I had made it this far, God would not leave me now.

"You don't have to live the way you've been living anymore. Come forward if you're in the need of prayer. Come forward if you're ready to lay down the burdens you've been carrying," the pastor entreated.

Without even thinking, I stepped out into the aisle, heart beating fast, knowing I had some burdens that I needed to lay down. But I could not make myself walk towards the front of the church. I hesitated at the end of the pew. I was halfway there. It would be so easy to turn left and walk the twenty feet or so to where the pastor and the prayer team stood expectantly. But, I was okay again. Everything that needed to be boxed up and pressed down and hidden away had been. There were no more flashbacks assaulting me behind my eyelids or in the recesses of my mind, so, instead, I turned right and headed toward the exit. I had gotten my blessing. The song had been beautiful and moving and had deeply touched me in a way that I probably had never experienced before. It was like a delicious appetizer followed by the perfect entrée. Between the song and the sermon, I was full. I felt confident that I was ready to tackle my week without any more breakdowns, nightmares, or late-night cleanings.

Chapter 10

The next morning, I walked into the office with energy and vigor. I was ready for the week and everything they had to throw at me. Sitting at my cubicle, I bopped a bit in my rolling chair. I was anxious for lunchtime when I'd be able to call the county to set up my first home study meeting. As my computer came to life, I pictured the onesie above my computer at home. Maybe I wasn't getting an infant, but I *would* become a mother.

"Hey, Sierra. What are you cheesing about?" Mikaela stopped at the opening of my cubicle, smiling knowingly at me. I didn't know what she thought she knew.

"Nothing. Why?"

"Mmmhmmm. Did you have a hot date this weekend?" Mikaela ran her fingers slowly along the top edge of my monitor.

I laughed. "No, no hot date. I guess I'm just in a good mood." And then I saw it. On Mikaela's left hand was a big, shiny rock. And not the kind of rock that women buy themselves, like I'd bought the expensive watch for myself for Valentine's Day. No, this was most definitely an engagement ring. An engagement ring from a man. An engagement ring from a man who loved her enough to declare his undying love and commitment. That kind of ring. I almost licked my teeth. And had that ring appeared even a week earlier, I might have done even more than that. But I was still full from the blessing I had received from church the day before; something in me really had changed. And so I smiled. I stood up. I hugged her. I oohed and ahhed and listened to every detail of how her boyfriend proposed. The crowd around my cubicle grew, and when someone suggested we go out after work to celebrate, I readily agreed. I was truly happy for Mikaela.

At lunch I made my call, then headed over to the break room. I knew everyone would be in there talking about Mikaela's engagement, and if I didn't join them I'd look like a jealous shrew, which I was not. Sure, Mikaela was only in her twenties, had only been dating her fiancée for a few months, and was probably living with him. And, yet here I was, doing everything God's way, and my hopes for a happily ever after seemed continually deferred. But I was not jealous. I had good news of my own. My home study was scheduled for three weeks. It was the last hurdle to being able to find out about Loveyouforever and starting my own family. Normally, I would have shared this update with Mikaela, but my news was nothing compared to hers.

We all sat at a round table in the break room, two microwaves whirring in the background.

"Did he get down on one knee?" one of the young interns asked with a dreamy look on her face.

"Yes," Mikaela gushed with an equally dreamy look, smiling down at her ring finger.

Someone asked where they were going on their honeymoon.

"Probably the Caribbean. Or maybe Costa Rica. I'd love to see a volcano." The conversation turned to ecotourism in Costa Rica, then adventure sports, and quickly to skiing. Somehow, the conversation at work always wound its way back to skiing, especially this time of year as spring was approaching. There were only so many weekends left, and even with a big snowstorm coming, winter activities would be done by April. I had gone skiing a few times when I had first moved to Colorado, but never really took to it. It always felt like something couples or families did together. I promised myself that once I brought Loveyouforever home, we would go skiing. I might even join a group, *Black Kids Ski, Too!* I must have had a faraway look on my face, because Mikaela turned to me.

"What's going on?"

I shrugged. "Not much. I just scheduled my home study."

Mikaela grabbed my hand. "That means you finished your classes?" I nodded, pleased that she remembered. "That's so cool. I'm really happy for you."

"Oh no," one of the guys said, "is Sierra getting married, too?" I guess they had reached their saturation point with wedding talk. Little did they know, it was just getting started, and they could count on wedding conversation for the next year, or as long as Mikaela's engagement lasted.

"No, I'm not getting married. I'm actually planning on adopting a little girl."

The oohs and ahhs repeated, this time with me at the center. Everyone was excited, but when I said that I'd be adopting from foster care, there were a few raised eyebrows. I ignored them, knowing that I, too, had done more than just raise my eyebrows when Carmen had brought up the whole idea. After a while, people started looking at their watches and we all headed back to our respective cubicles. I looked at my watch, too. The gaudy pink watch had grown on me. I didn't need a man or a fancy ring or a ski partner. I could- and would- have a full life, even without a husband.

On Wednesday, as I shoveled the heavy snow from my driveway, I was reconsidering my bold words. The snow was not a light powder, but heavy and wet. It was typical for this time of year. And while it wasn't exactly a blizzard, if I didn't shovel it now, it would turn into a thick block of ice. After an hour, I was only halfway done with my double driveway, which was fine since I only needed to clear one path behind my car. I contemplated going in for some hot tea and taking a break before starting on the sidewalk. It was cold, my fingers and toes were cold, and I wished there was someone I could hand the shovel off to. I looked up the street, hoping that a neighborhood teen would come walking by looking to make a few bucks. I would gladly part with $20 if it meant I could go inside. Just then, my phone vibrated in my pocket. I pulled it out, expecting to see Carmen's name pop up. She often texted or called during snowstorms to check on me. *Unknown.* I pressed the green button, tentatively saying hi, just in case I had to hang up on an overeager telemarketer.

"Hi, this is Crystal. I don't know if you remember me, but…"

I smiled. "Of course, I remember you! How are you? Have you had your baby yet?"

"No, I still have a couple more months." She paused, and I held my breath, waiting for her to say what she called to say. "Umm, I was just calling because…Well, you said I could call you if I ever needed anything."

"Of course! What's going on?" I asked, dragging the shovel behind me. I didn't want to stand out in the cold for the conversation.

"Well, my mom was supposed to pick me up, but she got stuck in the snow, so I'm stuck at this clinic and I was just hoping you could pick me up. It's too cold to wait for the bus, especially with all this snow."

I looked around. It would be hard getting out of the neighborhood until the snow melted, but the main streets might already be plowed and de-iced. But even if they weren't, I thought about being a 16-year-old girl, pregnant and cold with no one else to call.

"Where are you? I'll come pick you up." She gave me the cross streets of the clinic, and I was glad to stow the shovel away. Unfortunately, my prediction that the roads would already be cleared did not come to pass. Although the clinic was only ten miles away, it took over an hour to get there. The roads were icy and slick, so everyone was moving at a snail's pace. I passed dozens of cars that had spun out or slid off the road. And the snow was still coming down. My own tires slid as I approached every intersection. Having a four-wheel drive was practically mandatory in Colorado, but it didn't protect from patches of ice on the road. Finally, I reached the clinic and a cold, shivering Crystal climbed in the car.

When I had first met Crystal, I had been struck by how at peace she seemed. Now, just a couple months later, she looked tired. There were puffy, dark circles under her eyes. Her belly was much bigger, and she kept rubbing her lower back. She looked like she was ready to explode.

"How far along are you?" I asked.

"I'm seven months," she said with a weak smile. "I know, I know. I gained a lot of weight. People have been asking when I'm due since I was like four months pregnant. I'm gonna lose it quick, though."

"What did the doctor say?"

"I don't know," Crystal shrugged. "Nothing new. 'Eat right. Take your vitamins.'" Crystal impersonated a stern voice, which I imagined to be her doctor.

"That's good advice."

"Yeah, but it's not helping with the morning sickness."

"Still? I thought that was mostly during the first trimester."

"That's what they say, but I'm sick every day! You don't even know how bad it sucks. I hate being pregnant." Gone was the bubbly girl I had met in February. In her place was an exhausted pregnant woman. "And then he had enough nerve to give me this sh-." Crystal looked at me chagrined, like I was the profanity police. "Excuse my language. He gave me this *crap* about adoption." In the dark, I could read the title of the pamphlet that Crystal held up: "Making a Birth Plan: A Loving Choice".

I wanted to ask if she had ever *really* considered it, and what adoption might mean for her unborn child. I thought about Loveyouforever's mom. Had anyone sat down with her and talked to her about her options?

"There's no way I would give my baby to a stranger. That's just no." Crystal shook her head, answering the question I wanted to ask. She looked out the window and I squinted out the front windshield. The rapid swish of the windshield wipers was the only noise in the car for several minutes.

I remembered how to get to Crystal's apartment, so there was no need to say anything. I thought about keeping it positive and telling her how meeting her had inspired me to adopt. But I also wanted to be brutally honest and tell her that maybe she should consider the doctor's advice. Instead, I said nothing and focused on the road ahead of me. Crystal was the first to break the silence.

"You know, you should be the one having this baby, not me." I laughed nervously, glancing at Crystal. Did she know what she was saying? Was she just joking? I willed my heart to slow down, and forced a smile.

"Oh, really? And how do you know I don't already have a house full of kids?"

"Your car is too clean," she smirked.

I laughed. I didn't know if that was a backhanded compliment, but she was right. Carmen's car was always a mess of crumbs, toys, and booster seats. My car, on the other hand, looked the same as it had the day I drove it off the lot.

After nearly sliding into several rear ends, I finally pulled up to the curb in front of Crystal's apartment. We hugged as she got out of the car and promised to keep in touch. All the way home, the only thing I could think about was Crystal's glib comment that I should be the one having a baby, not her. I wasn't surprised when she called me a week later, asking if I could take her to her appointment because her mom's car was still out of commission from the snowstorm. Apparently, the doctor wanted to see her weekly. Since she had gained so much weight, she was considered a "high-risk" pregnancy and was at risk of developing gestational diabetes. I looked up the term on the Internet once we got off the phone. I also looked up foods that were good for morning sickness. When I went to the grocery store, I picked up a few items that might help her, too, like ginger candy, and also trail mix, which could be high in protein and low in sugar. I texted her to be sure she wasn't allergic to nuts.

When I picked her up for her next appointment, I handed her the bag of snacks. The streets were clear and what had taken hours the week before, only took twenty-five minutes. The next week, her mom was busy again, so I drove her to her next appointment, too. That week, I gave her a grocery bag full of healthy pregnancy-friendly treats that I'd found online. When I wasn't taking Crystal to appointments, I was praying and cleaning. I prayed and cleaned and prayed and cleaned my way through my house. I took out all the African décor and delicate trinkets from the guest room and exchanged them for the stuffed animals I had bought during the post-

Valentine's Day sales. The bright pink and red bears really didn't go with the blue and green theme in the room, but I wanted to go shopping with Loveyouforever and let her pick out her own decorations. I wanted her to be able to make it her home. I hoped the home study worker would not dock me for not having the room completely decorated. But even as I was making the full-size bed in the guest room for the hundredth time, I pictured replacing it with a crib. I tried not to let myself get too excited, but Crystal's words slowly played over and over in my head: *You should be having this baby, not me.* Maybe Crystal didn't want to give her baby up for adoption to a stranger, but maybe she would give her baby to me. I didn't know what she was planning to do, but I knew that God was doing something amazing and I was ready to accept whichever blessing the Lord had in store for me.

REY SIRAKAVIT

Chapter 11

Finally, the day had arrived. I swiveled in my office chair with a smile on my face. I was typing in code as fast as my fingers would move. I was in a groove. I remembered my conversation with my adoption class "besties", Yvette and Jessica. We had been so anxious about the home study, and yet here I was, not an ounce of tension. In just a few short months, I felt like two very real opportunities were all of a sudden in front of me. Although I still hadn't heard anything more about Loveyouforever, I felt drawn to her. Every time I prayed for her, I felt like I was praying for my own child, not a stranger. I didn't know if it was possible to fall in love with someone you'd never met, but I guess that's what pregnant women experience every day. Their hearts fill to overflowing for a creature whose face they've never seen, whose hand they've never held. But, their hearts are connected, as mine was connected to Loveyouforever.

On the other hand, there was Crystal. Everyday her belly grew more and more, and from being her personal chauffeur the past few weeks, I could see that the pregnancy was taking its toll on her, and all the support she thought she'd have, was not materializing. The baby had yet to be born, but Crystal was already experiencing the realization of what having a baby would entail. The fairy tale was being replaced by cold hard reality. Still, Crystal hadn't said anything more about me adopting her baby, but I knew that she was starting to trust me. I was no longer just a caring stranger who had helped her out during a snowstorm, or given her a few rides. We were becoming friends.

And, so, with both of these options before me I felt a peace in my spirit that "surpasses all understanding". I didn't know how God was going to work it all out, but I felt giddy with anticipation.

Positivity and confidence carried me through my workday, carried me through the ongoing news about Mikaela's wedding plans, and carried me through the awful Denver rush hour traffic. I practically glided into my house after work, doing one final pass through the house, smoothing pillows and wiping away any dust particles that had settled during the day. I pulled out a tray of veggies and glasses for water. I was ready. I sent a quick text to Yvette and Jessica, asking for their prayers while I counted down the minutes, then seconds, for the home study worker to arrive.

The doorbell rang and it was show time.

I greeted the social worker, Pamela Wilson, and invited her inside. She was an older woman with pale, dry skin, and what seemed to be a glued-on frown. She shook my hand limply and almost immediately started taking notes on a large legal pad. I was unmoved.

Pamela began by describing the process. We would meet 3-4 times over the next few months, and if I was going to be late or had to cancel, I had to inform her within 72 hours. Otherwise, I would be charged a no-show fee. What an intro.

"My purpose is to get to know you and the kind of family you would create for a child." She reminded me of a drill sergeant-sans the uniform-all business and formality. I gave her my warmest smile, silently inviting her to relax. Instead, she raised an eyebrow and wrote something else on her notepad. Still, I was not discouraged.

Within minutes, though, all my fears rushed back. Pamela was truly a viper in a polyester suit. She fired hypothetical, worst-case-scenario, doomsday questions at me and I could feel myself sinking.

"Do you expect your adopted child to take your name? What if they refuse to? What's your income? Is it enough to support a child all their life? What would happen if you lost your job? How would you support a child, then? Are you intending to use the adoption stipend to cover your living expenses?"

My honest answers did not seem to be honest enough for her. And was my positivity coming across as naiveté? Before I knew it, I was second-guessing myself, and every word I uttered felt canned and rehearsed. Instead of seeming composed, I was haphazardly regurgitating words and phrases I'd learned about trauma and parenting from the adoption class, barely forming a coherent thought or sentence. Ms. Wilson was not trying to make this easy for me. Deeper and deeper she went, until she pulled out my application. She flipped to a section toward the back and my heart sank. I took a sip of water, waiting for the next question, my heart beating faster than ever. *Be with me, Lord*, I silently prayed.

"It's very important to understand a prospective adoptive parent's childhood when considering how emotionally and mentally prepared they are to adopt. You, Ms. Harris, did not even attempt to complete this part of the application." The way she said "Ms. Harris" felt like a curse word. The hair on my neck and arms stood on end. I froze with impending dread. But she was not done.

"And from talking with you today, it is apparent to me that you have no experience and are trying to hide something. Your answers are completely superficial. In all honesty, I cannot imagine that your home study will be approved." Try as I might, I could not contain my frustration.

"You know, *Ms. Wilson*," I began, with the same intonation that she had used, "from the moment you came in tonight, you've been extremely hostile. This hasn't felt like a friendly interview. It's been an interrogation. Don't you want stable, healthy adoptive parents for all these kids who are in the system?" I looked pointedly at her, willing her to deny my accusation. "To be honest, this whole experience has been a turn-off."

"Oh, really? It's a 'turn-off'?" Pamela Wilson snapped. "Do you want to know what's really a turn-off? Having people like you think they can just waltz in and rescue a child." Ms. Wilson held up her fingers, making air quotation marks around the word "rescue".

"Excuse me? People like me?" I stood to my feet. I hoped she wasn't saying what I thought she was.

"Yes. You obviously don't take this very seriously at all." At hearing this, I almost dropped my glass. And it wouldn't have been accidental, either.

"How dare you say that I don't take this seriously!" Now, my blood was boiling. "I've been working on this for months. I've taken all the classes, I've been reading books, I've done a ton of research on your website. I'm completely turning over my home to welcome a child. And for what? So you can insult me? I will be contacting your supervisor tomorrow morning." I inched towards the door, hoping she would take the hint. This meeting was obviously over.

The worker looked as upset as I felt. "Look, I don't mean to be harsh, but until you're ready to deal with your issues, you will not pass this home study. So, I don't know what you're trying to hide, I don't know if you need to work through some of your issues in therapy, but I cannot in good conscience recommend you adopt until something drastic changes."

I walked to the door and opened it. Ms. Wilson picked up her legal pad, file folders, pens and stuffed them into her shoulder bag. I didn't care that the cold air was whipping through the living room. I just wanted this woman out of my house as quickly as possible.

It took several minutes after *Ms. Wilson* left for me to regain my calm. My heart was still racing. The insult! I picked up my phone. I wanted to call Carmen, but she'd be in the middle of putting dinner on the table for her kids. I thought about calling Yvette or Jessica, but I didn't want to scare them. They were already nervous enough about their own home studies without adding my horror story to their anxiety. So, I turned toward my office. I needed to pray.

I pulled Loveyouforever's profile from my office door. The red skunk onesie was still hanging over my computer, and I reached up and pulled it down. I laid both of them on the office desk. I re-read Loveyouforever's profile. I stroked the faux fur on the onesie as I had done a hundred times before. And I started to laugh.

REY SIRAKAVIT

START PRAYING

Chapter 12

The next morning, I emailed my supervisor letting her know that I would be in a little late. There was a phone call I needed to make, and depending on how it went, I didn't want to be walking around the office with a soggy face or steaming temples. I was still angry and shocked from my home study meeting the night before, but at the same time, I also felt peace. Was this a sign that Crystal was going to ask me to adopt her baby? I thought of that old saying, "When God closes one door, he opens a window somewhere else." I punched in the number to the county hotline, and waited impatiently to leave a message requesting a call back. By the time someone finally called me back, it was after lunch and I'd already decided to just take the day off. To my surprise, it was Ms. Pamela Wilson herself. She couldn't have heard from her supervisor yet, because I hadn't been able to reach anyone and had only left a few vague messages, hoping that her supervisor would take the bait and call me back. Just hearing her voice, though, my chest constricted and all the anger from the night before clawed at my skin. I was ready for another lecture about the sanctity of adoption, but instead of continuing the same themes from the night before, she immediately apologized.

"I'm sorry about my behavior last night," and "That shouldn't have happened." It was all quite calm, professional, and rehearsed,

95

much like she had accused me. Until she paused. I was too surprised to respond right away, and so the silence stretched out like a wet sheet on a clothesline. I wished I could see her face and read her eyes. Was she wearing the same frown? I wondered what had even compelled her to call me. I held my breath, waiting for her to say something, anything. I wasn't sure if she would ever speak again or had hung up. When she finally inhaled, I exhaled.

"It's no excuse, but yesterday was awful." She paused again, but this time I heard her swallow. "I found out from a colleague that two families I had approved have recently had their adopted children removed due to allegations of abuse." Ms. Wilson's voice broke on the word *abuse*. "At the time, I had some concerns that I just dismissed because…no family is perfect. But there were some signs I shouldn't have ignored." Her voice cracked, and I could tell that the cold and critical Ms. Wilson was crying. Was she in her office with her door closed? Or maybe, like me, she'd taken the day off, knowing that her emotions were raw and ready to spill over. She paused again, controlling herself.

"But, it was completely unprofessional of me to say, after just one meeting, that your home study would not be approved. I will tell you, though, that raising a child from foster care can open wounds you never knew you had. And if you haven't dealt with them, it could be a disaster for you and for your child. Please take my advice and get some counseling to deal with your issues. Come back in six months and we'll finish the home study then. There's no rush."

Ms. Wilson's words hung in the air, waiting for me to respond. To ask me to wait for six months showed that Ms. Wilson did not have the same sense of urgency as a foster child in the system. I thought about Loveyouforever. The reasons she gave for wanting me to wait were exactly why I felt the need to move quickly. Loveyouforever needed me now, not in six months. God only knew what she was experiencing in her foster home. Yet, here was Ms. Wilson still threatening to deny my home study if I didn't start counseling. I pictured myself doing as she said, going to counseling, digging up old wounds. And, for what? I was okay. I had a good job, I had good friends, and a nice house. I didn't need someone taking me back to the awful past that I had worked so hard to leave *in the past*. I couldn't do it.

"Look, I won't close your file, I'll just put it on the bottom of my stack."

Not knowing what else I could or should say, I reluctantly agreed. I was sorry for those families whose children had been removed, sorrier for those children, but their stories weren't mine. I would never abuse a child. And so I hung up the phone, knowing that I would not be adopting through foster care, knowing that I would not be adopting Loveyouforever. And my heart broke. I fingered the now crinkled paper that her profile was printed on, with the grayed-out square where her picture should have been. To say I was disappointed was an understatement. My disappointment was so tangible it felt like someone had ripped my heart from my body. I knew that if God was saying no to Loveyouforever, then he must be saying yes to Crystal's baby, but that was no easy consolation. My heart was big enough to love both of these children, and one of them was being torn from me.

This time after talking with Ms. Wilson, there was no laughter. I sank to my knees in the middle of the kitchen with my face on the floor, crying about what could have been, crying about an unfulfilled promise.

I don't understand, Lord! Why do you keep telling me no?

I sat on the tile floor with my knees folded under me and my hands rubbing against the ground.

I'm not going to move until I hear from you, Lord.

The chorus of an old gospel song came to my mind and I sang it out through my tears in a hoarse, raspy voice with lifted hands.

Speak, Lord.

I don't know how long I knelt in the middle of the kitchen, wiping my face on my sleeve. Eventually the sun faded and it was dark inside. I had no more words to say, so I just knelt. And waited.

Speak to me, Lord. Speak Lord.

And, then, my phone rang.

It was Crystal.

* * *

As we wove through the aisles of the big box baby store, I was a little overwhelmed. First of all, the lights were ridiculously bright, especially for someone who had spent the better part of the day lying on the floor crying in the dark. Not only did the lights burn my eyes, but I knew my face must be puffy- even after the quick shower I'd had. On top of that, the store was huge. There were a hundred aisles with every kind of baby item for every kind of budget. There were baby bottles and bottle liners and bottle warmers and bottle sterilizers and even special baby bottle drying racks that looked like rubber grass.

Crystal's birthday/baby shower was fast approaching, and she wanted to create her registry. So we walked up and down aisles, sat in recliners, squeezed nursing pillows, pulled and pushed drawers open and closed. She didn't really know what she needed, so we took the generic list from the customer service rep and started there. The list had all the basics and more.

Crystal said she was going to get her cousin's old stroller, so she didn't need that. But, her cousin had been a bit of a flake, so maybe she did need one. Crystal stood with the registry gun in her hand, indecisiveness etched on her face like the ridges of Pike's Peak. She bit her lower lip.

"Look, why don't you just get it? If you don't need it after all, the clerk said you can return anything from your registry, even if you don't have the receipt."

Crystal pointed and squeezed the plastic trigger. The lines in her forehead smoothed out and we moved on. Next there was the baby carrier. Crystal really wanted a cheap backpack-looking thing with a funky -"fun"- design: purple and silver lightning bolts interspersed with pink skulls. It looked like a baby carrier for teen moms. But the ergonomically designed one with adjustable straps that "grow with the baby" looked best to me. Crystal took the adult one and put it back on the rack, saying it looked "boring", then scanned her high school version. I tried not to roll my eyes. And if that wasn't bad enough, there was the crib. I quickly fell in love with a beautiful oak crib with storage drawers at the bottom. It was rated E for safety, the highest rating for cribs. I pictured the crib across the room from the window with the early morning sun casting a gentle glow on it. It would fit just perfectly. Crystal walked by the crib and pointed her gun at a cheap, plastic play yard, a foldable crib that was supposedly good for babies and toddlers. I sighed. She seemed to be just picking things at random. Nothing matched or coordinated. And while the rational part of my mind knew that choosing a consistent color scheme or theme were not the most important factors in raising a happy and healthy baby, it annoyed me nonetheless. How could she be so cavalier? I wanted to wail against her and all the other accidental mommy-to-bes who were clueless about raising a baby. I glanced at my watch. It was past dinnertime. Maybe I was just hungry and cranky from an emotionally exhausting day. But maybe it was also true that Crystal was completely unprepared to be a mother. Did she not deserve to be a mom just because she was young? Because she was poor? Or, because I wanted her baby? As hard as I tried to wrap my mind around it, it just didn't seem fair that God had said no to marriage for me, then no to adoption, but yes to a 16-going-on-17-year-old girl. But maybe this was all part of God's plan. Knowing that Crystal wasn't ready to be a mother, knowing that she wouldn't give her baby to a stranger, maybe God had chosen me to adopt her baby. Maybe that's why our lives were becoming more and more entwined. Maybe all I had to do was be patient and continue to build trust with her and she would give me her baby. So what if she picked out mismatched décor? So what if she got the play yard and the funky baby carrier if I was going to be the one bringing the baby home? For the first time all day, I smiled. I teased her about the mismatched items. I sat beside her in every glider. I bought her more trail mix to snack on and keep the "morning sickness" away.

And in the back of my mind, I made my own list. I pictured myself hanging gray and purple owl curtains and spreading out the coordinating crib sheets in the beautiful oak crib. They even had the perfect owl wall hanging. I picked out a diaper bag, changing table, stroller, and car seat. When I came back, or went online, I knew exactly what I would get. And no one would accuse me of allowing my newborn to begin life with a haphazard assortment of mismatched items.

Crystal must have picked up on my lightened mood because when I offered to take her out to dinner once we were all done, she said, "Are you finally out of your funk? You were walking around here like your dog died."

"It was a hard day," I admitted.

"Hard?" Crystal smacked her lips. "What's so hard about your life? You don't have any kids, no family, you've got plenty of money."

"Doesn't mean I don't have problems," I responded sharply.

"Okay, sorry. No offense. I'm just saying, your life seems pretty perfect to me."

I thought about what she said. My life seemed perfect? I had to laugh. If only she knew the truth. "Well, everyone has problems. But I know God is in control. So, I'm not gonna worry about it. At least not any more tonight. So, where do you wanna eat? Anywhere you want. My treat."

"Are you sure?" Before I could stipulate no expensive restaurants from Restaurant Week, Crystal continued, "I've been craving brats."

"Brats?"

"Yeah, there's this place that has spicy brats with fried onions on 'em." Crystal's eyes rolled back in her head. "Better than sex."

I raised my eyebrows. "Really?"

"Umm-hmm. You know what I mean?"

I thought about saying, *No, I don't know what you mean because I am the world's oldest virgin who hasn't taken a vow of celibacy*, but instead I just smiled knowingly like I always did when I wasn't in the mood to tell all my business.

"Okay, brats it is." Thirty minutes later, we were eating the most delicious, fancy hot dogs I had ever eaten. But were they better than sex? I couldn't say. If they were, I would be incredibly disappointed.

REY SIRAKAVIT

Chapter 13

For the next few weeks, I vacillated between being confident that Crystal was going to give me her baby and wondering whether I should just start therapy. But I knew I was not going to pay someone to tell them all about my problems that had happened years ago, just like Crystal wasn't going to give her baby to someone she didn't know or trust. And, I felt more and more assured every day that Crystal didn't want to keep her baby. The pregnancy was wearing her out. Her so-called family "support" had all but dwindled away. And to top it off, she had no one to go to birthing classes with.

Crystal and I had begun texting each other.

TO CRYSTAL:

When do your birth classes begin?

FROM CRYSTAL:

I don't know. Not doing it anyway.

TO CRYSTAL:

What do you mean? Why not?

FROM CRYSTAL:

Nobody to do it with

Crystal had never mentioned the boy who'd gotten her pregnant, but I knew that he wasn't involved and wasn't an option.

TO CRYSTAL:
What about your mom?

FROM CRYSTAL:
NOOOOOOO! I'm not taking birthing classes with my MOM.
smh
ugh
Besides, she's busy.

It seemed like Crystal's mom was always busy. Ever since the snowstorm, she'd been unable, or unwilling, to take Crystal to any of her doctor's appointments or even shopping.

TO CRYSTAL:
Well, what about your cousin?

FROM CRYSTAL:
She don't wanna do it. Says I need to get my baby daddy to step up.
But I'm not even gonna waste my time asking him.
For every two words I typed, it seemed like Crystal typed 20. I could barely keep up.
I decided to change the topic.

TO CRYSTAL:
Is the plan still for your mom to watch the baby for you while you work?

FROM CRYSTAL:

Yeah, I guess.

TO CRYSTAL:

Well, if you really don't have anybody else, I'd be happy to go with you.

FROM CRYSTAL:

Really????? Y?

Why? I didn't really have an answer, at least not an answer she was ready to hear. I stared at the phone, hoping that God would just type my response for me. *Crystal, this is the Almighty. You will give birth to a child, and shall call its name....*What? Crystal still didn't know what she was having. My fingers finally started moving again.

TO CRYSTAL:

You shouldn't have to go through this alone.

And that was true. I couldn't imagine not having anyone to call on. Even though I didn't keep in touch with my family, I had my best friend Carmen and her family, my good friend from work Mikaela, the ladies from the adoption class, and many friends from church. I could think of at least a dozen people I could call on. And that's how I wound up sitting on the floor in yoga pants with a pregnant 16-year-old girl seated between my legs.

I rubbed Crystal's back, practiced breathing techniques, and helped her try different positions to minimize birthing pain. The instructor encouraged all the moms-to-be to practice each of the techniques, whether they were planning to have a natural childbirth, an epidural, or a C-section.

From the beginning, Crystal had insisted she wanted a C-section. "I'm not trying to go through all that pain. They can just cut this baby out of me." Yet, she rolled to her knees and lifted herself up on her palms, arching her back rhythmically and hee-hee-heed, mirroring the instructor. There she was, stretching and pushing herself.

I swallowed, hoping to push the feelings away.

Crystal paused, looking at me over her shoulder. "Are you okay? Are you crying?"

I shook my head, smiled, and swiped quickly at my eye. "I'm just...I'm really proud of you. You're doing great."

"I thought it was pregnant women who were supposed to be crying all the time for no reason!" Suddenly, Crystal's eyes bulged. "The baby's kicking!" She grabbed my hand and for a second, I didn't feel anything, but then there it was. My hand jumped against her tee shirt.

"What's it doing in there?"

"Jumping jacks." Crystal shook her head ruefully.

"Does it hurt?"

"Not really. It's mostly uncomfortable." This time, Crystal looked away and I could tell she was trying to hold back tears, too. "Sierra, thank you again for coming with me. You really didn't have to do this. Give me your phone."

I raised my eyebrows, but complied.

"I'm putting the baby's due date in your phone, so you won't forget about us."

Before I could respond, the instructor interrupted and pushed a bowl of ice cubes toward us. "Try to keep your hand in the bowl for at least 60 seconds," she said. This was supposed to give the moms a small taste of the pain they would experience during labor.

I poked the ice with my index finger. Crystal reached her whole hand in, but after 19 seconds she grimaced, pulling her hand out.

"Oh my God, that's cold!" She rubbed her fingers together, then nodded at me.

"It's ice," I laughed. "Of course it's cold."

"No, but it like legit hurts. You do it, if you don't believe me." Crystal held the bowl out to me. All around me, other women were gritting their teeth as they submerged their hands into their icy baths. I plunged my hand into the bowl that Crystal held out to me. My hand quickly numbed, and I wanted to pull it out.

"Try to find an object to focus on. That will help you so you're not just focused on the pain." The instructor walked by, giving me an encouraging pat on the back. My eyes locked onto my pink watch, which was sticking out above the line of ice. I didn't look at the second hand, or the minute hand; instead, I stared at the solitary diamond in the center of the watch face. It shined and sparkled and reminded me that while my path was not straight, I didn't need a husband to reach my dream of being a mom. What did they say about coal and diamonds and pressure? I would be the piece of coal; I would withstand the pressure. I would not give up or give in. No matter how long it took, I would not give up on my dream to be a mom. I flexed my fingers and clenched my hand into a fist. I could feel the cold and the pain, but I was stronger than it.

Eventually, Crystal patted me on the back. Around the room, I could see other moms-to-be were already all dried up. Crystal passed me a towel, with a look of admiration on her face. "Man, you should be the one having this baby," she muttered. Taking the towel she held out, I couldn't agree more.

* * *

"Sierra, are you crazy?"

Carmen and I were once again sitting in our favorite coffee shop. Carmen needed to get out of the house, and I needed a hot chai. The spring weather was flip-flopping from the low 70s to the high 40s on a day-to-day basis, and a sweet, hot drink sounded divine. I took a sip, pretending not to hear or understand.

"Sierra, you don't even know this girl. Doesn't she have family to help her?"

I shook my head no, keeping my face close to my steaming mug.

"So, you went to her birthing class with her? I don't know. That just seems so intimate. You're the godmother to both of my babies, but you didn't go to my birthing classes with me."

I lifted my eyebrows. "You're married. That's what your husband is for."

"So, she doesn't have anybody? No boyfriend, no baby daddy, no mom? Nobody?" Carmen sounded incredulous.

"I already told you, no one who's willing to step up."

Carmen bit her lip.

"Don't get mad, but can I ask you a question?"

I could see her eyebrows knit, and I knew what she was going to say before she even said it.

"Are you just doing all this because you think she might let you adopt her baby?"

I sipped my chai while I thought about how I wanted to respond. Did she mean all the shopping, rides, texting, and birthing class? Or, the constant praying? Either way, I wanted to say yes, obviously, but I knew that was the wrong answer. I didn't want to seem like I was scheming or manipulating, not even to my best friend. But I also didn't think she would understand why I felt so certain that I was doing the right thing. So, I went with a half-truth.

"I don't know." I shrugged. I stared off at the stage, at the wall of books, everywhere but at Carmen. What was so wrong about wanting to adopt a child whose mother couldn't take care of them? What was wrong about helping a young girl who had no other help?

"I've been praying so much for this girl and her baby, and I just feel like God brought her into my life for a reason. I mean, it was from meeting her that I even started thinking about adoption."

Carmen's lips parted for a second. "Have you thought more about going to counseling like the social worker suggested?"

I could feel Carmen's eyes trying to lock with mine, but I avoided her gaze. Here she was, once again, trying to play the role of the spiritual mentor. Well, God could talk to me just as much as he could talk to her.

"Why would I go to counseling? For them to tell me I had a crappy childhood? Well guess what? I already know that. It's pointless. And if Crystal gives me her baby, I won't need a home study, just a good adoption lawyer."

Carmen's face crinkled at my words. "Something about this whole thing just isn't sitting right in my spirit."

I responded quickly, before I could check my words or censor myself. "Well, that's odd because I'm feeling a lot of peace in my spirit. And at the end of the day, that's really all that matters." I took a breath, trying to change my tone. I really didn't want to fight with my best friend. She was smart and funny and a woman of faith. But she didn't know everything, and I was an adult with my own relationship with God. I needed her to understand that.

"You know I love you, but if you can't respect my decision, then let's change the subject. How are my god-babies doing?" I pretended to smile. And I really did want to hear about the kids and their latest antics. I had been so busy with the adoption classes–and then with Crystal–that I really hadn't been able to spend as much time with them as I generally did.

Carmen allowed me to change the subject, telling me about trying to take a shower and one of the kids spilling sticky juice all over her right after she got out. We both smiled half-heartedly at the story.

Even as Carmen continued talking, my mind replayed Crystal's words and hints. There were times when I was absolutely certain that she was going to ask me to adopt her baby. But we had never talked about it. And I wasn't certain. As much as I hated to admit it, the anxiety, the uncertainty, the not knowing was killing me. Crystal had me on pins and needles. But that was something I would never be able to share with my best friend.

Chapter 14

For some reason, I waited until the night before Crystal's baby shower to go shopping for her gift. It was past the time where I could buy anything online, so I returned to the baby depot where Crystal had registered. Of the dozens of things on her list, only one had been purchased. The backpack. I rolled my eyes. Walking through the aisles, I felt torn. What was the point in having a baby shower? In just a few weeks, Crystal would be handing her baby over to me, so why even have a shower? What would she need? Wouldn't any gift she received just serve as a reminder of the child she had given up? And, truth be told, there wasn't much on the list that I would want passed along to me. Except a car seat. I wouldn't be able to take a baby home without a car seat. For the first time since entering the store, I smiled.

Crystal had registered for the cheapest basic model, a boring black and gray model with stiff plastic armrests and plasticky fabric lining. I quickly stepped around it to see what else the store had. Besides the thousand-dollar crib, which I had been wanting from the first moment Crystal and I had entered the baby warehouse and which I definitely was not going to buy, getting a car seat was a great choice. Somehow, I got into a conversation with the very pregnant mom-to-be next to me who was looking at the same car seat.

"Okay, this one has to be good. It has the word 'safety' in its name and it says it has over '70 safety features, comfy armrests that pivot, and thick, luxe lining'," I said reading the side of the box. I pulled the one on display off the shelf, testing just how comfortable and easy to use it really was. I clicked and unclicked every button, ran my fingers over the fabric, knocked on the frame. I squeezed the pillowy headrest. At that moment, I could have been a paid spokesperson, except I wasn't getting paid and I, hopefully, didn't have that trademark plastic grin. Still, the mom-to-be wasn't sold, and walked off with a cheaper car seat.

After she was long gone, I still stared at it. The design was bold, modern, and sleek. Unlike the one on the registry, I could picture it perfectly in the back of my SUV. And the colors were gender neutral, since Crystal still didn't know the sex of the baby. I carried the floor model back and forth up the aisle, testing it for comfort and portability. I loved it. Although it was pricey, it was exactly what I would want.

But would Crystal?

At that thought, I set the car seat down on the ground in the middle of the aisle and just stared at it. Could I picture this soon-to-be 17-year-old mom wielding this luxury car seat on the bus? Or, hauled from one borrowed car to another? With its multi-point harness system, it would be a veritable nightmare to load and unload from the backseat of whomever was giving her a ride.

I tried to think back to the kind of stroller Crystal said her cousin would give her, and sure enough it matched the car seat from the registry. With a sigh, I put the Cadillac of car seats back on the shelf, and grabbed the much lighter one from the registry. I also chose a board book featuring an African American baby on the cover. It was a sweet empowering story, and perfect for chubby little fingers. Lastly, I grabbed a onesie with a funny saying, because no matter how much you spend at a baby shower, it's the onesies with funny sayings that get the most attention. With a heavy heart, I pushed my cart toward the checkout, leaving the beautiful car seat behind.

I was minding my own business, standing in line, ready to check out, when a sales display caught my eye: *40% OFF ALL CRIBS*.

Immediately, I wheeled my cart out of the line and toward the crib section which I had purposely avoided earlier.

And there it was, the beautiful, thousand-dollar oak crib, marked down to six hundred dollars! While I couldn't afford the $35,000 infant adoption price tag, six hundred dollars for a crib wasn't going to break the bank.

Be practical, I told myself, looking back at the car seat I had already picked out.

Be generous, I rebutted, stroking the glossy crib railings and fluted posts. I don't know how long I stood there, staring at the ridiculously overpriced crib with its tufted upholstery. I read and re-read the side of the box: converts from infant crib to toddler bed to full-size bed. It also had a changing table and drawers for storage. And it was on sale. And wasn't it just as ridiculous to buy a car seat, but not a crib? *And it was on sale!* And I could always bring it back. So, I flagged down an employee and told them I wanted the crib.

I hoped I wasn't like one of those over-eager women who buy a wedding dress before they're even dating. I wrapped my hand around my wrist. Just like I didn't need a man to buy myself an unnecessary piece of jewelry for Valentine's Day, I also didn't need a baby to buy a crib. Because I was under no pretext that I was going to give that crib to Crystal. That crib was going home with me, into the guest room that would soon be transformed into a beautiful nursery.

But instead of feeling that boost of dopamine that I usually had after going shopping, I felt shame.

My mood did not improve as I stared at the car seat and crib in the back of my trunk. Both boxes were huge, and I had had to drop the back seats in order to get them to fit. My mood did not improve as I lugged the heavy, unwieldy boxes out of said trunk, up the driveway, and into the living room. Nor did it improve when I wrapped one box in bright yellow paper, and stored the other in the guest room. So, I prayed. Or vented. But I still couldn't kick my gloomy mood. It was not until I walked into Crystal's cousin's living room the next afternoon that my mood began to lift.

It was a beautiful spring day; in fact, it felt more like summer than spring. The sun was strong, and the temperature was climbing. I was glad to be in a sleeveless sundress. Loud music met me on the steps. I didn't recognize the artist, but it was something popular and trendy and filled with expletives. It didn't strike me as baby shower music, but not 17-year-old party music, either.

A cheerful cellophane sign on the front door said "Welcome," so I entered without knocking. The door opened into a dark living room. A couch was set up facing the door, and kitchen chairs lined the other wall. On the other side of the living room was the kitchen. There was a round table and a baker's rack. Crystal was seated in the corner of the living room, crying, being comforted by about six other girls around her age. They were all wearing various shades and styles of the same uniform: tight tank top with spaghetti straps and short shorts. Each of the girls' brightly colored bras peaked from beneath their tanks. Apparently, this was the style.

The woman who I assumed was Crystal's mom sat in the opposite corner on the couch. She was a slightly older version of Crystal, with the same eyes and nose. The only difference was the cigarette hanging from her mouth. Besides her, I didn't see any other adults.

There was a tall tower of boxes of diapers by the wall, so I dropped the wrapped car seat next to it. Before I could turn around, I felt arms arounds my shoulders and a big bump in my back. Crystal. I returned her hug.

"I'm so glad you're here!" she rasped.

"Of course! I wouldn't have missed this for the world. What's wrong?"

Crystal wiped her nose with the back of her hand and I waited. Had she gotten into a fight with her mom? Or cousin?

"I don't know. Nothing's turned out the way it was supposed to be." For months, Crystal had been talking about the baby shower/birthday party that her cousin was going to throw for her. But from the placement of the balloons to the menu, she had wound up doing "everything" while her cousin had flaked. In fact, her cousin had disappeared an hour earlier and still hadn't returned, leaving Crystal to cook the hot dogs for the party in the microwave by herself.

"Your friends didn't come for the food; they came to celebrate you! I know everything hasn't turned out the way you wanted, but it's gonna be okay. We can play a few games, open your gifts, and just have a good time."

From the corner of my eye, I could still see Crystal's mom puffing on her cigarette, staring off into space and Crystal's friends milling around the kitchen. How many people did it take to set out a plate of hot dogs and a bowl of nacho chips? I could understand why Crystal was so disappointed. This *was* turning out to be a sad party.

"Where did your cousin go?"

"To pick up this girl who was gonna do the games."

I looked at my watch. It was only twenty past, but with every minute that passed, Crystal was only going to freak out more. My first instinct was to go into the kitchen and help organize whatever was going on in there, but the need for respect won out.

"Crystal, introduce me to your mom."

Crystal rolled her eyes, but complied. "Mom, this is Sierra. Sierra, this is my mom, Lavondra."

Lavondra didn't move from her spot on the couch, but I reached my hand out, and Lavondra took it limply with her left hand, not bothering to exchange her cigarette to her off hand. Again, I was struck by how much she looked like Crystal, albeit a much thinner version. They could have been sisters rather than mother daughter. I wondered how old Lavondra was when she had Crystal. Probably not much older than Crystal was herself. I tried to make small talk, but Lavondra just grunted, so I excused myself and headed to the kitchen.

Most of the girls were on their phones, the swollen hot dogs growing cold on the counter. They didn't look very appetizing. After introducing myself, I asked, "Who's in charge of the food?" I tried to use my most upbeat, least critical voice. I craned my neck, looking from left to right around the girls and over their shoulders as if I was hungry and couldn't wait.

One of the girls sheepishly raised her hand. "Me, I guess. I mean, I just volunteered to help when I got here."

"What a good friend you are!" I exclaimed. "Do you know if the hot dogs are still hot, or do they need to be warmed up?" While we examined the eight little dogs, I sent the other girls out of the kitchen with the bowl of chips and instructions to cheer Crystal up. I knew that Crystal loved a good, loaded hot dog so I took the liberty of looking through the cabinets for a can of chili or baked beans. By the time I found the chili and a can opener, I could hear laughter coming from the living room. I washed out a bowl, then dumped the can of chili into it. And for some reason, *my* mood improved. I wasn't thinking about how the refrigerator needed a deep cleaning or how few people there were or how late Crystal's cousin was. I wasn't even thinking about how different the day would have been if Crystal had already announced that she wanted me to adopt her baby. It just felt good to be a help. In fact, with every task my heart grew lighter, and I prayed.

Lord, bless this food. May this one can of beans feel like a feast.

Father, wrap your arms of love around Crystal. Let her know that she is your daughter and you love her more than she could ever imagine.

God, wherever Crystal's cousin is, I pray that she is safe.

When the chili was piping hot, I pulled it out of the microwave and set up a serving station. Paper plates. Buns. Warmish hot dogs. Bowl of chili. Shredded cheese. Ketchup. Mustard.

"Okay, who wants a plain dog? Who wants loaded?" I called out, taking orders and preparing plates.

When the hot dogs were served and sprinkled with cheese, I prayed for the "meal" and prayed a blessing over Crystal. Peace, protection, wisdom, favor, obedience, love, faith. It was my voice, but God's words. I had changed so much since the first time I had met Crystal and prayed awkwardly for her.

As we all sat around the living room with plates in our laps, there was a lull in the conversation. I said, "You know, I just met Crystal not too long ago. Tell me your funniest Crystal story." The girls clamored over each other, cutting in on each other, crisscrossing stories about secret crushes, rotten cafeteria food, mismatched shoes. I could barely understand where one story ended and the other began, but the girls were happy to talk and even act out the scenes that they all seemed to share. Everyone laughed and giggled-especially Crystal-who relished being the center of attention. Everyone except Crystal's mom. She had barely taken a bite out of her food, but she regularly took long drags from the cigarette that was clasped between her index finger and middle finger.

Even though I didn't have a great relationship with my family, I was shocked at how small Crystal's support network was. All she had was her mother, who was probably young enough to be her sister; a cousin who had barely made it out of her teens; and her classmates, friends who were sweet, but just as silly and carefree as could be. There were no aunts, no godparents, no church mothers, no teachers. Would I be as courageous if I were in Crystal's position?

But Crystal was shining.

Eventually, Crystal's cousin sashayed into the room, arms in the air, obviously expecting a huge reception. Crystal just licked her teeth.

"It's about time. We're about to open gifts."

"Y'all should've waited. I told you I had to go get my girl."

"Whatever. Let's get back to the gifts!" Crystal's eyes widened in expectation. The first gift was a box of diapers. As was the second and third. "You're gonna need a lot of diapers!" One friend presented a 2-pack of bibs. And then it was my turn. Everyone oohed at the size of the brightly wrapped box as it was brought to Crystal. But it was the onesie that stole the show: *Straight Outta Mommy* in the same font as the movie it referenced. The girls passed the onesie from hand to hand as everyone had to read it and touch it for themselves.

Before I left, Crystal grabbed my hand. "Thank you for everything. It was awful before you got here."

"All I did was open a can of beans."

"No, it was way more than that. It's like you know what needs to be done and you figure out how to make it happen." Crytal leaned forward to give me a sideways hug, her belly between us. "Sierra, you're gonna be a great mom!"

My heart screamed.

"Happy birthday," I said, squeezing her hand back. I walked to my car empty-handed but full of expectation.

Chapter 15

That night, I laid across the guest room bed, the little red onesie on my chest, and stroked the faux fur. If I had a project to work on, maybe I wouldn't have obsessed so much over it. But I didn't have a project to work on. I didn't have any more adoption classes to take. There weren't any books for me to read. TV was blah. I just wanted to hold my baby in my arms. I pictured us at the hospital, Crystal sweating and exhausted from delivery. Me leaning over her, wiping her forehead. Her holding the most beautiful, perfect baby up to me, putting the baby in my hands. Me taking the baby and tears falling down my face, even though I was trying not to cry. Her telling me how grateful she was to have met me, and that she knew I would be the perfect mother to her baby.

I could see it all happening, as if I were watching the video of it in high definition. So, why hadn't Crystal said anything? And why was I afraid to call the adoption lawyer I'd found online? I had even bought the oak crib. Although I had bought the pink watch as a declaration to myself that I didn't need a husband, I questioned my wisdom in buying the oak crib. It wasn't like the $10 onesie that I could fold up and put in the bottom drawer if I couldn't adopt Crystal's baby after all. A $1,000 crib, even if it was on sale, couldn't be hidden in the bottom drawer if things didn't go the way I knew they would.

I pulled out my laptop. At the very least, I could contact the lawyer. I pulled up the website for the adoption and family lawyer I had found online. I typed my information into the "contact us" box and pressed submit before I could change my mind. There. It was done.

Feeling bolder, I pulled out my cell phone to text Crystal then immediately thought against it. No. This was a conversation that needed to be done live. In person. She needed to see my face and know that I was not trying to pressure her, and that I genuinely cared about her. I might even give her a little gift, a small memento for her to treasure, like a poem about adoption and love. And I would tell her how I was willing to have an open adoption and that I would never prevent the baby from knowing Crystal as his birth mother.

I had read through countless adoption agencies' blogs, joined social media groups dedicated to adoption, followed a few popular adoption advocates. I felt like I was being invited into a brand-new world and the entry ticket was a willingness to have an open adoption. And based on the relationship that Crystal and I already had, I could easily agree to that.

I imagined us exchanging letters and pictures, and maybe even spending holidays together. I pictured us all around the Christmas tree: me, the baby, and Crystal. Crystal might even have another child. And everyone was smiling. We were one big, happy family. Not a traditional family, but a family nonetheless. I could see it all so clearly, but the clock was ticking down. Crystal was already eight months pregnant and she still hadn't said anything. Was she nervous? Was she unsure of how I would respond? Maybe she was sitting at home, too, staring at her phone, wondering what to say and confused about the process. Whatever happened, I would reassure her that she was making the right decision. For what felt like the umpteenth time, I closed my eyes and prayed. *Lord, help Crystal to not be worried or stressed. Let her know that she's making the right decision. Assure her that I will be the best mother to her child.* I reached for my phone and it vibrated in my hand just as I picked it up. My heart fluttered as I read the caller ID: It was Crystal!

I took a deep breath and answered the call. Right away, I could hear Crystal breathing hard, as if the air had been knocked out of her lungs. Something was wrong.

"What's the matter?" I asked, skipping the pleasantries.

"I-I-I-" Crystal gasped, and I sat up, dropping the onesie to my side. I immediately went into task mode. Problem, solution.

"Are you going into labor? Is there anybody who can take you to the hospital?"

"No, I'm okay. I'm just so- mad!"

Mad? Not going into labor? I let myself breathe, but didn't relax my grip on the phone.

"What's going on?"

"My mom is getting at me about who the baby's father is 'cause he should be helping. Ugh. Why can't she just stay out of my business?" I pursed my lips, glad that Crystal couldn't see the look on my face. I had been curious, too, about who the father was. Crystal didn't talk about any boys or guys or men. I hoped it was not a man. I didn't know what I would do, but a protective anger started to rise up in me.

"So, you haven't told her who the father is?"

"Um, if I haven't told you, I'm definitely not telling her. She's just gonna trip."

"You know, you can tell me. Whoever it is. I mean, your mom is right. He should be helping."

From Crystal's tone, I knew she wasn't going to say any more. And as hard as it was, I wanted to respect her decision.

"So, what did your mom say?"

Crystal started to gasp. I could tell she was crying again. "She said if I don't tell her who the father is, I have to move out."

"Wow! I'm so sorry, Crystal. What are you gonna do?"

"I don't know. I'm glad I already had my party, though, so at least she can't cancel that," Crystal sulked. Once again, I was struck by the absurdity of this child having a child. Here she was, practically homeless, and her biggest concern seemed to be whether or not she had been able to have her baby shower/17th birthday party.

"I guess it's just me and Khalid now."

"Khalid?" Wait, was that the baby's dad? I was confused.

"Yeah, I decided to name the baby Khalid."

She had decided to name my baby Khalid? In that moment, my brain stopped working, but not my mouth. I knew what naming the baby meant, but I didn't understand.

"Why would you name the baby?"

"Oh, I forgot to tell you. I decided to go ahead and find out what the baby is. Everybody was telling me it's a boy anyway, so I just wanted to know for sure." Crystal's voice sounded light and happy for a second. I smiled, too. It was a boy, just like I had seen in my mind.

"I have an important question to ask you," Crystal hesitated. My brain was still not working, and neither was my mouth. Only my heart. *This is it*, it screamed. The moment I had been waiting for. I clutched the red skunk onesie. There would be a baby wearing it after all. My eyes filled with tears. *Thank you, God. Thank you, God.*

"You've been there for me like no one else. I don't even know what I would have done without you all these weeks. So, I was wondering if you would be willing to…"

Yes! I wanted to shout, but I willed myself to be quiet, to wait, to let her ask. It was an honor, and I would be sure to tell her that. I didn't take it lightly. After all this time, my dream of being a mother were finally coming true. I could finally make an appointment with the adoption lawyer I'd found online, I could finally unbox the beautiful oak crib, and I could finally tell Carmen that she was wrong, I *was* going to be a mother. I was going to be a *mother!* I almost laughed from the pure joy that welled up in me.

"So, could I stay with you for a few weeks? I just need some time to figure things out."

"Yes, and…." I waited. Waited for her to finish her sentence. Waited for her to ask me to provide the life for Khalid that she couldn't. "Khalid"? Was that her condition, that she be allowed to name the baby? From the blogs I had read, many birth moms made that a condition of the adoption, that they be allowed to name their baby. Khalid wasn't what I was thinking of, but it was a fine name. That was not a deal breaker.

"And…thank you?" Crystal paused, and so did I. I forced myself to come back to the present, to focus on what she was saying. What did her words mean? What was she asking me?

"And?"

"And…I promise I won't mess up your house. It'll only be a few weeks. Way before the baby is born, don't worry."

In truth, the baby could come any day now and it'd be considered a full-term pregnancy. There was no "way before the baby is born" anymore. She could easily stay with me until the baby was born. Didn't that really make the most sense? That way, I could be there when she went into labor. And then I could bring the baby home from the hospital. My baby. Yes, everything was coming together.

"You can stay with me until you have the baby," I said, happy to be able to relieve at least one burden from her.

"Thank you, Sierra! You're the best! Oh my gosh, I really don't know what I would do without you. You're going to make a great mom!"

Tears- happy tears- flooded my eyes. A year ago, I would never have imagined that such simple words would have such an impact on me.

"That's so sweet, especially coming from you. And don't worry about anything you didn't get at the shower. I'll take care of everything we need."

"You don't have to do that. Why are you being so nice to me?"

"Well, I can't even imagine how hard this decision has been for you. I just want you to know you're not alone and Khalid will always be your son. I would never try to replace you." The words were out before I could stop them. I reached out my hand as if to pull them back, but it was too late.

For a second, I thought Crystal hadn't heard me, but then her voice came through the phone slowly and quietly. "What do you mean?"

My silence must have told Crystal everything she needed to know. But this was not the plan. This was not how the conversation was supposed to unfold. We were supposed to meet in person so Crystal could see my face and see how much I cared about her and Khalid. I was supposed to present her with a memento. And I was going to tell her all about open adoptions.

"Are you joking?" For the first time, I was glad that we weren't in person. Crystal's voice was barely above a whisper, but I could still hear the venom that dripped from every word. "Did you think I wanted to give my baby up? And why would I ever choose you?"

Crystal's words began to sink in. Immediately, I thought back to all the conversations we'd had. I analyzed every hint. I circled very clue. I wasn't crazy. Was I?

"I know you said you didn't want to give the baby to a stranger, but I thought–"

"You thought what?" she interrupted.

"I thought we were becoming friends and that you were beginning to trust me."

"So, everything you've been doing is just because you want my baby?" Crystal's voice was at least an octave higher, but I didn't respond. What could I say? I thought back to the first time I'd seen Crystal at the bus stop in the snow. Or the times that I had given her a ride or took her to her doctor's appointments. I couldn't pinpoint exactly when my motives had changed, but hearing Crystal's characterization of me was a blow.

"Is that why you bought the most expensive things from my registry? You want to buy my baby. Sierra, I told you I was not giving my baby up for adoption, especially not to some sad, pathetic so-called woman who don't got a man and can't have a baby!"

"Listen," I cut in, but Crystal was just getting started.

"No, you listen! I don't care how much money you got, I don't care about your nice house or car. You're trying to use me, and that's messed up. My mom always told me to watch out 'cause boys only wanted one thing from me. But she really should've warned me about desperate old hags who are fake friends." Crystal made each point with an f-bomb, and called me out of my name more times than I could count. But by that point, I wasn't listening anymore. The only thing I could hear was the sound of my own heart breaking. I was not going to be a mother. In my mind's eye, I could see Carmen, warning me to be careful, to watch out. But I hadn't. I had been so desperate, so hopeful that I had put aside all reason and put all my hope in this one girl and her baby. Crystal was right. I, Sierra Harris, was a sad pathetic hag. I let the phone drop to the floor before collapsing in tears onto the bed.

REY SIRAKAVIT

The next few days were a blur. I went to work. I cried. I ate. I cried. I went to the bathroom. I cried. I drank water (because my head hurt from all the crying), which only hydrated me so that I could cry more. Which I did. I tried not to think about Crystal or Khalid. Khalid!

I replayed the conversation in my mind. I replayed the past months. Had my desperation really led me to make such a fool of myself? I swallowed my pride and called Carmen.

Carmen would come over and sit with me, let me rest my head on her shoulder. She was a good friend. She wouldn't say "I told you so." She would pray with me, console me, tell me I wasn't crazy, just a little too trusting and optimistic.

As soon as Carmen walked through the door, I settled in. And, just as I expected, Carmen fulfilled the role of the dutiful best friend. She made me some chamomile tea, offered tissue after tissue, and listened for what seemed like hours. Finally, I had run out of tears.

"I just can't believe God would do this to me! I've been praying so much for this girl. I felt like God was pointing me in this direction and now...I don't know. I just feel so used." I rubbed my hand over my forehead, as if the pressure of my palm could push the truth back.

"So, do you know what Crystal's going to do now?"

"What do you mean?"

"Well, it sounds like she's getting kicked out and she was hoping she could stay with you. What are her options now?"

I hadn't thought about that, and frankly, I didn't really care. It wasn't my problem. "She's gonna have to figure that out on her own, I guess," I hmphed.

"Sierra, this whole time as you've been talking...I can't help but feel you're right. It does seem like God brought Crystal into your life for a reason. But maybe not for the reason you thought."

I hmphed again. And rolled my eyes. "And what reason might that be?"

"Well, it sounds like Crystal really needed a friend and you were that friend. You took her to her birthing classes, you took her grocery shopping for healthy foods, you modeled how a responsible adult might approach having a baby, and that's exactly what she needed. A role model. A mentor. A friend. This girl has like zero support. And, she's on the verge of being homeless..."

"So, are you saying I should let her move in, even though she's been leading me on all this time, letting me think she was going to let me adopt her baby?" My voice rose in anger and frustration.

"I don't know if she led you on. Remember, I told you I didn't think-"

"I can't believe you're about to say I told you so!" My eyes bulged.

"No, that's not what I meant," Carmen said, shaking her head with a frown. "I just meant that I think there's another way of looking at this, that's all."

"I can't believe you're taking her side! You're supposed to be *my* friend, you're supposed to take *my* side."

"This isn't about taking sides, it's about what God wants, and God wants –"

"Don't even try to tell me *you* know what God wants! It's so easy for you to sit there and judge me, but if you're so holy, why don't you take her in? What, she might upset your perfect little family? Why do you get the perfect kids and perfect husband, but the best I can hope for is either a drug baby or taking care of a crazy, pregnant teen? You get the easy life; but, for some reason, you just know that God is calling me to the hard road. That's pretty convenient, don't you think?"

"You're not the only one whose life hasn't gone exactly like you hoped. Grow up! Stop focusing on yourself for just one minute and you'd realize how blessed you are."

"Blessed? Whatever, Carmen. I don't want to hear it."

"You know I love you, but don't take your frustration out on me." Carmen glared at me, but I couldn't meet her look. Instead, I looked out the window just above Carmen's left shoulder. The sky was clear blue. It had been a beautiful early spring day, with lots of sun, but I had barely noticed.

We sat in awkward silence, me pondering the weather and Carmen picking at the pill on her sweater. Eventually, she made some excuse about having to pick up the kids from their grandparents, and with that, Carmen slipped her feet into her leather ankle boots, pulled her jacket off the hook, and slid out the door all in one motion. All of a sudden, I was alone. Really alone. A voice in the back of my head said pray, but I just couldn't bring myself to. What was the point? God obviously didn't care. He wasn't listening to me.

I stomped around the house, picking up pieces of Kleenex, putting the tea kettle back on its stand. I filled a bucket with hot, soapy water, letting the familiar scent of cleaning soap massage my senses, even as I held on to the anger welling up in me. For as long as Carmen and I had been friends, I had never envied her. Not when she got married before me, not when she got pregnant and I got to be the godmother. Or when she got pregnant again, even when she wasn't "trying"! I wasn't jealous when they bought a big, beautiful home in the suburbs. Every Christmas I put her holiday card on my fridge door, and left it there for months because I was genuinely happy for my friend. Her happiness was my happiness. But when would it be my turn? It wasn't fair that some people had such perfect lives, and others seemed to struggle from day one.

I carried the bucket out to the driveway, careful not to spill a drop on the floor. The spring evening was cool, but the sun was still shining brightly. I started scrubbing the outside of my car, hoping to maximize the light before it got too late. I made big, broad circles, letting my anger sweep over the car. Eventually, exhausted, and no closer to an answer, I squeezed the rags out and dumped the water onto the grass. I rubbed my thumb over the ridges that had formed on my fingers. Even though it was only my hands that had been in the water, my whole body felt wrinkled and shriveled up.

I tried to convince myself to cheer up. Hadn't I gotten my life back? No more chauffeuring an immature, ungrateful teen around. Once again, I had my evenings completely to myself. But night after night of sitting on the couch alone, I still ached from Crystal's punch in the gut. The sting of rejection still burned. And I had no one to commiserate with.

Eventually, I called Jessica, my friend from the adoption class. Even though we had promised to stay in touch, we hadn't. We spent a few minutes catching up, but her excitement oozed through the phone.

"We got our first placement. A little girl!" Jessica proceeded to tell me all about her foster daughter. Even as I oohed and ahhed, I had to admit that the only reason I had called Jessica was because out of the three of us from the adoption class, her situation seemed even more hopeless than mine. No one-except Jessica-really believed her husband would ever take his classes. But, apparently, we'd all been wrong.

Finally, the conversation moved around to me.

"So, has the county called you about any possibilities?"

"Actually, I haven't been approved yet."

"Are you serious? I knew they were backed up but this is ridiculous. It's been months."

"Actually, I never passed my home study," I was ashamed to admit.

"What? The system is so ludicrous. They won't give someone like you a license, but they return thousands of kids to dangerous, drug addicted parents every year. I'm so sorry. What are you going to do?"

Finally, someone who understood *my* side. "I don't know. I met this pregnant teen- she was actually the reason I was even thinking about adopting to begin with- and we hit it off and—"

"Don't tell me you were thinking about adopting her baby!"

"Actually, I was."

Jessica laughed. "Oh no! Did you get a lawyer? Those situations can be so messy."

"Yep, you called it." I tried to seem nonchalant, as if my heart hadn't been ripped out of my chest by Crystal, stomped on by Carmen, and was oozing on the floor in the corner.

"Well, have you thought about doing the home study through a different county? You'd have to take the classes all over, but it might be worth it to get a different worker for the home study."

"Well, the social worker said she wanted me to do some counseling before she'd approve my home study. But I have no desire to do that."

"Why not? You know, after Jack and I kept not getting pregnant, and then had several miscarriages, I started seeing a therapist. It really helped."

"I don't know. Maybe it's just a cultural thing, but I've never been comfortable with the idea of paying someone to listen to my problems. That's what friends are supposed to be for!" I laughed half-heartedly, remembering how I had alienated my best friend, prayer partner, and most honest confidante.

"You know, times are changing. For a long time, my husband said men don't go to counseling, either. But I think it's a cop out. At a certain point, you have to be willing to face your demons. Especially if it involves what's best for kids. These kids in the system don't just exist so we can have the experience of being a parent. They've been traumatized, victimized, abused, neglected. They need us to work out all our issues so we can help them heal theirs. If I had never gone to counseling to deal with my pain about losing my babies…" Jessica's voice cracked, but only slightly. "If I hadn't gone to counseling, I wouldn't be able to say we're gonna be parents!"

I let Jessica's words sink in. Maybe she was right. Maybe it was time to stop letting fear rule me.

The next day, I got up earlier than normal, even before my alarm went off. I thought about lying in bed, pretending to pray, while really just staring at the ceiling feeling sorry for myself. If I got up right away, I could be on time to church. Maybe even before the service started. I pursed my lips. It wasn't that I was mad at God, but I felt as if God had written me a bad check. And when I took it to the bank, it bounced. Obviously, I didn't have the emotional energy or spiritual fortitude to remind myself of God's love or faithfulness, so I really needed to go to church. I pulled myself out of bed and got dressed.

Plain black trousers and a thin black sweater. Black socks. Black loafers. And a black head wrap. The only thing I was missing was black lipstick, but the black circles under my eyes more than made up for it.

When I stepped into the sanctuary, early for the first time ever, the worship team was chatting off to the side of the stage. The drummer was beating his sticks in the air, and the guitarist was strumming chords. The altar was open.

A few people were already at the altar, on their knees, rocking back and forth, deep in prayer. I hesitated only for a moment, just long enough to drop my purse in a pew, then stumbled forward to the carpeted stairs at the bottom of the stage. The altar. There was nothing magical or supernatural at the altar on its own, but for some reason I knew I needed to plant myself at the feet of Jesus and not move until the Lord spoke. I don't know how long I stayed there, with my hands clasped and my head bowed and tears streaming down my face, but eventually I heard the music that signaled the service was about to begin. I walked back to my seat with a lighter heart.

Nothing about my situation had changed. I was still single. Still childless. Still confused and disappointed. But not hopeless. I wished the Lord would speak and tell me exactly what to do. But he didn't. At least not in the way I wanted.

However, from the very first note, the worship team reminded me over and over that God was in control.

Help is on the way.

Worship through your pain.

Don't look at your situation, look at God.

By the time the pastor took the stage, my heart was almost ready to hear from the Lord.

"When you ask, you do not receive, because you ask with wrong motives," the pastor said, quoting James 4:3.

"Umm," I said, nodding my head the way people do when the pastor has said something true that somebody somewhere needs to hear.

"Your motives are wrong," he repeated, "just straight up bad!" He practically yelled these final words, and for a second I felt like he was talking specifically to me, right there in row seven, at least ten rows in front of my usual seat.

This is what I get for coming to church early, I thought, longing to be back in my usual spot in the back that gave me a good enough view to see, but not be seen. My eyes wandered, and I looked around to see if the pastor was staring at everybody else so intently, or just me. All around me, heads were nodding. I reluctantly looked back towards the stage, but purposely kept my eyes averted.

"How can God bless you? 'You desire but do not have, so you kill. You covet but you cannot get what you want, so you quarrel and fight.' Why don't you try obeying God, not because of what you can get, but because that's the right thing to do? God knows your desires. God knows your heart. Obey him, and he will fight the battles for you."

At that, Sister Johnson, the church secretary and Women's Bible Study teacher, stood up and shouted, "Hallelujah!" Several others waved their hands. For a second, I felt like maybe I was just being paranoid and the pastor wasn't talking only to me, but then his words really began to sink in.

You covet but you cannot get what you want, so you quarrel and fight.

Isn't that exactly what I had done? I coveted Crystal's baby, so I quarreled not only with her, but with Carmen, too. I didn't want to go to counseling, so I quarreled with the home study worker.

Every prayer I prayed was about me, what was best for me, what I wanted. I wasn't trying to seek the Lord. I was trying to twist the Lord's arm. I was trying to pray him into a corner, where he'd be forced to give me exactly what I wanted because I had prayed the right number of times, had used the right combination of words and scriptures, and had cried enough tears to get his attention.

I didn't see Crystal as a young girl who needed help, I saw Crystal as a common convenience. She had something I wanted, and I thought I deserved it more than she did.

I didn't even see Loveyouforever as an abandoned child who needed a family; her history of abuse and neglect was just the necessary evil for me to become her mother.

"When you ask, you do not receive, because you ask with wrong motives," James said.

Even Carmen had said almost the same thing.

I'd spent most of my adult life in church, and I had heard countless sermons on asking *with faith*. Asking *in the name of Jesus*. But for what seemed like the first time, I was being told to ask *with right motives*.

Instead of seeing how the Lord might want to use me to meet Crystal's needs, all I could see was how Crystal was going to meet *my* need. My stomach began to churn and my skin crawled. I was everything that Crystal had accused me of, and worse. I was a bloodsucking vampire.

Was this what the Lord was trying to say to me?

With my head bowed, I sat back in my seat, rubbing my hands together and biting my lip. *Forgive me, Lord.* For the umpteenth time that morning, I swiped at the pool of tears on my cheeks. And then I felt a jolt against my thigh. My eyes flew open in surprise. What was that? There was another vibration against my thigh. My heart slowed to normal as I realized it was just my cell phone. I wondered who it could be, because pretty much everyone knew that I was at church. I pulled the phone out and glanced surreptitiously at the screen. It was not a call, but a notification. I read the screen: "Crystal's Due Date".

Chapter 17

My heart pounded as I sat in the car, thinking back to the day when Crystal had put her due date into my phone. It was during the birthing class. Was she at the hospital right now, preparing for a c-section? Or, had she gone into labor naturally? *I should be there*, I thought. But would she want me there? After all that had happened, I couldn't imagine her allowing me to stroll into her hospital room, regardless of how completely my intentions had changed. I was not naïve enough to believe that she would want anything to do with me after the way I had broken her trust. By the time I pulled up into my driveway, I had made up my mind. I called her, but wasn't surprised when the phone went straight to voicemail.

I changed into sweats, rolled up my sleeves, and grabbed a fresh notepad. It was time to clean house- my spiritual house. I made a list of all the things I needed to do: *make an appointment with a therapist, return the crib, call Carmen, pack the little red onesie away. Call Crystal.* I double-underlined that one. Then circled it. That one would be the hardest. I had no idea what I could or would say. She still hadn't answered any of my calls or texts since church, but I knew I had to keep trying.

And then there were some things I had to add to my list because at 33 years old, I was completely lost. I wanted- no, needed- to figure out how to pray. I had lived my whole Christian life praying occasionally, praying in emergencies, praying at church, praying with wrong motives. My hands were outstretched, not to worship, but to welcome every blessing I could get my hands on. I was spiritually greedy, praying "gimme" prayers.

Gimme a house.

Gimme a job.

Gimme a husband.

Gimme a baby.

My pencil stalled on the pad. If I said I loved God, then my relationship with Him needed to be bigger. I had created a "genie Jesus" who was supposed to grant all my wishes, instead of seeing him as the suffering servant whom I was supposed to emulate.

I picked up my pencil.

Pray. Everyday. For 30 Days. For others. NOT FOR SELF! I added with bold letters. My relationship with God had to be about more than what I could get from Him. But it seemed impossible. Excluding blessing my food, I knew I hadn't prayed every day for 30 days, ever. And definitely not focused on others. Yet, I knew that was just what I needed to make an abrupt, dramatic change in my prayer life.

Read a book about prayer. Go on a prayer retreat. With those additions, my list was long and I felt good. I felt almost as good as when I was up to my elbows in a bucket of hot water and suds. And I knew exactly where to begin. Prayer. Day one. I looked back up at Crystal's name. Had I prayed one prayer for her that didn't somehow wrap around and impact me? If I was honest with myself, I had to say no. Every prayer for protection, wisdom, and comfort would inevitably lead to a healthy birth and a healthy baby for *me* to adopt. I exhaled.

Lord, I pray for Crystal. Sitting at the kitchen counter, I prayed for her as a mother and parent, I prayed for her housing situation, I prayed for her relationship with her mother, I prayed and prayed and prayed. And my heart hurt a little less and a little more. This was real. I was not going to adopt Khalid.

Khalid.

Help her to be the mother Khalid needs for her to be.

Several times I felt my gaze slipping inward. What I needed, I wanted, how this all was impacting me. *What about me, Lord?* And while I didn't want to be legalistic, I also sensed that my capacity to selflessly love was being strangled by my incapacity to genuinely intercede.

I remembered Carmen's parting words from days earlier about how blessed I was. I remembered the speaker from months earlier about "being love". Did Jesus give me everything I had just so I could hunger for more? Or, was my blessing positioning me to be a blessing to someone else? I picked up my phone again. This time, a raspy voice answered.

* * *

I paced back and forth in the hospital waiting room, waiting for Crystal's mom to take me to Crystal's room. Even though Crystal had gone into labor the night before, Khalid still hadn't made his grand entrance.

Crystal's mom, Lavondra, walked down the hall toward me, pulling her jacket over her shoulders. She must have read the question on my face.

"Look, I've gotta go to work. I'm working the second shift this week, and now that you're here, I can just about make it on time," she paused. "Crystal told me all about you wanting to adopt her baby."

My heart stopped. Would she yell and insult me as Crystal had? I instinctively took a step back, squared my jaw, and prepared myself for whatever might happen next.

"Well," she continued, "I think you should. She's got no business trying to have a baby. I was fifteen when I had her, and it ain't easy. She thinks it's going to be all unicorns and rainbows. She has no idea how hard it is to raise a baby all by yourself." Did I? Before I could respond or convince her to stay, she told me Crystal's room number and was gone.

I followed the nurse's directions to the third-floor birthing center. The colors on the walls were warm and featured huge prints of smiling babies. Lavondra's words still whirled around my head. My heart leapt at the thought that even Lavondra thought I should adopt Crystal's baby. A week ago-a day ago!-I would have taken that as a sign and allowed my mind to run off making plans that my heart would have to endure the disappointment of.

Lord, I pray…. My heart was overflowing with longing and hope, but I cut the prayer off. Instead, I reminded myself of the horrid and humiliating conversation with Crystal where she unequivocally denied ever considering giving her baby up for adoption. Regardless of what her mother thought, this was Crystal's decision.

The Lord knows what you need, I told myself.

So, I turned my attention to Crystal, who at that very moment was alone in her delivery room, without a friend or birth coach or mom to hold her hand and get her ice or rub her back. My heart went out to the girl whose mother hadn't attended birthing classes with her, who hadn't had time to take her to doctor's appointments, who had barely showed up to her baby shower, and had just left the hospital before the baby was even born…Whose mother had only been a child herself before becoming a mother.

Lord, I pray for Lavondra. I didn't know what else to say, but God knew exactly what she needed. He had a future and a hope for Lavondra and Crystal and their relationship, even if I didn't know what it was.

When I came to Crystal's room number, I stopped and looked through the open door. There was Crystal, leaning over her hospital bed, face drawn and sweating. She must have seen me out of her periphery, because she looked up, lips curled in anger.

"Where's my mom?" she demanded, as if maybe I had kidnapped her and was setting in motion an elaborate plan to isolate her and eventually rob her of her baby. I shook the thought off.

"She had to get to work. But I'm here for you and I'll stay with you for as long as it takes," I said, walking into the room. I didn't know if I should hug her, put my arm on her shoulder, or touch her hand. So, instead, I let my arm drop awkwardly to my side.

"Why are you here? You know I'm not giving this baby up for adoption. Not to you or to anyone." Her eyes pierced mine. There was so much I wanted to say, had been planning to say, but now the words didn't seem to fit. I did want Crystal's baby. And even now, I would take him if she offered. So what could I say to convince her that that wasn't why I was there?

"I can't begin to tell you how sorry I am and how wrong I was. I'll leave if you want me to, but you and Khalid mean so much to me. You don't have to go through this alone. I promised you I would be here for you; please, let me keep my promise." My face was wet with tears and sweat, the same as Crystal's. Finally, the edges of her mouth lifted, not quite a smile, but also not the death glare she had given me when I entered the room, either. I happily took that as a sign and wrapped my arms around her shoulder for a side hug. I sent up a quick prayer of thanks that Crystal didn't make me grovel, and somehow, before long we were talking and chatting as if nothing had happened.

She complained about the nursing staff who ignored her and didn't take her complaints seriously. She complained about the bland food. She complained about the dressing gown and the lack of privacy. I helped her cinch the gown a little better from behind, but much of her backside was still exposed.

For the next few hours, Crystal paced the halls of the hospital. I walked beside her, mostly listening as she talked and careful not to touch her because her skin, quote, "felt like melted fire". She said the contractions were like being hammered with a nail, and described in excruciating detail the difference between that and just being nailed with a hammer. But the contractions had slowed down and, by morning, the baby still hadn't arrived. During one of the few moments that Crystal was resting, I emailed work, letting them know I wouldn't be coming in.

As I was about to put my phone away, it rang. At first, I assumed it was Mikaela or someone else from work, but I didn't recognize the number. I thought about letting it go to voicemail, but hit the green button instead. Even if it was just a telemarketer for a local business offering to clean my gutters or check my roof for hail damage, I needed a mental break. As I had predicted, it *was* a local business, but not one who was offering to work on my house.

As the caller introduced himself, all I could think was, *Why me? Why now?* Immediately, I started sobbing. Sitting in the hallway outside Crystal's hospital room, the river of tears that I'd been holding back sprang from my eyes uninhibited. I cried about what was, what could have been, what would never be. I cried because I was a selfish woman trying to be selfless and it was hard. So hard. And it didn't feel fair. And as much as I wanted to be strong and obedient and focused on Crystal and what she needed, how could I when even her own mother thought I should adopt her baby? And now, here was the adoption lawyer I had contacted the week before everything fell apart, when I was still hopeful and confident and willfully deluding myself. He paused in his spiel about wanting to protect my interests, the importance of expertise and experience. Blah blah blah.

"Are you okay?" he asked, his voice calm and smooth.

"I'm at the hospital *right now*," I whispered, "but, she's keeping the baby." I covered my face with my hands and cried into this stranger's ear. And for some reason, I told him everything, from meeting Crystal on a cold night in February all the way to sitting outside her hospital room in June, supporting her as she transitioned into motherhood. He didn't tell me I was stupid. He didn't call me crazy. He didn't laugh. He just listened.

Finally, my tears subsided. "I'm sorry. I can't believe I told you all that," I sniffled, wiping my nose on the back of my hand.

"Don't worry about it. You don't know how many people have been right where you are, only they go to the hospital with the car seat and baby carrier, not knowing the birth mom is going to change her mind. Don't be embarrassed for being disappointed. God knows your heart and he sees your pain. Trust him and he'll take care of you."

I was encouraged at how simply this stranger, a man I had never met, was able to express everything I needed to hear in just a few short sentences. I treasured his words, folding them up and putting them in my pocket. Thanking him for the call and the kind words, I hung up, feeling oddly refreshed and encouraged.

God is good, even when I don't understand what's going on in my life!

I went to the bathroom down the hall, washed my face, and shook my hair out before pulling it into a fresh bun.

When I stepped back into the room, nurses were milling around and Crystal held her hand out to me. I took it eagerly. The nap seemed to energize Crystal and Khalid, because once she woke up, all the action started. The pain began in earnest, and Crystal begged for an epidural. I watched as the anesthesiologist inserted the needle, I watched as a look of a peace eventually washed over her face, I watched as she grunted and pushed and Khalid finally slid out and into the doctor's hands. And, yet, I felt so incredibly proud of my incredibly small role in bringing this baby to life. And when Crystal asked me if I wanted to hold Khalid, I could not hold my tears back. Here was the child that had captured our hearts and hopes for months.

"Thank you for letting me be here," I whispered, not ignorant of how close I had been to missing out on this moment.

"Thank *you* for being here," Crystal murmured, exhaustion and joy etched on her face. "Didn't I tell you he was going to be perfect?"

I smiled, watching her count his fingers and toes, stroking his face, and had to agree. He was perfect.

REY SIRAKAVIT

Chapter 18

It is a truth that must be universally acknowledged that sometimes things happen and you have no idea how. Even though you may have been there when it happened. You were there. You *know* you were there. But you can't piece together the how or the why. Like a train that jumped its tracks and ends up in a mess of metal and iron. Or, those speed painters who throw colors on a canvas in an almost haphazard way, then "Voila!" They spin the canvas and the portrait is complete. What happened at the hospital was either a terrible train wreck or a beautiful, unexpected work of art.

After Khalid and Crystal were settled, I used Crystal's phone to call her mom, but Lavondra didn't pick up. I assumed she was sleeping off her late shift, but would come as soon as she could to see her grandchild and daughter. All throughout the day, I kept looking at Crystal's phone and the door and the baby. Phone, door, baby. Phone, door, baby. But Lavondra did not call. She did not text. Lavondra showed up with the car seat. And a duffle bag.

She looked ready for a fight.

"I don't have room for a baby, so if you're grown enough to keep this baby, you're grown enough to figure out where you're gonna live."

I stood on the sideline, wanting to jump in and interrupt the mother and daughter argument that had obviously been repeated many times before, but not knowing how. I wanted to shout that this wasn't the time or the place, and that the focus should really be on this new life. The baby started to whimper, so I picked him up out of the bassinet. I bounced him, sang to him, hoping to screen him even as the voices rose around us. I dared not take him out of the room, but hoped to stand as a human shield to guard him from words like abortion, adoption, and homeless shelter. At that last word, I looked over my shoulder at the two mothers behind me, one who would not give up her child for anything, and the other who seemed only too eager to do so. And, yet, I could not judge either one. I had never been pregnant and alone and afraid. Or, a mother of a mother.

"You can't just kick me out," Crystal wailed. "Where are me and Khalid supposed to go?"

"That's not my problem. I've been trying to tell you, you're not grown. Stop trying to act like it. You don't have a penny to your name, so what kind of life can you offer this boy?" Lavondra lifted her chin toward Khalid, but still had not looked at him.

"You did it. Why can't I?"

"Yeah I did it, but if I had known—" Lavondra's lips curled, ready to say something she would forever regret.

"Okay, ladies, let's calm down," I interjected, finally finding my voice. Lavondra looked at me, over Khalid's head. Behind the anger, there was sadness…and fear. Without another word, Lavondra walked out, leaving the duffle bag and car seat behind. The car seat that I had not wanted to buy. The plain, basic model car seat that would not look good in the back of my SUV.

"What am I gonna do?" Crystal cried, covering her face with her hands.

I thought about the deluxe crib in my guest room at home, still in its guilty package. I looked down at little Khalid in my arms. I looked over at Crystal's tear-soaked face.

"You're coming home with me," I said.

After handing Khalid to Crystal, I grabbed my cell phone and headed to the hall. What had I just agreed to?

* * *

"So, what did you agree to?" Carmen asked.

For the second time since I had been at the hospital, I was grateful to not have to grovel. Carmen accepted my apology as easily as if all I had done was step on her toe instead of insulting her family and faith and friendship. I thanked the Lord for her, even as I pleaded with him to give me wisdom.

"That's the thing, I don't know. All I said was she could come home with me, but I don't know what that means. What do I do?" I paced the halls of the hospital, down a flight of stairs, around a series of corners. All of a sudden, I was in a different wing from the birthing center. I looked around me. I was completely lost.

"First, calm down," Carmen said.

"How can I calm down? I haven't slept in like two days."

At that, Carmen harrumphed. "Well, if you're going to have a newborn houseguest, get ready for many more sleepless nights! Seriously, though, I think you're doing the right thing." Of course she did. As grateful as I was for my friend, I couldn't pretend that I was not annoyed. I didn't know, though, if I was more annoyed at the situation or at the fact that my friend had been right all along.

"They're discharging Crystal in the morning. I probably just need to go home and get some rest. Eat something that didn't come out of a vending machine. Put the crib together." I told Carmen about the thousand-dollar crib I had gotten on sale, smiling at the memory, yet feeling slightly aggrieved. The irony of the situation was not lost on me. Even though I had bought the crib for Khalid, I still resented unboxing it for him. "It's just sitting in my guest room..."

"How about we come over and help you put it together?"

I jumped at the offer. With a renewed lightness in my heart, I found my way back to Crystal's room. She thanked me again and assured me that she wouldn't stay with me for long. Then, I went home to prepare.

I bypassed the kitchen and went straight to the shower. Even with the warm water pulsing down on me, I could have slept right there. Somehow, I managed to summon just enough energy to crawl into bed and sleep. After what seemed like only minutes, I heard the doorbell ring. And ring. And ring. Carmen's boys must have been playing with it. It was still light out, but according to the clock on my nightstand, I had been asleep for at least three hours. I pulled myself out of bed and shuffled down the hall. I needed more sleep. But I was not going to get it, as two very excited boys rushed at me as soon as I opened the door.

"Josiah, James, be careful," Carmen called out as two whirling dervishes whizzed past me. "These boys. Sorry," she said. As Carmen and I wrapped our arms around each other's shoulders, I repented of every evil thought, every hateful word that had crossed my mind in the past week. But all I said was, "I'm sorry. I'm really sorry," glad to be able to finally apologize in person.

"You don't have to keep apologizing. I'm the one who should be sorry. I was being pushy. I was in mommy mode instead of just being your friend." She squeezed my shoulders then released me, letting the warm June air blow in behind her. "We're allowed to disagree. Sometimes," she added with a smile.

"Well, I never want you to feel like you can't tell me the truth," I said, knowing with all my heart that that *was* the truth. I didn't want or need a shallow friend who would only tell me what they thought I wanted to hear.

Before Carmen could respond, Travis walked through the door, arms overflowing with an assortment of gear.

"Is that everything?" Carmen asked her husband, eyebrows raised.

"Yep," Travis said proudly, motioning us aside as a playpen, bouncer, baby carrier, and tool belt all tumbled to the middle of my living room floor.

"Don't just drop it!" Carmen reprimanded her husband, but he only laughed.

"It's been through worse," he countered.

"No, it's just well-loved. We cleaned everything thoroughly," Carmen said quickly with a knowing grin to me.

Travis picked up the tool belt and held it out for me. "I know you're an independent woman and have your own tools, but I brought this just in case you need anything," he smiled.

I missed this. Missed them. The easy banter. The warm smiles. I sat down on the couch and called the boys to me, planting my "trademarked" loud wet kisses all over their cheeks and head. I felt ashamed at how long it had since I had seen the kids. Aside from a few quick glimpses at church, I hadn't really spent time with them all spring.

"Oh my gosh, look at how big you guys have gotten. Are you in college yet?" I asked Josiah. He giggled.

"I'm a college, auntie!" James said, arms waving in the air, wriggling on my lap. The adults laughed. Even though he was more than a year younger than his brother, James already had a strong sense of humor and talked circles around everyone. Carmen liked to say that he came out of the womb talking and cracking jokes.

"So you're a college, huh?" Travis picked James off of my lap with one hand and tossed him playfully in the air.

Even though he had no idea why we were laughing, James knew that he had said something funny, so he just kept repeating it over and over. "I'm a college, aunty! I'm a college!"

I hadn't noticed before, but Carmen also came bearing gifts. She set a bag of foil-wrapped burritos on the countertop.

"I don't know if you already ate, but you can always microwave it later." Before the words were even out of her mouth, one of the burritos was already in mine. I was ravenous.

"Aunty," Josiah shyly tugged on the oversized tee shirt I had quickly thrown on earlier. "Are you having a baby?" Unlike his younger brother, Josiah was cautious and slow to speak. Although he had just as much energy.

I swallowed the mouthful of burrito I was chewing, then used my wrist to wipe the corners of my mouth. The time I took to answer his question must have felt like an eternity for a five-year-old, but Josiah waited patiently, his curious eyes never drifting from mine. Finally, I said, "Nope, but my friend just had a baby, and she's going to stay with me for a little while." I was proud at how the words seemed to roll off my tongue matter-of-factly, even if my heart did constrict the tiniest bit.

"Well, she can use my stuff 'cause I'm a big boy now. It's good to share." And with that, Josiah ran back off to play with his brother.

After devouring the burrito, we set the boys- and Travis-up in front of the TV with some snacks while Carmen and I pulled the crib out of the box and got to work putting it together. Between the two of us, we fastened the front rails, side rails, back rails, bottom rails, safety rails. I began to question the wisdom in choosing a crib that had quite so many features. But by the time it was all put together it was fit for a prince. Prince Khalid.

There were no fun nursery theme decorations.

There was no rocking chair and ottoman.

There was just a full bed still draped in an African print comforter, an elegant crib pushed against a wall, and a hand-me-down baby bouncer.

In all its mismatched glory, it was beautiful, and Crystal agreed.

When she walked into the bedroom the next day, her eyes brightened and bulged.

"Wow, this is so nice! Your friends just gave you all this stuff?"

"Yeah, mostly," I said looking around at the baby gear I had set out for Crystal and Khalid.

"I can't believe it. And look at this crib! It's gorgeous! I can't believe someone would just give this away. It looks too beautiful."

I considered telling her the truth, that I had actually bought the crib when I still thought she was going to let me adopt Khalid. But that did not seem wise. So, I just smiled, glad that Travis had thrown all the packaging material in the trash outside.

After giving Crystal a tour, I decided to go into work. A half day would be better than not at all. Plus, I didn't want to hover. I didn't know how much longer I could watch her bonding with her baby, stroking his thick curly hair, playing with his toes and fingers. All while I tried not to pick apart her every action, from the way she held the baby to the way she covered him with a blanket. Yes, even though I was still exhausted, I needed to work.

REY SIRAKAVIT

Chapter 19

I sat in my cubicle at work thinking about Crystal and Khalid, at my house, sleeping in my guest room, Khalid in the crib I had specially picked out for him, but not for him. *Let it go, Sierra,* I told myself, but the words lacked conviction.

I thought about God, but could not think of any words to pray. I hadn't even made it two days in my prayer challenge, and already I was feeling sorry for myself.

I turned my attention to work and all the unopened messages in my inbox that were waiting for me. There were messages about reports due, recent retires and new hires. There was a reminder from HR to take advantage of our employee benefits. "Three free therapy sessions with a licensed counselor." I sighed. Even work seemed to be conspiring against me. How many times had HR sent this same exact message? And how many times had I ignored it, clicking delete without a second thought? But this time, I couldn't.

Even though one part of me had decided to go to therapy, there was another part of me, a much bigger part, a stronger part, a more independent part, that was still resistant. At the mere thought of the idea, that part of me roared up.

It's too expensive.

It's nobody's business.

You are what you are.

You don't need therapy, you just need to pray more.

There's a lot going on in your life right now.

But hidden just below the surface of each excuse was a lie: *you are not strong enough.* The truth was, I could not bear the thought of getting sucked through the window of the past. Reliving past mistakes, rehearing past lies.

I had so many excuses, but now I had to at least cross the first one off my list, because thanks to HR, it was free. And I wanted to be free. Free to move on. Free to adopt. My desire to be free just barely outweighed my fear. So, I clicked through the links, and entered my contact information in the required boxes. I didn't bother to check the details, though, on the off chance that if I entered the wrong digit here or there, they would not be able to contact me and I would be free.

Pressing submit did not remove the invisible weight from my shoulders and I still could not bring myself to focus on any of the tasks before me. So, I got up and walked towards the break room. Maybe a cup of tea and mindless conversation would do me good. Mikaela must have seen me stand up, because she popped up, too. I considered turning around, heading back to my desk, sure that the conversation would inevitably turn towards her wedding preparations and I really didn't feel up to it. I was tired. Tired of pasting a smile on my face and being happy for everyone else. Tired of pretending that nothing bothered me. I just wanted to have a light, empty conversation where I wasn't being reminded of anything from the past I wanted to escape, or anything from the present that I couldn't capture.

But it was not to be. Mikaela came in behind me, perky and ready to chat. She spent fifteen minutes telling about the extremely rude service she and her fiancée had received at the jewelry store where they had bought their wedding bands. I was indignant in all the right places, and laughed when it was appropriate. And then my phone rang, rescuing me from the story that would not end. I smiled at my friend, held the phone up to my ear, and said, "Hello?"

"Hi, this is Leon Baker from Baker and Associates." The name didn't ring a bell, so I waited, glad to have any excuse to end the conversation with Mikaela.

"We talked a few days ago," he continued. Still, I couldn't place his name or voice, so I said nothing and just smiled over the top of the phone at Mikaela as if I was taking a very important call from a very important person about a very important topic.

"While you were at the hospital," he added. Finally, the lightbulb went off. I stood up and walked to the doorway of the break room as if the six feet between us would magically prevent Mikaela from hearing every word I said.

"Yes, yes, I remember you! Um, what can I do for you?" I asked nervously. I barely remembered the conversation with the adoption lawyer, only how overcome with emotion I had been, and how kind he was. But I felt fairly certain I had made it clear I no longer needed his services. Or, more accurately, that I had never needed them.

"Well, I just wanted to follow up and see how you were doing. A lot of people really struggle when they get home from the hospital."

I laughed. I had struggled more than enough at the hospital, too. "Is that supposed to be reassuring?"

"No, I just meant…"

"I'm just joking with you, Mr. Baker. It's very…considerate of you to call, though." My shoulders relaxed slightly, relieved but still curious as to the purpose of the call. I chose my words carefully, not wanting to get ahead of myself. I didn't want to make any assumptions. "Your firm has excellent customer service. Are all the attorneys at your firm so…attentive?"

He laughed. "I'd like to think so."

For some reason, I *didn't* think so.

"And, do you always pray for your prospective clients?"

Mr. Baker laughed again and I found that I could quickly become used to it. "No, not usually. But when God places something on your heart, you have to obey him."

Amen! I agreed, even if I felt too empty to pray in that moment. "You know, Mr. Baker, you are kind of breaking every lawyer stereotype right now."

"Call me Leon."

I smiled to myself. Was this really happening? Right now, in the middle of the break room? I didn't know how I felt about a lawyer I had never met, who knew the biggest disappointment of my adult life, flirting with me at work during my break. I could feel Mikaela's curious eyes boring into my back. "Well, Leon, I really appreciate the...follow up, but I really should be getting back to work."

"I understand. Would you mind if I gave you a call later tonight?"

"Uh, sure," I shrugged, not knowing what else to say. After tapping the red button, I turned back toward Mikaela.

"Who was that?" Mikaela asked, practically bouncing out of her seat.

"Just this adoption lawyer I was thinking about hiring," I answered, not wanting to reveal too much. Even though Mikaela knew I had taken the adoption class, she didn't know about my foolish plan to adopt a pregnant teen's baby. I groaned to myself. That sounded so predatory.

When you see your reflection in a mirror, no matter how bad you look, you can't blame the mirror. The situation with Crystal held up a mirror to me, and I was not proud of what I saw. I vowed to myself that I would show more emotional restraint, and not let hope consume me. No, it was not just hope. It was desperation. Fear that time was passing me by and I would end up sad and alone. My longing to have a family had made me see signs and read between the lines of a play I had penned the lines to.

I would not allow myself to be so desperate again.

"Were you flirting with him?" Mikaela asked, staring at me quizzically.

"No, he was flirting with me," I snapped, perhaps more forcefully than I intended.

"'Me thinkest thou doth protesteth too much'," Mikaela intoned in her best old English accent, waiting for me to laugh. "Anyways, is he cute?" Unsatisfied with my shrug, Mikaela grabbed my arm and led me to her cubicle.

"What's his name? I want to look him up."

"We shouldn't be doing this at work," I protested, even though I told her his name and the name of his firm. I crossed my arms and pursed my lips, trying to blow out the first flickers of excitement. I would not turn nothing into something.

"I'm not going to a social media site. But, luckily for us, most lawyers post their pictures," she said clicking through a series of links until she found the website for Leon Baker and Associates. "Completely professional." After a few more clicks, she yelled "Bingo!" We scanned the page. He owned the firm. His name and picture were posted prominently at the top.

He was clean-shaven, wearing a black suit with a red tie. "Oooh," Mikaela crowed. "He's fine!" She dragged out the "i" just so I would know she was serious. And I had to agree- he looked very handsome. But more importantly, the first thing I noticed about him was his eyes. He had kind eyes. His smile reached up to his eyes and pushed the corners up. I could remember hearing the kindness in his voice when he had consoled me at the hospital.

"Not bad, Sierra, not bad."

I rolled my eyes. But I smiled as I walked back to my cubicle. Maybe God had something in store for me after all.

Chapter 20

When I got home that night, it was still bright outside. Maybe laying in the sun for a bit would help relieve the throbbing in my temples. I thought about taking a nap on the chaise on the back deck, but Crystal met me as soon as I opened the door. Apparently, she was hungry and hadn't eaten all day. All. Day. I was appalled. I stepped over piles of boxes and packaging that were strewn around the living room, and headed to the kitchen with Crystal trailing after me. I opened the refrigerator door. There was plenty of fresh fruit and vegetables; yogurt, and meat. More than enough for a seventeen-year-old girl and a newborn infant.

"I'm starving," she whined. "You don't have any noodles or anything. Nothing I know how to make."

My head was pounding. I was exhausted. All I wanted was a nap in the sun. Maybe some watermelon lemonade. I slumped onto a stool at the kitchen island. For "not having eaten all day", the kitchen was as bad as the living room, with a mess of plates and cups and silverware. Even as my stomach churned looking at the disarray, I decided to ignore it. To ignore the crumbs, the smudges, the open cabinet doors. Well, at least I tried. I quickly walked around the kitchen, softly shutting all the cabinet doors, then sat back down.

"Okay, so what do you usually eat?" I forced cheeriness into my voice, not wanting to make Crystal uncomfortable. But she didn't seem to notice anything more than her own grievance.

"Noodles, hot dogs, chips. You know, regular people food. Not this fancy, healthy crap."

"Junk food isn't really great for the baby. He needs you to…" I stopped at the look that Crystal gave me. I wanted to say, *My house, my rules*. But I knew that wouldn't come across as very welcoming. At the same time, I didn't think I should have to stock my cabinets with junk food just because she couldn't fry an egg or boil a potato. I pursed my lips. If we were already having conflict after just one day, I couldn't imagine what it would be like after a week. Or two. And, realistically, I had no idea how long she'd be staying with me. Would she and Lavondra patch everything up quickly? And if they didn't, what other options did Crystal have? It wasn't like she was going to be able to quickly get a job with a newborn son who kept her up all night. What had I agreed to? I wasn't going to let the girl starve. Should I cook for her, teach her how to cook, or just buy her the junk that she was used to? My mind was whirling. Until I got some sleep, I couldn't think straight.

"You know what, give me an hour. We can talk after I take a shower and a nap, okay?" Without waiting for a reply, I walked to my room. Foregoing the shower, I just stripped off my work clothes and collapsed into bed.

If I was tired, I could only imagine how tired Crystal must be, but that didn't change the annoyance I felt. *Lord, help me to be patient. Give me wisdom.*

When I awoke to a light tapping on my door, I felt refreshed. I pulled on shorts and a tee shirt. Crystal was outside my door, my self-designated alarm clock, Khalid in her arms. I held out my hands for him, and she passed him to me. I happily cradled his tiny body in the crook of my arms and walked and bounced with him down the hall back to the kitchen that looked the same as when I'd left it.

"How was your first day home with the baby?"

"It was all right. He slept for a little bit, but he wanted to eat all day! And I'm almost out of the diapers that the hospital sent me home with, so I called my mom and she brought over the stuff from the baby shower." That explained all the cardboard and trash by the front door. "And I was starving," she threw in, "so I barely had any energy to do anything."

She sounded like a whiny teenager, not a mother. I had to remind myself that she was both. She was still a teen who was having to live with the very adult consequences of her decisions. But that didn't mean she didn't need help. We both did. It wasn't fair to expect her to learn how to be a mom and how to cook healthily all at once. And even if I didn't know how long she would be living with me, I would do my best while she was there.

I pulled out a legal pad and pencil and handed them to Crystal, all the while I kept walking and bouncing.

"Okay, what do you usually like for breakfast?" And from there we made a menu for the upcoming week. Things I could cook and leave her for lunch, things she could easily warm up herself. When Khalid fell asleep, I laid him in his crib, then I put rice in the rice cooker, fish in the oven, broccoli in the steamer, and finally made the fresh watermelon lemonade I had been craving all afternoon. I poured a glass for Crystal, too, and she agreed that it was far better than any of the powdered drinks she was used to. As we sat on the deck, waiting for dinner to cook, I realized that in a way, I had exactly what I said I wanted. To have people who needed me. To have a child sleeping in that beautiful crib. To not be alone. Yet, for all the similarities, it was not the life I had imagined. We sat there in silence until I heard a gentle snore. I looked over at Crystal. Her eyes were closed and she looked so peaceful. I should have been happy, but I was not and I could not force myself to be.

My phone buzzed. It was a notification for a new text message. I read the 3 short messages that had come in quick succession.

FROM UNKNOWN:
Hi, it's Leon Baker.

The adoption lawyer.

How are you?

I had forgotten all about Leon Baker's call, but when I saw his name, the picture of him from his website popped into my mind's eye. He was following up *again* and I hadn't even decided if I wanted him to or not. Regardless of how "fine" Mikaela said he was, here was a man who had an almost front row seat to my meltdown at the hospital.

But, he was a Christian. Like, *"I'll pray for you without even knowing if you're a Christian and this could potentially cost me a client"*, type of Christian.

And, he was handsome.

And obviously successful.

And kind.

I went through my mental list. The little that I did know about him was positive. And what if... *Stay in the moment, Sierra, don't get ahead of yourself.* I reminded myself of my vow, but at the same time I wondered, *When should I respond?*

Immediately. Otherwise, I would just obsess over what to say and do and probably dive into deep house cleaning to distract myself. And I already knew the kitchen needed to be cleaned. At that thought, I stood up, grabbed my phone and lemonade and headed to the kitchen. I set my glass down on the edge of the countertop, then I looked at the screen one more time. Why was he even interested in me? He had never seen me. He had only heard me ugly cry into a phone. Maybe he was a rescuer, attracted to the "damsel in distress." I reminded myself of my vow again: *Sierra, don't get your hopes up! Play it cool. He could be a crazy stalker.* So, I decided to respond with something light, detached, and noncommittal.

TO UNKNOWN:
Great, thanks for asking.
Just about to have dinner.

I pressed send, then set the phone back down and opened the dishwasher. It was halfway full. I added Crystal's dirty dishes, making sure every plate was lined up in parallel rows. Then I pulled out a bottle of cleaning spray. One of those all-natural kinds that smell like actual lavender. I breathed deeply as I scrubbed the inside of the sink. Then I sprayed the counters and wiped them down. I could see sticky fingerprints on the microwave and refrigerator, so I wiped those down, too. I got lost in the task, wiping down every surface, taking occasional sips of my watermelon lemonade, but mostly just looking for crumbs and smudges and stickiness. How many times had I cleaned the kitchen and it didn't even need to be cleaned? But this time it did. I smiled. I would not complain about having a reason to do what I would normally do whether or not Crystal was staying with me. When the timer on the oven dinged, I pulled the tray of fish out and set it on the stove. I ignored the repeated dinging of my phone letting me know I had a new notification. I added fish, steamed rice, and a side of vegetables to two plates. On another night, when I wasn't so tired, I would make something more elaborate, but for our first dinner as housemates, I was satisfied.

I placed the plates on the table, and went to get Crystal, finally glancing at my phone as I walked towards the guest room. There was a new message from Leon. Just three little words.

FROM LEON BAKER:

So you cook?

I hmphed to myself. Everybody, male or female, should know how to cook. It was a basic life skill, one that obviously no one had taught Crystal. I quickly typed back:

TO LEON BAKER:

Of course.

Almost immediately a smiley face popped up on my screen. I set the phone face down, then waited for Crystal who sleepily stumbled into the kitchen and to the table. She rested her face in her hands as I blessed the food, thanking God not only for the food, but also for the provision and having someone to share it with. Words that I had been at a loss for earlier, now seemed to flow like a waterfall, gathering momentum, tumbling forward, until I heard Crystal clear her throat. I didn't know how long I had been praying, but I took the hint and said amen.

I looked at Crystal across the round table. She stabbed at her plate, picking up a piece of fish, examining it as if it was something she had never seen before.

"What is this?" she asked, forehead creased.

I smiled with pride. "Salmon," I said, putting a bite of the perfectly seasoned, moist fish into my own mouth. She stared at her fork disbelieving. "It's a kind of fish," I added, not wanting to insult her, but also not sure why she was looking at it as if it was covered in Khalid's diaper.

"I've never seen fish like this before," she rotated the fork, sniffed it, looked at it again, then scraped the bit of flesh onto the edge of her plate.

My smile wavered. "You don't like fish?" I couldn't believe I hadn't bothered to ask.

"I like fish, but not this kind of fish. Why is it pink? Shouldn't it be yellow or brown?"

"Well, yeah, fried fish is yellow but you don't really fry salmon."

She just oomphed, and took a bite of rice. "Your rice is good," she said as if sensing that my ego was fragile and needed a boost. After adding seasoning salt and pepper, she ate all the rice, but did not touch the vegetables. And definitely not the "pink fish". She probably would have been happier with a plate of frozen fish sticks, I thought sourly, instead of my expertly seasoned and grilled salmon. I wanted to tell her how healthy salmon was, and how unhealthy fried fish was. Especially for a nursing mother. But, I decided to take the win. *At least she likes the rice*, I thought, and added fish sticks to my mental grocery list. Sure, it was kid food, but there was no use in wasting money on salmon if she wouldn't eat it.

"Somebody's calling you," Crystal said, pointing to my phone with her chin. I hadn't even heard the notification. I flipped the phone over. There was another text from Leon.

FROM LEON BAKER:
Tell me about yourself.

"Tell me about yourself?" I laughed. Why did getting to know someone so often resemble a job interview? I started to type back, What are your strengths, but then deleted the characters I had almost instinctively swiped. What did I really want to say? He already knew more about me than even many of my closest friends.

TO LEON BAKER:
What do you want to know?

FROM LEON BAKER:
Why a beautiful woman like you is single...

I paused. I couldn't stop myself from grinning.

TO LEON BAKER:
How do you know I'm beautiful?

Or single?

FROM LEON BAKER:
I may have stalked your social media sites...

What a confession! My mind filled with questions: Should I be worried? Was he really a psycho serial killer? In all honesty, I had looked him up online, too, though. And I appreciated that he was upfront. But immediately, my mind jumped twenty steps ahead. Was this how our love story would begin? Would he one day be my husband? It was easy to picture him in a black suit based on his profile picture.

I reminded myself of my vow and recent humiliation.

TO LEON BAKER:
Waiting on the Lord to bring the right person into my life.

What about you?

I put the phone back down, and smiled at Crystal. "Do you want me to go check on Khalid?" He had started whimpering, but Crystal didn't show any sign of moving. I stood up, but Crystal shook her head.

"I've got him," she said, then walked toward the guest room. Her room. From my seat at the table, I watched as she gently picked Khalid up, careful to support his head as the nurses had shown her. "I think he's hungry again," she called out. She adjusted her shirt, and almost instantly Khalid was suckling away. She sat on the edge of her bed, cradling Khalid with one arm and resting her head in the other. Even after her nap, she still looked like she might pass out at any moment.

"Here, let me help you," I said, walking to her side. "Sit back against the headboard, and let's prop this pillow under the baby's head."

"That's better," she sighed, then stroked his fine, curly hair.

And just like that, we fell into a pattern. I went to work, came home, cleaned up, helped Crystal with Khalid. I responded to the occasional flirty text from Leon. Like most lawyers, he worked long hours. He didn't have a lot of time for dating, and didn't seem impatient to meet in person. And, honestly, neither was I. I was busy, too, with my houseguests. I didn't tell him about that, though, knowing it would sound crazy. And I tried to pray, but didn't really know what to say or ask for.

Once, I went to the bathroom in the middle of the night and heard the sounds of crying. I opened my door, expecting to see Crystal attempting to soothe Khalid, but found her alone on the couch.

"I'm sorry, was I too loud?" she muttered, wiping her nose with the end of her sleeve. "I didn't wanna wake the baby," she whispered through her tears.

"No, I was just gonna get some water." I walked to the couch and instinctively put my arm around her shoulder. "What's wrong?"

Crystal was silent for a second before responding. "I don't know. I just feel so overwhelmed. And I feel bad asking for help 'cause you've already done so much for me."

I thought about what she said. I was happy she realized how much I was doing, with all the cooking and cleaning falling to me. But I also knew that being up multiple times a night with a newborn was exhausting, too. Every day her eyes got blearier and the dark circles had taken root. I wanted to tell her about sleep training and getting the baby on a schedule, but I didn't want her to think I was trying to take over, so I just listened.

She complained about muscle spasms in her legs, constipation, and sore nipples. "Nobody tells you this stuff!" She wailed. "And your place is nice, but I haven't left the house in a week!" I wanted to say, *"Take the baby for a walk!"* but again I clamped my mouth shut. This three-a.m. conversation/meltdown/breakdown was not the time for problem solving. It was the time for listening. Especially since the only advice I could offer was sourced from observing friends and reading blogs online. There was nothing worse than pouring your heart out to someone and having them give you a soundbite or a nugget they read from some book. So I sat there, silently agreeing how tough it was not to be able to leave the house and have nowhere to go.

"And everybody knows you would be so much better at this than me, which makes me resent you, but then I feel bad for resenting you because you've done so much for me."

Her words were a punch to my gut. *She* resented *me*? I wanted to jump up, push her away, lay out all the reasons why *she* didn't get to resent *me*, no matter how insecure she may have felt. But before I said anything, I let her words hang in the air for a second, then five, then ten. I don't know if it was due to my spiritual maturity or sleepiness, maybe a combination of both. Yes, she resented me, but she also felt bad about it. *Don't get offended, Sierra.* What was she trying to tell me? "Wow, I had no idea all this was going on," I murmured soothingly. "Except for the constipation. I was suspicious about the constipation because you never eat your vegetables," I lightly teased. I was rewarded with a small smile, glad that I hadn't fallen for the bait of being offended.

"Seriously, though, how do you...how do you handle all this? I mean, do you ever still think about..." Her words trailed off, but even in the dark on the couch, not seeing her face, I could see her words as clearly as if they had been written in the sky. She wanted to know if I still thought about adopting Khalid. About being a mother.

"Do you ever still think about adopting Khalid?" She whispered. I could feel the tension around Crystal's shoulders, as if she were holding her breath. I knew that I had to choose my words carefully.

"Honestly, I don't. And when I first met you, I just wanted to help you. I wasn't even thinking about adopting. But you were so brave and knew exactly what you wanted. I really admired you for that. That's what gave me the courage to even think about adoption. *You* inspired *me*.

"You're a great mom, Crystal, and Khalid is lucky to have you. Everybody feels overwhelmed at the beginning. No matter how old you are, rich or poor. Even if you had a full-time nanny. It's just the nature of being a mother for the first time. You're responsible for a whole other life. Plus, your hormones are all over the place. It's tough. But you can do this. I believe in you."

"But, I mean, you must have been disappointed, right? How did you move on?"

I was silent for a second. How had I moved on? And regardless of what I said, had I moved on?

"You have such a deep relationship with God. That's it, huh?" Crystal looked at me longingly. I didn't know what to say.

"Did God tell you to help me?" she pressed.

I thought about that. "In a way, yes. God tells us to help those who need it. It's never wrong to do the right thing." That sounded good and spiritual, but I knew something was missing.

"But you could have helped me in lots of different ways. You could have taken me to a hotel, you could have called social services, you could have given me a hundred bucks and said good luck," Crystal sniffled. "But you didn't. You opened up your house to me. Not everybody would do that. My own mom wouldn't do that for me. I'd be homeless right now if it wasn't for you!" At that, Crystal began to cry again in earnest. I squeezed her shoulder. I didn't know what to say. I didn't have any magic words that would take her pain away. So, I just wrapped my arms around her shoulders and let her cry. And I thanked God that Crystal wasn't alone.

REY SIRAKAVIT

Chapter 21

The next morning, I woke up feeling like I had the flu. My body ached. Every muscle was tight. I felt like throwing up. A tiny patch of sunlight filtered through the blinds, shining straight into my eyes, and I pulled the covers up over my head and buried my face into my pillow. But I was not sick. Nor was I just tired from staying up late talking, though that had been emotionally draining.

Today was the day.

I sighed, tucking the edge of the comforter around my head and behind my ears, leaving a small gap around my mouth and nose. A feeling of dread pressed down on me. I lay in bed, considering not getting up at all. Calling in sick. Cancelling my appointments. But that was the fear talking. I replayed the conversation with Crystal from the night before. Why *had* I helped her? My eyes landed on the red onesie in the corner. Did I still want to be a mother? Instead of being wrapped in a queen-sized cotton comforter, did I want to be wrapping my arms around a small child? Instead of pretending to be sick in bed, did I want to be the one coaxing a child out of bed?

Lord, I don't know if I can do this.

Was I going to let fear prevent me from moving forward? No. So, I forced myself up. I released my death grip on the edge of the comforter and swung my feet over the side of the bed. I had finally

179

been able to schedule my first therapy session for after work that day, and every cell in my body protested. On top of being tired and drained, I was tired and drained. I wanted to go on a day when I had had a full night of sleep and knew exactly what to say and how to say it. When I was fresh.

Even though I felt better after a quick shower, the feeling of dread still did not disappear. I stared at myself in the mirror, still fogged up. *You can do it,* I said. *You aren't alone. God's with you.* But was that true? The words from the popular Christian song popped into my head. "Even when you can't see him, he's working." I picked up my cell phone from the edge of the counter top and began typing a message to Carmen.

TO CARMEN EVANS:

Sorry it's so early but can you pray for me? Therapy is today and I'm not feeling it.

Almost instantly, my phone beeped.

FROM CARMEN EVANS:

Praying. Read 1 John 5:14.

I asked her to pray, not give me a homework assignment, but I walked back to my bedroom anyway and picked up the Bible off the edge of my nightstand. Flipping through the pages, I stopped in 1 John:

This is the confidence we have in approaching God: that if we ask anything according to his will, he hears us.

For some reason, the verse didn't comfort me. Sure, God hears us, but he doesn't always give us what we want, or I wouldn't have had to go to therapy at all!

I plopped onto the edge of my bed. Was there something wrong with me? I just wanted what most other women throughout history, including my best friend, had. A husband. Children. And no matter how much I asked the Lord, door after door continued to close in my face. I had "named it and claimed", but it just wasn't happening for me. Was that how Sarah felt when Abraham told her the Lord would bless them with a child? Way beyond the age of conception, but hanging on to a promise that seemed far-fetched? Like Sarah, did I just need to have faith and hang on to the promise of God?

But had he made that promise to me? Every promise that God made in the Bible didn't apply unequivocally to every believer. The only way to know would be…to ask. Maybe instead of just asking God for what I wanted, maybe it was time to ask God what he wanted.

I bowed my head and exhaled. *Lord, you know my heart. I want a family so bad I can taste it. But, is that your will for me? I have tried to do things your way, I have tried to obey you…I don't want to be like Sarah, coming up with my own plan. I want to do your will, Lord.*

And then I forced myself to stop talking. To quiet my heart and mind.

A car rumbled down the street.

Khalid whimpered.

A dog barked.

And barked.

And barked.

Khalid's whimpers turned into full-fledged cries.

Instinctively I stood up, but Crystal must have quickly gotten to him, so I sat back down. Trying to hear from God was hard. There were so many distractions, inside and outside of me. I picked up the Bible, still open to 1 John 5. My eyes scanned the page and fell upon a sentence a few verses up. "Perfect love drives out fear."

Was I allowing fear to stop me following my dream of being a mom? Of providing a safe and loving home for a child who didn't have one? "Perfect love drives out fear." Whose love? God's love for me? My love for Loveyouforever? I hadn't thought about her in so long. Or prayed for her. Where was she at that moment? Still waiting? I pictured us in heaven one day, meeting for the very first time, me trying to explain that I had not been able to adopt her because I was afraid of talking to a therapist. God's perfect love, and a little bit of shame, propelled me to my feet. Even if God had not spoken the way I wanted, he had spoken. *Thank you, God.* I glanced down at my watch. *Now get moving Sierra.* Pulling a sundress and cardigan over my shoulders, I headed to the kitchen, resolved to not let fear dictate my destiny.

Crystal met me at the kitchen table with a grin. While I still hadn't been able to convince her to eat something that didn't come out of a box, I was happy to see her eating some relatively healthy granola. She held the box out to me but I shook my head. I wanted something hearty and filling, even in the summer. I turned on the tea kettle, then pulled out some eggs, veggies, and cheese to make an omelet. I shook my head at myself. Just fifteen minutes earlier I had been pretending to be sick. Now, I was ready to scarf down a high-protein breakfast for bodybuilders!

Crystal and I glided around each other, pulling ingredients out, opening and shutting cabinet doors. Well, she did more of the opening and I did most of the shutting. But it was like we were in sync. A team. A family.

My mind drifted back to that afternoon's appointment and whether or not I should tell Crystal. Would knowing that I was still pursuing adoption make her feel uncomfortable? The words from 1 John came back to my head. *Perfect love drives out fear.*

"Um, I'm going to be late tonight," I began, still unsure of how much to share. I arranged the vegetables and knife and cutting board, avoiding Crystal's inquisitive gaze.

"Do you have a date?" Even from the corner of my eye, I could see her big smile. She leaned so far forward over the kitchen island that I had to take a step back.

"What? Why do you ask that?" Did Crystal know about Leon? Not that there was much to know.

"Well, I know you've been texting someone. You start smiling all big," she smiled. I couldn't hold my own smile back. "And it's not just your friend Carmen," she added knowingly. I was surprised that she hadn't brought it up before, and a part of me wanted to just talk about the man I was texting and the fun of flirting and the excitement of possibilities. But that wasn't the purpose of the conversation, so I steered us back to my original topic.

"No, it's not a date, just a… doctor's appointment." I sighed at my cowardice. That wasn't a lie. Therapists were doctors, weren't they? But no matter how I tried to justify it to myself, I knew that I was not being completely honest. But I couldn't bring myself to just come out and say, *"Hey I'm going to therapy tonight so that I can be certified to adopt. Not your child, of course, as we've already discussed, but someone else's child."*

So, instead, I filled my mouth with cheesy eggs while Crystal filled the silence with chatter about Khalid's upcoming doctor's appointment and wellness visits and shots.

* * *

Somehow, the day flew by, and before I knew it, I was standing outside a brown brick office building on Colorado Blvd. The force of the cars whipping by were like an invisible hand pushing me towards the entrance even as I considered heading back to the parking lot. I stood in front of the glass doors for a full minute before pulling the stainless-steel handle towards me. According to the sign, there were a handful of businesses inside, including a massage therapist, nail salon, and Suite 201: *Circle of Serenity*. Foregoing the elevator, I chose the enclosed concrete stairs, dragging my feet up each one as if I were heading towards the guillotine. It smelled like rotten eggs and urine, but even that did not compel my feet to move any faster. I just kept my hands wrapped around my purse and held my breath.

At the top of the stairwell, I used my elbow to push through the door. I followed the signs pointing left toward the therapist's office. And then I was there. I stood hesitantly outside suite number 201. A drab brown door with a six-inch black sign and basic white block font. I took a deep breath, then opened the door. Instantly, I was transported to a whole new world. A large black and white tapestry of an elephant on a wall. Water fountain in the corner. Fake LED candles "flickering" on shelves all around the room. There were two chairs along the wall. I reminded myself of why I was there. I asked God for strength. I tried not to think about what would happen if I just walked out and didn't come back. There was no receptionist and the room was completely empty. I could leave and no one would be the wiser.

You can do this.

I let the door handle go and walked over to the plastic chairs.

Calm down.

I repeated these words to myself, long enough to breathing, but not so long that I grew impatient and left.

Pray, Sierra. I blinked. The words were my own, but somehow not my own. Audible, yet silent. I was commanded to pray, but I didn't know what to say. No spiritual words or scriptures came to my mind. No heavenly voices or angels on high. Just me. Sitting on a plastic chair, seconds away from bolting. Heart pounding. Lightheaded.

Father.

Our father. *My father. Yes, call on him, he cares for you.* Again, the words seemed to be my own, but not my own. A prayer within a prayer.

Who art in heaven. *He is in heaven. He has all power.*

Hallowed be thy name. *Even his name is holy. Even his name has power to save.*

Thy kingdom come, thy will be done, on earth as it is in heaven. *Lord, show me your will.*

Give us this day our daily bread. *You are a provider, Lord, and will meet all my needs.*

And forgive us our debts, as we also forgive our debtors. *Let my character be like yours.*

And lead us not into temptation. *I will follow you, Lord, not my fear, not the world; you, and you alone.*

But deliver us from the evil one. *Deliver me, Lord. I can't keep walking around with this weight on my shoulders, this fear holding me back!*

For thine is the kingdom and the power and the glory forever. *Amen.*

I opened my eyes and took a deep breath. A sense of peace washed over me. I had never prayed the Lord's Prayer like that before. It had always just been something I had memorized and recited, but it never had real meaning until that moment.

Within minutes, or maybe just seconds, an older white woman with long, thin blond hair breezed into the room and immediately the hairs on my arms and neck stood on end. All the peace I had just had disappeared. This was a mistake. A very bad mistake. A very bad, awkward mistake that I had no idea how I was going to extricate myself from.

Chapter 22

I fumbled with my purse and stood.

It wasn't that I was racist. Or even prejudiced. I mentally pulled out my racial resume: I had several close white friends, including Jessica from the adoption class. I worked in an almost all-white office. And, I lived in Denver, Colorado, for crying out loud! But instead of my racial resume reminding me of how open and accepting and tolerant I was, I just felt guilty. I was judging her before she'd even opened her mouth. For some reason, all I could see was her pale skin. Her pale hair. Her pale *teeth*! Her whiteness.

Going to therapy, being forced to open up to a total stranger, needing to win their approval already felt like an impossible task. And, on top of that, potentially having to deal with any subtle racism would be unbearable. I had plenty of experience being seen as a stereotype by people who pretended to "not see color". Like the realtor who'd assured me she was colorblind when she first met me, but kept calling me "girlfriend". Or, the hiring manager who had told me about the last time he had hired a Black man he'd been fired for coming in late too often, but he would take a chance on me anyway. They were telling me that even though I was Black, they wouldn't hold that against me, as if my ethnicity were a deficit that they were kindly ignoring. *Be on your best behavior, prove to us that you deserve to be here,* they seemed to say. Were they expecting me to fawn over them for their alleged kindness and altruism?

I was already exhausted just thinking about it. I should have done more research. Checked out the website. Looked at the staff pictures. Even if they weren't African American, a therapist who was a person of color would be more likely to understand me. The decision to go to counseling had been hard enough, and this only cemented the feeling that I had made the wrong decision. That was the last time I would just go with something because it was "free". I stood to leave, but my feet didn't move.

And then the woman pulled up a chair beside me and smiled. Not knowing what to do, I sat back down, too. Was she going to be one of those super spiritual, mother earth types with the affected voice who would try to hug me? I shuddered. *Lord, please don't let her hug me.* How was I going to get out of that office without embarrassing her or myself?

Then she introduced herself: Frances Anne Rogers. She thanked me for coming and then went immediately into her spiel about her philosophy of counseling. Wholeness. Acceptance. Removing roadblocks. Slowly the hairs on the backs of my arms and neck relaxed. My heart responded. Those were all good things that I knew I wanted and needed, even if I kept running from them. And then Frances Anne Rogers said something that I have never heard a white person say. Ever.

"You are an African-American woman and I am a white woman. Because of that, there may be things that we see differently, but please know that I am here for your healing and growth ...." As much as those earlier experiences had angered me and wearied me to my core, this was different. Frances Anne Rogers was actually saying that she recognized my ethnicity as *one* part of my identity, just as she recognized me as a woman. I don't remember everything she said, but she calmed me. Reassured me. *I see you,* she seemed to be saying, and she was asking that I see her, too. I felt my shoulders relax.

When she stood and headed down the hall to her office, instead of making a mad dash for the door, I followed her. As we walked, she asked all the things Denverites who were not native Coloradans talk about when they first meet. How long had I been in Denver? What was my favorite season? Did I ski? Didn't I just hate the atrocious traffic? She motioned for me to sit and eventually, the conversation lulled. She smiled gently, and I knew it was time.

"Well, at my work they offer to pay for three counseling sessions…"

She nodded, legs crossed, leaned forward. And waited. Obviously, there was more. As much as I had thought about coming and not coming, I had never really considered what I might say. Or how.

"Umm, so," I continued, filling the silence with more silence. "So, I, well, I-" I looked around the room, hoping the perfect words would jump off the walls and into my brain. Unfortunately, the framed degrees and more paintings of elephants didn't spark me.

"Why don't you start at the beginning?"

The beginning? Where was that? Meeting Crystal? Failing my home study? Going to the singles event? My humiliating conversation with Drisk? Or even further *further* back? Not yet. Hopefully, not ever.

"Well, I recently decided to adopt." She nodded, encouraging me to continue. "And I took all the classes and everything, but when I had my one-on-one interview with the social worker who was doing the home study, she seemed to think that I was not prepared to parent a child with trauma." I paused, unconsciously waiting for affirmation. Surprise. Indignation. *Based on the seven-minute conversation we just had about traffic and weather, I can't understand how anyone could say you wouldn't make a great parent!* I would accept that. Or something along those lines. But Frances Anne Rogers did not say that.

"It's never too late to heal from our own trauma," she murmured reassuringly. I wanted to laugh. I may have. "Heal"? To "make like new"? No. I would never heal. I could cope. I could try to forget. I could try to move forward and pray that memories from the past wouldn't consume me and eat me alive, devouring my flesh and heart and soul from the inside out.

But heal?

No.

"So," I continued, as if I hadn't heard her, "I don't know how this works, but I guess I need proof that I came to counseling and that I'm ready to move forward with adopting. Is there a form or something you can give me?"

She smiled. "No, but we can figure that out when the time comes."

"When the time comes"? What did that mean? How long did she intend on seeing me? I returned her smile, even if mine did not reach my eyes.

"Why do you want to adopt?" she asked. She leaned back in her chair.

That was a question I was prepared to answer.

I told her the short answer, the one reserved for acquaintances and strangers. "I'm ready to be a mom, and I have enough love in my heart for a child, even if I didn't birth him." I thought about Khalid.

"You seem really sure," Frances said, and I smiled, glad to have nailed at least one question.

"I am. I've been thinking and praying and planning and I just feel like this is the best thing for me."

"And what does your family think?"

191

Immediately the smile dropped from my face. I licked my teeth, then waited for my breathing to regain its tempo. My family? What did they have to do with anything? *Keep it light, Sierra*, I told myself. Should I lie? That would be the easiest thing to do. Just say they're supportive. And who's to say it wasn't the truth? Maybe they really would be supportive, if I'd given them the chance. I tried to think if there was anyone adopted in my immediate family, but there wasn't. I tried to imagine what Debra would say. Would she be the doting grandmother? Would she be supportive and fly out to Denver to attend the adoption ceremony? Would I even want her to?

"Umm, it's really just me."

Then there was a quiet chime in the background, and I knew our time was over. I breathed a sigh of relief. We set up a time to meet again the following week, and as I walked back to my car, I felt relief wash over me. I had survived. True, I would have to go back again, but I had survived. Maybe if I just did this for a couple more weeks, convince her that I was normal and okay and didn't need therapy, she'd write a little note or letter to the social worker, they could add that to my file, and I could move on.

That night, when I unlocked my front door, I was emotionally exhausted, but oddly hopeful. Crystal was sprawled out on the couch with Khalid on her belly. There were pillows spread out on the floor all around them. In case he fell? I picked him up, and Crystal barely moved. I sat with him in the armchair across from Crystal, cradling him in my arms. His dark brown eyes blinked up at me. He drooled and I wiped his mouth. He was a beautiful boy. He still had that fine baby hair that would eventually curl up. I tried to picture him as a toddler stumbling around, then a young man. My heart swelled with love for this child who I had not carried. Aside from his mom, he had spent more time in my arms than anyone else's. And even though he was not mine, I hoped that I would always be able to be in his life. I kissed his cheek. I blew raspberries on his belly. I changed his diaper. I sang him a song. I placed him back in his mother's waiting arms.

REY SIRAKAVIT

Chapter 23

Before I knew it, another week had passed and I was sitting in the therapist's office again. I wasn't as nervous as I had been the week before, but I wasn't exactly relaxed, either.

"So, tell me a little more about yourself. Are you married? Seeing anyone?"

I held up my ringless left hand. "I'm 33, single, never married."

"And you're thinking about adopting, right?" Frances picked up a notepad and scribbled a few notes, then set it back down. Her eyes never seemed to leave mine, though. "That can be really expensive."

"Infant adoption, for sure. But I'm actually adopting through foster care, so there have just been a few nominal fees. Nothing major," I smiled. If I could come across as normal as possible, then maybe she would write that letter even sooner.

She didn't speak, and neither did I. In a negotiation, whoever speaks first loses. I thought that might also apply to counseling. The goal was to not oversell myself or look desperate. I would answer all her questions, but I wouldn't volunteer any information.

"Are you interested in dating?"

"Sure." I paused, willing my face to look open and light. Frances nodded, but said nothing. "I'm not opposed." I looked at her, she looked at me. I continued. "I'm just at that season where I'm not getting any younger, so adopting just makes the most sense."

Frances nodded.

"I mean, adopting isn't like my last resort," I added. Frances nodded at me again. "It's just that it wasn't my first choice. It's not exactly how I thought my life would turn out, but I'm not resentful," I shook my head, willing my mouth to stop moving, but I only dug myself deeper into the hole I was digging. "What do I have to be resentful about? It's a privilege to be able to adopt and to offer a loving home to a child who has nothing. Not that they have nothing. Or that I'm their savior or anything... I just..." I stopped, catching my lower lip between my teeth. And just like that, I lost and Frances Anne Rogers got the "W".

"You seem nervous," she stated kindly.

"What was the question again?"

She shrugged nonchalantly, "Are you interested in dating?"

That seemingly innocent question had produced a river of tears over the years.

"I'm not opposed. I was seeing someone for a while, but it didn't work out."

"Why do you think that is?"

"Umm, well I think a major part is that I take my faith very seriously, and some men can't handle my...celibacy." There, I had said it. For some reason, I felt just as nervous as when I was bringing it up on dates.

"Do you usually date men who share your faith?"

"Definitely."

"Then why do you think it's so hard for them to accept?"

I thought about that for a second. I wanted to say, *Because I'm just a stronger, more faithful Christian.* Or, *Men are more driven by their physical needs than women are.* But I knew that neither of those were completely true. Godly men who took their faith seriously enough to be celibate did exist. Drisk had complained that we lacked chemistry, not that he resented being celibate. Would other exes have agreed? I racked my brain. Since college, boyfriends had come and gone, most not lasting longer than a few months. Each ended things with an excuse about needing to focus, being busy, or just wanting to stay friends. But maybe those were all just smokescreens. Maybe they were all good guys who didn't want to hurt my feelings by telling me I was a bad kisser and they didn't feel a spark with me. And how to put all that into words to someone I barely knew?

"You know, all this time, after every breakup, I've blamed the guys. They were weak. They weren't willing to obey God. They didn't love God as much as I did. And I was never surprised when it ended. But maybe it wasn't them. Maybe it was me."

"Well, it's rarely all one person. What does celibacy mean to you?"

"Sex is intended to be between a husband and a wife. In the confines of marriage," I added hoping I didn't sound as self-righteous to her as I did to myself.

"When you say 'confines', it makes me think of a prison. Would you mind if I just changed one little word?"

"Sure," I hesitated.

"Instead of 'confines', how about 'boundaries'? Like, the lines on the freeway serve as boundaries. Stay in your lane, keep up with the flow of traffic, know you're heading in the right direction. But when you veer out of your lane, when you cross over your boundaries, then you're headed for danger."

Boundaries. Huh.

"So, in a relationship, the boundaries protect you *both*; but there's something wrong if the boundary is erected to protect you *from* the other person. Sometimes we can use celibacy as a shield, as a way of not getting too close. What do you think?"

"I can see that."

"So where do you think this need to protect yourself comes from?"

The harp sounded in the background, cutting Frances off.

"Well, our time for today is up. Same time next week?"

"Sure," I agreed.

"For next week, I'd like you to be thinking about why you protect yourself and how you might take a risk in your next relationship. One that- obviously- doesn't involve you compromising your faith, but maybe that pushes you out of your comfort zone. Sound good?"

I nodded. "Sounds good," I said letting the words roll off my tongue with the ease of someone who was carefree and not carrying around twenty-five years of baggage. But Frances didn't know my life. *"Take a risk"* sounded good and easy, but risks were...well, risky. By definition. A risk could lead to heartache and sorrow and pain, and I had more than enough heartache, sorrow, and pain to last a lifetime. I picked up my purse and cardigan and walked to the door. My purse was filled with tissues, various sizes of bandaids, a multipurpose pocketknife with 8 blades, pepper spray, feminine products, extra makeup and lip gloss, SPF-50 sunscreen even though with my complexion I probably only needed SPF-30, and fuzzy socks for if I went to someone's house who had a no-shoes policy and my feet were in need of a pedicure. Unnecessary risks were not a part of my life. Even the coordinating cardigan that I draped over my arm was more than a fashion accessory. I never left home all summer without a cardigan because most office buildings kept the AC turned up so high that you were in more danger of frostbite in the summer than in the winter! No. Risks were not good.

But wasn't adopting a risk? Wasn't taking Crystal in a risk? Wasn't going to therapy a risk? All risks that I had taken. I pulled myself up a little higher. This year had been one risk after another, and though everything hadn't worked out exactly like I hoped, I knew that I was stronger.

On the drive home, I replayed Frances' words.

When I got home, Crystal was in her room with the baby and the kitchen looked like a hurricane had blown through. Where to begin? My large soup pot was on the counter top.

"I made hotdogs for lunch," Crystal said. Hot dogs in a soup pot? Not in a saucepan or small pot. The soup pot. The 20-cup capacity soup pot with carrots, onions, tomatoes, and potatoes clearly painted on the outside. I narrowed my eyes at the counter strewn with dishes beside the empty sink. The dishwasher was probably empty, too.

I shook my head to myself in frustration. How would I have responded back in college when I had a roommate- just clean up everything myself, or leave it for them to handle? But how could I cook when there wasn't one square inch of counter space? Crystal bounced the baby in her arms as she asked me about my day, chatting blithely while I could feel my temper rising. I made a decision.

"Why don't I hold the baby while you clean up a bit? Then I can make some dinner for us."

Crystal bounced Khalid, looking around at the mess. "Um, okay," she said, reluctantly placing him in my outstretched arms.

I turned all my attention to the cutie pie in my arms, feeling all my frustration melt away as he smiled. What a risk that had been, to invite someone I barely knew to stay in my home…and what a reward. My chest filled with love as Khalid looked me in the eye and smiled. As I bounced him a little higher, his smile widened and he waved his chubby fist in the air, finally finding his mouth and shoving it in. He hadn't giggled yet, but I was ready. I couldn't wait. I tickled his chubby belly, tickled his chubby cheeks, and he gurgled. Not exactly a giggle, but close enough. None of the risks that I had taken could compare to the reward in seeing Khalid's smiling eyes.

I decided to do what Frances had suggested. Take another risk.

Chapter 24

TO LEON BAKER:

> *Are you busy this weekend? Wanna grab dinner and finally meet in person?*

I ran my finger around the edge of my phone case as I waited. The message was delivered. I waited. What if he wasn't interested? What if he just wanted someone to occasionally flirt with? What if we met, but he wasn't who he said he was? My mind latched onto that possibility, and the titles of a dozen false identity movies- all involving dark parking lots- flashed across my mind. Dinner was a bad idea.

I stared at the phone, searching for the recall function that didn't exist. Then, the phone beeped in my hand.

FROM LEON BAKER:

> *I have a big case coming up, but how about coffee?*

Mentally, I gave another point to Leon, and allowed my breathing to settle. A coffee date was a great idea. Even though I didn't drink coffee, I loved the idea of a public place filled with potential caffeine-induced warrior/witnesses who could step in if necessary.

Leon suggested a date, time, and location, and just like that, our first date was scheduled. I set the phone down face down and turned my attention back to the one who was exactly as he appeared, beautiful and full of light and ready to receive as much love as anyone could give.

When I told Crystal about the coffee date, she practically erupted from her chair with excitement.

"Are you nervous?"

"It's just a coffee/tea date," I said. And said. And said again. Having a teenage roommate was exhausting.

" in the middle of prepping for a case and can only steal away for about an hour. And since the point is just to meet in a low-key atmosphere, with very little financial investment if either party does not meet the other's preliminary expectations, a coffee date is quite shrewd."

Ha! I'm already starting to sound all lawyerly- or British. Maybe a British lawyer? The voice in my head had morphed into the queen's English towards the end of the sentence. I pictured a British lawyer with their white wig and long black robe. And for some reason, he had Leon's face. At least, Leon's face from his website. And he was holding his arm out, like he was beckoning me into his embrace.

But Crystal didn't laugh. She just raised her eyebrows at me.

I shook my head. *No more British romances for you, Sierra.*

"So, how do I look?" I stood to show her my outfit. Nothing fancy, just jeans and an embellished tank with strappy heeled sandals.

Crystal nodded her approval. "You're so pretty. Why don't you date more?"

The question was one of those double-handed compliments/insults that teens were notorious for. I decided to not be offended, and just shrugged. "I've been busy."

Crystal did not seem convinced.

"I've had a houseguest for the past month," I added, hoping that she would cease and desist with her line of questioning. I smiled. I just hoped I didn't slip into my lawyer voice at the coffeehouse. It was definitely too early to introduce him to my cheesy humor.

But as I stood in the packed coffeehouse, trying to protect my exposed toes from the foot traffic, I was worried about a few other words slipping out. At least the man wearing trendy boots, golf shorts, and floral print shirt paused to say "Sorry."

The new coffee shop was very different from the one that Carmen and I went to. Everything here was shiny and bright. And sterile. No warmth. No personality. A sign of the gentrification occurring in many previously "undesirable" neighborhoods. The change always seemed to start with a coffee shop, before new, more expensive housing was built. I sighed. But the coffee must be great, because the line was long and every seat was filled. I looked around, butterflies filling my stomach, wondering if Leon was already there. I couldn't decide which would be better: if he was watching me attempt to weave my way through the tables? Or, if I were already seated and happened to look up casually just as he approached?

When I got to the front, I ordered my standard coffee house alternative, chai, and hoped it would be more than some bland box mix with a heap of cream on top. Taking my cup, I turned and there he was at my elbow.

"Hi. Sierra?" His smile stretched from ear to ear. It immediately pulled me in and I was smiling, too.

His face was so smooth, I wanted to run my hands across his cheeks. I rarely felt such immediate attraction to someone, especially someone I hardly knew. *Snap out of it, Sierra.* I captured the thought, folded it up, and tucked it away. *Lord, be with me.* Holding the cup of chai in front of my chest like a shield, I nervously followed Leon to the table he had already commandeered. He moved books and folders to the side and motioned for me to sit.

I tried to remind myself of first date etiquette. I had plenty of practice, but having a lot of practice did not mean that you were any good at it, either.

Leon made some small talk about the coffee shop, the brand, and skipped right over the weather and traffic and straight to the most important question every Denverite wants to know.

"What high school did you go to?"

"Oh, I'm not from Denver," I confessed. "I'm actually from California," I added, before he could start listing all the suburbs outside of Denver.

"Yeah, you and half the state."

I laughed.

There did seem to be more Californians in Denver than Coloradans. "How about you? Are you originally from Colorado?"

He smiled big, with the pride of a local who knew he was quickly becoming a rarity. "Yeah, I went to East. Go Angels!"

"So you're a local boy. Did you ever think about leaving?"

"Not really," he said. "My mom got sick in college, so I decided to stick around. And I'm very involved in my church, so that was really important to me, too."

I squinted and nodded, trying not to roll my eyes. Almost every Black man I met said he was "involved" in his church. But oftentimes that just meant he was involved with someone *at* the church. I had met enough men who could have their Masters of Divinity for how "involved" they were.

"What church do you go to?" I asked.

"It's this small church south of Denver. I've been going there since I was a kid."

I nodded, waiting for more details, but none came.

"Small churches can be nice, but I feel like everybody knows everything about you. There's nowhere to hide."

"What are you trying to hide?" He asked, wriggling his eyebrows.

"No, I just meant-"

"I'm just messing with you," he said, smiling. "The great thing about going to a small church is everybody knows everybody. The bad thing about going to a small church is everybody knows everything *about* everybody. It's a family. Flaws and all."

"So you're a lifer?" I asked.

"I am. I feel like people choose churches based on superficial reasons. How good the pastor preached, how well the choir sang. As if the church is there to entertain you. And then as soon as the pastor preaches one sermon you don't like, you just bounce."

I nodded as if he were "preaching to the choir", but inwardly, I felt a tinge of conviction.

"You've never wanted to try something different?"

"Of course. We've only had three pastors in the twenty-five years I've been there. And when my pastor's wife died, he cried through every sermon for months. It was depressing! But you don't leave family when they're down." He shrugged as if it were obvious. "Okay let me get off my soapbox."

"No, you're right. We're too quick to up and leave." I was impressed. Maybe he was more than just the typical pew-warmer, someone who treated church like a social club at best, and night club at worst. Was I?

By the time our cups were empty, we had talked about church, sports, work. In fact, it was exactly what a coffee/tea date should be. We'd laughed and found we had a few things in common. I didn't know if abstinence was one of those things, but hopefully there would be a second date, and a third, and maybe more, to find out. I reluctantly picked up my cardigan.

"Can I just say, you are so beautiful. My cheeks are gonna fall off my face you've got me smiling so much!"

My lips automatically curved upward in response. One of the things I had missed about being in a relationship was that external affirmation that you were special. And even though Crystal had said almost the same thing earlier, it was very different hearing it from an attractive man.

"Thank you," I replied, then stood. "Well, I know you're busy," I said, eyeing the books and folders that had been pushed to the side. "I'll let you get back to work."

"Yeah, until I can bring on more staff, I'm swamped. But, I'd like to take you out to dinner sometime."

Once again, I found myself competing with Leon over who could smile the biggest.

"I'd love that."

REY SIRAKAVIT

Chapter 25

Crystal wanted to know if we kissed.

Mikaela wanted to know if he was as cute in person as he was online.

Frances Anne Rogers wanted to know if I could ever open myself up to someone and be truly vulnerable with them. Apparently, smiling so much that your cheeks hurt didn't count as being vulnerable.

After such a great date, and what I thought had been a great connection, I didn't hear from Leon for a few days. No smiley face texts. No emojis. Radio silence. Maybe I *had* smiled too much. Been too eager. What did Frances Anne Rogers know about dating as a Black woman? I was fighting against statistics, time, and stereotypes. Don't be too eager. Don't be too strong. Don't be angry. Don't be needy. And one false move was the romantic equivalent of stepping on a landmine.

I analyzed and re-analyzed every word and every look until I had convinced myself that his smile of pleasure was really just a smile of pity, and I would never see him again. Then finally just three words:

FROM LEON BAKER:
Dinner August 3?

That was almost 3 weeks away.

Maybe he was not as interested as I had thought. But I agreed, eager to reassure myself that I hadn't just imagined the spark between us.

Eventually, August 3 came.

For our second date, the plan was to go to dinner and a movie. He suggested we meet at one of those trendy restaurants that were featured in City Magazine. It was full of traditional romance, complete with white tablecloths, flickering candles, and a string quartet playing in the corner. Definitely outside my price range. The most expensive thing on the menu was the same as my grocery budget for the week. I went with a conservative option. Stuffed chicken breast.

Leon ordered the steak.

"So, you've been really busy. You're a hard man to catch up with."

"Yeah, all of my free time goes toward building my practice and my commitments at church."

I nodded, not wanting to appear suspicious.

"What?"

"I didn't say anything,"I replied with a shake of my head. But I couldn't stop the edges of my lips from sneaking upwards a bit.

"Your look says it all."

"What does my look say?"

"That I sound like some sketchy dude who's running game."

"I didn't say that." I raised my hands in innocence.

"Well, how can I prove to you that I'm an upstanding guy? You wanna talk to my mom? I'll call her right now." Leon pulled his cell phone from his jacket breast pocket.

I laughed. I wanted to ask how serious he was about dating, or if he was just having fun. But that would sound needy and desperate, and regardless of what Frances Anne Rogers said, opening myself up did not mean I had to put all my cards on the table. So far, he was like a magical unicorn, a single Black Christian man, handsome, and successful. There had to be a catch.

I asked all the questions I had skipped on our coffee date: When did you become a Christian? How important is your relationship with God? What's your favorite book in the Bible? Well, all the *Christian* first date questions. But there were no red flags. Just an honest, funny man who seemed too good to be true. Maybe God really had heard all my prayers over the years, prayers that I had thought were stamped RETURN TO SENDER. Maybe they had been delivered after all.

"What are you thinking about?" He leaned forward, arms on the table.

"Just how much fun I'm having." I looked around at the restaurant, then back at Leon. "The food is incredible. And the company is pretty good, too."

"Good," he said, squeezing my hand. He rubbed his thumb along mine. My heart fluttered and I met his eyes. I pulled my hand away and nervously picked up a napkin. I made small circles on the glass table, wiping up every bit of moisture, every crumb, every smudge. All of my attention zoned in on the small motions my hand was making and the feeling of panic started to subside. I guess I was lucky that I didn't grab a rag from one of the servers and start scrubbing tables. Or the floor. For how expensive the restaurant was, there were sticky stains on the floor that had been left unattended for more than one night. Even the salt and pepper shakers had little bits of food encrusted on them. I just stopped myself from scraping it off with my thumb when Leon put his hand on mine again. I finally looked up at him.

"How about some dessert?" From the look in his eyes, I couldn't tell if he meant a sweet treat, or me. I tore my eyes away and picked up the menu.

"Everything looks so good. Any recommendations?" I willed my breathing to slow down and tried to sound as normal as possible.

We decided on a pecan tart, which, according to the waitress, was big enough to share.

As he put a forkful of the sweet gooey confection into his mouth, I imagined what it would be like to trade places with that fork.

"So, you ready for that movie?" He asked.

I looked guiltily away from his lips, and I questioned the wisdom of being in a dark room with him, whose presence -and thumb- were causing all kinds of sensations up and down my spine. As much as I didn't want our date to end, I needed to catch my breath.

"I think I'd better call it a night, actually. I'm sorry."

"No, not at all. I hope this won't be our last time." He stood to go.

"I don't see our waitress," I said, looking around.

"I already handled the check," he said. "You modern women, always fighting to pay."

"Oh, I just didn't want to get arrested for 'dining and dashing'," I teased, standing beside him. "Although I do know a good lawyer, so…" I shrugged. "Seriously, though, I had a lovely time."

"Oh, 'lovely'," he smirked as he slid his hand lightly against the small of my back. As we walked toward the exit, I could feel that small bit of pressure, and I liked it. "I know what that means."

"What do you mean, 'you know what that means'? I had a lovely time," I repeated.

"No, that's the kiss of death. The friend zone."

As we approached my car, I pulled out my key, then turned to face him. "What are you talking about? Saying I had a 'lovely' time isn't the friend zone."

"So then you won't mind if I do this?" He leaned in, but his lips stopped just a millimeter before touching mine. His breath was warm with a scent of nutmeg and cinnamon. My arms went stiff at my sides. Should I put my hands on his chest? On his shoulders? Behind his head? Lean forward? Lean back? Tilt my head so our noses didn't bump?

Had I always been so awkward? Or, was I once again just being self-conscious since this was my first kiss since Drisk's comment that kissing me was like kissing a cold fish? Gross. Unappetizing. Too wet. No chemistry.

But this wasn't Drisk, and I was sure I felt enough chemistry for the both of us, even if I couldn't force my arms to move. *Just kiss me already*, I wanted to shout. Instead, I leaned forward, my lips meeting his.

Did he feel a spark? Did I? To be honest, I didn't know. I didn't know what I was supposed to feel. Was I supposed to feel fireworks? And what about Leon? Would he say that kissing me was like kissing a cold block of ice?

When he pulled away, there was a smile in his eyes. I breathed a sigh of relief.

"You don't have to be nervous," he said. "I don't expect anything."

"Was it that bad?" I wanted to fade away. Just disappear. Drisk was right and I was going to die alone.

"No, I just wanted you to know I wasn't going to pounce on you."

"Sorry, I think I'm just nervous because…" Because, what? How could I possibly explain what I was thinking without scaring him off or giving him a mental image of me having cold, fishy lips? That image would be stuck in his head- just like it was in mine- forever. No. I was definitely not going to say anything about my ex thinking I kissed like a cold fish. But, I also didn't know if I was ready to tell him the big reason, the reason that sent most men running within seconds. Maybe my delivery was off. If I didn't use the dreaded V-word, maybe it wouldn't be so off-putting. "Because I made a commitment to the Lord that I wouldn't have sex outside of marriage." I waited for the laughter, impertinent questions about the full extent of my sexual experience, and the awkward goodbye.

Leon dropped his hand from my arm and took a step back. I wasn't surprised. I looked toward my car, the ground, the crowded parking lot, anywhere but at Leon. Another relationship over before it even began. I pulled my keys from my pocket and clicked the unlock button, ready to escape the increasingly awkward moment. Why did dating have to be so difficult? Why couldn't Christian men-

"Wow," Leon interrupted my train of thought. "I've never met a woman who takes her faith so seriously. It's refreshing." I looked up into his eyes, not sure if he was joking or serious. "Usually I'm the one..." he trailed off, as if reconsidering, then kissed me on my forehead. "Text me when you get home." Was Leon saying what I thought he was saying? I nodded and slid behind the driver's seat of my car.

Chapter 26

TO LEON BAKER:
I hope I don't have to wait another month before seeing you again.

Delete. Delete. Delete.

You're a wonderful kisser.

DELETE. DELETE. DELETE.

Thanks for a LOVELY evening.

SEND.

I replayed our after-dinner conversation over and over in my mind. I couldn't help but gush about the date whenever I got the chance. Mikaela asked every day if I had heard back from Leon. Before I knew it, a week had gone by but my answer still had not changed.

"Nope," I smiled.

"Why don't you text him again?" Mikaela leaned over the cubicle divider, her whisper more of a regular voice in the busy office.

I shrugged.

"I thought you said you liked him?"

"I do. If he's interested, he'll respond." I wheeled my chair back toward my computer, hoping Mikaela would take the hint.

"Some guys need a little more encouragement. Send him a dirty text and see what he says." She wiggled her eyebrows suggestively.

"Are you crazy?" There was no way I could do that, especially after the way our date had ended.

"Sorry, I forgot who I was talking to." Mikaela rolled her eyes, a very bad habit that she had gotten from me.

"Besides, I don't want him to think that I have no life and that I spend my work day thinking and talking about him." Even if it were true.

"What if while you're over here, trying to play it all cool, he meets some other woman who isn't playing it cool, and she keeps sending him all these flirty texts and they go out and fall in love and get married and have a family? All because you couldn't send just one more text!" Mikaela breathed triumphantly, as if she had just made a closing argument before the Supreme Court.

"I'll think about it." I pulled up the latest program I was working on, confident that we had had a connection. Leon would call or text when he had time.

Like Mikaela, Carmen was not convinced.

"You're both adults. There's no need to play games. If you like him, call him."

"He's probably busy with work or a case or something. He'll call me when he can."

Carmen looked doubtful, but didn't press it.

Even Frances Anne Rogers had an opinion.

"You said that you've been wanting to date for a while. You wanted to meet a nice guy, and poof. A nice guy practically falls in your lap! Why do you think you're not actively pursuing it?"

"I am. I'm just not trying to rush into anything."

"Hmm."

"I mean, I don't want to mess this up."

"Umm hmm."

"Like I've messed up all my other relationships." I pressed my lips together, startled once again by how my temporary therapist managed to get me talking about things that I did not want to talk about.

"How have you messed up your other relationships?"

"I don't know," I shrugged. "Maybe I had too high of expectations."

"For you or them?"

"I don't know," I repeated, feeling caught in a web of my own making. I really didn't want to reminisce about all the ways I had ruined my previous relationships. I just wanted to focus on the here and now, the present- and the future- with Leon. "Maybe my expectations for both of us were too high. I just feel like I've been here before, you know? Everything starts off great and then before you know it you're being dumped and told you have no chemistry. Maybe I just want to savor this season…where everything is fun and light."

"And there's no pressure."

"Yeah, no pressure. I mean, we've only gone out a couple times."

"But you really like this guy?"

I smiled. I couldn't deny that.

"I know it's only been a week or so, but do you think you might be hiding? You put the ball in his court and that way if things don't work out, you can feel like you did your best, but at the same time never really opened yourself up to the possibility of being hurt."

"Why would I open myself up to being hurt?" I crossed my arms and narrowed my eyes.

"Whenever you open yourself up, there's always a risk you might get hurt. But you also might find love. It's really hard to find love with someone, though, who hides behind walls and protects themselves at all costs."

I mulled her words over. "So you're saying I should call him?"

She leaned back. "No, I'm saying I want you to really think about *why* you don't want to call him. I don't think it's as simple as you've been telling yourself."

I thought about her words, working them over in my mind. It made no sense to me why I would want to purposely open myself up to being hurt. On purpose. That seemed like the exact opposite of what a sane person would do. I sighed. I felt no closer to getting my letter of clearance than I had at the beginning of the summer. Even though I didn't hate therapy as much as I thought I would, I was having a hard time understanding her logic. My motto had always been to make sure I didn't get hurt. Regardless of everyone's advice, I saw no reason to change.

Before bed, I glanced at the phone again. No new notifications or missed calls from a certain individual. I plugged my phone into the charging station and rubbed lotion into my hands. My skin was almost raw from the heavy cleaning I had spent the evening doing. Cleaning up Khalid's spit up from the carpet and other random places around the kitchen and living room that Crystal didn't seem to notice. But instead of just cleaning, I had prayed. And I felt peace. Leon would call. I was sure of it.

The next morning, I woke with a lightness that I could not explain. It was like someone had pulled the shades open and let light into a room that had been left dark for too long. I rolled out of bed and stretched my arms over my head.

On Sunday, I even thought about visiting Leon's church, but realized he had never told me the name of it. "It's a real small church south of Denver." That was vague. Maybe he didn't want anyone just showing up and messing up his action? I glanced at the clock on the nightstand. I only had 20 minutes before my own church service started. I pulled on my thin cotton robe then headed to the kitchen and was surprised to see Crystal already there. She was scrolling through her phone. Probably waiting for me to make breakfast. I sighed. Was this what it was like being the mom of a teenager? Ugh, I grimaced. If Crystal were my daughter, that would make me a grandmother! I raced around the kitchen, pulling out butter and eggs to make a quick egg and toast breakfast for Crystal and myself.

As always, I asked Crystal if she wanted to go to church with me.

"It's gonna take me forever to get Khalid ready," she frowned.

"I can help you," I offered, "if you want to go." I set a plate in front of her. "I'm going to go get dressed. Let me know."

By the time I was dressed, Crystal was wearing a clean tee shirt and jeans, and Khalid was in a fresh onesie.

"It's so hot. Should I leave him like this, with no pants?" She held the baby up, letting his tiny legs kick at the air. Before I could respond, she pulled a pair of cotton shorts out of the backpack baby-bag she was carrying on her shoulder. Even with the backpack baby-bag that I had looked down on, she looked like a real mom. She *was* a real mom.

At church, we found a seat toward the back in my usual row with the other latecomers, which also just happened to be perfect for a new mom who needed to slip out periodically to nurse or change a stinky diaper.

Even though I was happy that Crystal had decided to go to church with me, a part of me wished I was sitting beside Leon, and instead of holding someone else's baby in my arms, I was holding my own. For the first time in a long while, I really believed that God was finally going to answer my prayers. So what if Leon hadn't called or texted or emailed in a couple weeks? Everything about him felt right. Easy. One day, I'd be going to church with him instead of with my young housemate. Would I like his church? He had said he'd been going to his church for over twenty years. I pictured an old-fashioned, small church building with peeling paint and worn-out carpet. Leon would wear a suit, of course, with a large gold cross, like a televangelist. He said he was very involved in his church. Was he a deacon or elder, helping to collect the offering? Did he preach occasionally? I felt myself get a little giddy inside. I, Sierra, was going to marry a deacon!

Before I knew it, it was the end of the service and I had only caught a word or two of the sermon. I couldn't even tell what the topic was. But there I sat with my Bible open on my lap. I had heard myself say "Amen" along with everyone else, but my mind had been miles away, serving at Leon's church.

As the pastor opened the altar for prayer, I felt a little tug on my heart. I hesitated, feeling like I was supposed to go forward, but not sure for what. I looked around. Several people were walking forward down the center aisle of the church. I looked over at Crystal who was bouncing the baby on her knee. What did I want prayer for? I didn't feel stressed or unhappy or worried. In fact, I felt hopeful. But for some reason, I felt the urge to stand and go forward anyway. So I did.

As soon as I stood, Crystal popped up beside me, with Khalid on her hip.

"Are you going forward?" She asked.

When I nodded, a look of relief swept across her face. I walked down the aisle, Crystal beside me. She was walking so close to me that I could feel her heart pounding. I looked down at her. She looked nervous, but I had no idea why. Did she think she had to go forward? I wrapped my arm comfortingly around her shoulder, just like the wife of a deacon would do. In front of us was the prayer team. Sister Johnson, who was in charge of the women's ministry, another woman I did not recognize, and a man who looked familiar. He was wearing a wedding band on his left hand. He had long locs and a slightly

221

arrogant look. As Sister Johnson called us forward, it clicked. He was the guy I had seen at the Valentine's Day event. Mr. Vegan. Well, good for him, I thought. Just a few months since the singles event and he was already married.

Bless you, God. If you can do it for him, I know you can do it for me. I remembered his slightly condescending air and added a prayer for his wife, whoever she was. *Lord, give her patience and grace with this man.*

Once we got in front of Sister Johnson, Crystal unglued herself from my side and stepped forward. From the look on her face, it seemed like she wanted privacy, so I took a step back, even as I smiled encouragingly at her. Sister Johnson put her hand on Crystal's shoulder and whispered in her ear. Then Crystal leaned forward and whispered in Sister Johnson's ear, all while keeping Khalid balanced on her other hip. As I waited, I noticed the altar filling up all around me. What had the pastor preached about that had compelled so many people to come forward for prayer? Finally, Crystal and Sister Johnson were done. She squeezed Crystal's hand and glanced at me over Crystal's head, who was brushing moisture from her cheek. I smiled as we walked back down the aisle. What in the world had I missed?

START PRAYING

Chapter 27

Though Crystal was usually chatty and had a habit of oversharing, she didn't bring up her sudden urge to go to the altar for prayer, so I didn't either. Instead, as she buckled Khalid into his car seat, she looked over at me like she had a confession to make.

"I've been staying with you for a couple months now and I know I'm not helping out financially. But I'm exhausted. I can't imagine getting a job right now. And school is about to start in a couple weeks."

"Your senior year!" I said excitedly, though it was hard to reconcile the image of a free-spirited teen whose only worry was picking out a prom dress with the teen mom in front of me.

"Yeah, my senior year." She rolled her eyes, not buying my attempt at optimism. She hopped into the passenger seat as I clicked my buckle." Nothing is how I thought it would be. And you have been so amazing, but I know I can't live with you forever. I need a plan, but I have no idea what to do."

I wished for a magic wand that I could twirl and make all her problems go away.

"I know I don't say it enough, but thank you. I'd be homeless if it weren't for you."

I reached across the center console and gave her hand a little squeeze, unsure of how to respond. As had become my habit when I didn't know what to say, I prayed. *Lord, give me wisdom.* "I'm always here for you if you want to brainstorm options."

"Well, my cousin said I could stay with her, but I would have to pay half of all the bills."

"What about your mom? Have you talked to her?"

"Yeah, I send her pics of the baby every once in a while, and she likes it when I post about him on social media...but she's relieved you let me stay with you so she doesn't have to feel guilty. And anyway, she has some new dude who's staying with her, so I can't move back there." I wondered how often Crystal had been displaced because of her mom's boyfriends.

"We never really talked about how long I could stay with you and I don't want to just assume that you're cool with me staying with you forever."

I laughed. "Forever is a long time."

Part of being an adult meant figuring out some problems on your own, problems that she had ignored and glossed over when she was pregnant. But part of being a friend meant giving a helping hand when needed.

Again I prayed, *Lord, give me wisdom,* hoping I wouldn't regret my next words.

"Why don't you just stay with me? You can use this next year to come up with a plan for what to do after you graduate."

"Are you serious?"

"Of course," I said. *Right, Lord?* It felt like the right thing to do, the right thing to say, but even as I said the words, my heart pounded at the huge commitment I was making.

Months more of middle of the night feeding and crying?

225

Nonstop chatter from Crystal?

A house covered in crumbs and toys and dishes?

I smiled as Crystal thanked me, hoping that my face looked more confident than I truly felt.

"When I went to the altar, I asked God to help me 'cause I honestly had no clue what to do next. I didn't know what to expect, 'cause I've never really prayed before, but he answered my prayer so quickly!" Her face was a mixture of shock and happiness. Mine was a mixture of shock and...something else. But definitely not happiness.

She had prayed, had asked God for help, and he had answered. I should have been pleased and proud at the show of faith.

I wasn't.

"God had answered her prayer"? I almost laughed. What about me and my prayers? Even though just a few minutes earlier, I'd felt happy and content, it was all just a fantasy. A happy fantasy that kept the fear and doubt away, but just a fantasy nonetheless.

Was God answering everyone but me? Even as I repented of self-pity, I couldn't help asking, *God have you forgotten me?* There was no answer. Not even silence. Just Crystal gushing about newfound faith and answered prayers.

But maybe the answer was right in front of me. Leon. Maybe a life with him wasn't just a fantasy. And if he was the answer to all my prayers, what would he think about me letting Crystal live with me for a year? Would he think I had too much baggage, too much going on as the surrogate mother to a teen mom? Wouldn't I think the same thing?

As I pulled into the driveway, I licked my lips. I would just tell Crystal I had changed my mind. I didn't owe her anything, but the sooner I told her, the better. I unbuckled my seatbelt just in time for Crystal to lean over and hug me. As she pulled away, she smiled.

"A year ago, I never would have guessed that I'd have a baby and no place to live. But meeting you was the best thing that has ever happened to me." She brushed her cheeks, then continued with a smile. "I'm gonna go make a list," she said, her eyebrows going up playfully. "A Sierra list. With checkboxes and due dates. By this time next year, I'll have my diploma and my own place. You'll see. All because of you!" And with that, she pulled Khalid out of his seat and they disappeared into the house.

With all my questions, one thing I knew for sure was that I couldn't refuse to show love *today* just because I hoped something might happen in the future with Leon. Leon, who still hadn't called. I sighed.

Just like Crystal, my life looked nothing like I thought it would or should. But unlike Crystal, I had done everything I thought God wanted me to do to get what I wanted, lists and all.

But had I?

Everyone was telling me to follow up with Leon. To take more risks. And if I was honest, I couldn't really think of any good reason for not calling him.

Before I could second-guess myself further, I pulled out my phone and looked at the time. Most people would be out of church. My finger hesitated over the green button next to his name. It wasn't that I hadn't called a guy before. I had called plenty of guys. But after the way our last date ended...this felt different. I took a deep breath and pushed the button. The phone rang and rang and I debated hanging up. Finally, I heard the click.

"Hey, I was just thinking about you!"

He didn't say "Hello?" with that way your voice rises at the end of the word, the question implicit. *Who is this? What do you want?*

No, he had recognized my name and number and voice and was happy to hear from me. I let out the breath I had been holding.

"Really?"

"Yeah. I've been swamped, but I was thinking of taking Labor Day off. Maybe we could go on a picnic?"

I chastised myself for waiting so long. What had I been trying to prove?

"That sounds fun." I relaxed my grip on the phone and leaned back in the car seat.

Leon said he knew the perfect park and would handle the food.

"Unfortunately, I'm still at church. This deacon's meeting is just getting started so I can't really talk. But it was good to hear your voice."

In less than two minutes, the long-awaited, much-anticipated conversation was over, and I still had so many questions for Leon. *Relationships are a marathon, not a sprint, Sierra. That's the whole point of dating and getting to know someone. You don't have to figure everything out on day one.* But, I had been right about one thing. He was a deacon. I slipped my phone back into my purse with a self-satisfied smile, already beginning to count down the days until our romantic picnic.

But life didn't pause. Between work and caring for Khalid at all times of the night when Crystal needed an extra pair of hands, I also helped her sign up for her online classes. I fell into bed physically and mentally exhausted each night. When Crystal received her textbooks in the mail, she plopped down on the couch and ripped the package open.

"What class are you most excited about?" I sat beside her, looking over her shoulder as she scanned the covers of each book.

"Early Childhood Development." She pulled out her weathered *"Sierra list"* that she had taken to carrying in her back pocket and pointed to one of the bullets near the bottom of the page. "See, it says get a job at a childcare center, go to college, and become a teacher."

"That sounds like a good plan," I nodded, impressed and hopeful that she would stick to it. "I picked up the textbook from the table, flipping through the pages. "This has a lot of great information about taking care of an infant. Childhood Development was a smart choice for an elective." As I continued flipping, my finger stalled over one page: *Recognizing Signs of Abuse.* I dropped the book as if it were on fire, my mind instantly filling with unwanted images and memories.

Not right now, Sierra, I warned myself, but it was too late. I could already feel my skin crawling with a thousand pincher bugs. My throat closed.

Just breathe. But telling yourself to breathe when you can't breathe doesn't actually help you breathe. And the more I thought about how I couldn't breathe, the harder it was to find my breath. I leaned forward, and before I knew it, I had lost my breakfast all over the floor. Crystal jumped up from the couch, pushing her textbooks aside. She said something, but her voice sounded far away. I couldn't breathe, and now I couldn't hear. I could barely see. Chunks of half-processed food and bile crawled across the carpet. The smell wafted up to me. I had to clean it. Now. I pushed past her and ran to the kitchen sink. I grabbed a handful of paper towels and gloves and cleaning spray bottles and went to work. My eyes blurred as I sopped up the mess. And the smell made me heave more. I wiped my mouth across my shoulder, leaving a trail of spittle on my shirt.

Breathe.

But the sound of screaming in my ear was deafening. I had to make the noise stop. So I did what I knew. I shoved the coffee table aside, and picked up all the packing scraps. I shoved them into a trash bag, along with all the paper towels. I pulled out the vacuum and as the noise outside grew, the noise inside me began to subside. As I moved back and forth over the carpet, I could feel my body begin to relax. I forced myself to focus on the six inches of carpet in front of me. Just push and pull. Push and pull all the memories away.

Breathe.

Once I vacuumed the living room corner to corner, and back again, I sprayed the carpet with a deep cleaner and scrubbed. By the time I was done, my knees were wet and my face was dry. And I could finally breathe. I looked over the living room to survey my work and was startled to see Crystal. Khalid was in her arms, crying. She patted his back, but simultaneously looked at me as if I had two heads. Her lips were moving, but I couldn't make out what she was saying. My eyelids fluttered. I couldn't handle talking, or the inevitable questions. I needed a shower and sleep and then I would be okay. Then I could handle it. We could talk tomorrow. I walked past her and into my room. As soon as the door closed behind me, I ripped off my clothes and fell into the shower, letting the stinging hot water wash away the last few memories.

When I woke up the next morning, my head was pounding, my mouth tasted vile, and I was starving. I lay in bed, grateful that I had to go to work. If I were quiet, maybe I could sneak out before Crystal was awake. In fact, I could avoid her altogether and just grab breakfast on the road.

I opened the faucet gently, wet my toothbrush, then immediately turned it off, hoping the dripping water would not echo through the sleeping house. Shirt, pants, sandals...I pulled each article on slowly and silently. I wrapped my hair into a quick bun, then dropped lip gloss into my purse. I would add that after breakfast. I opened my bedroom door, ready to begin the walk of shame through my own house. Unfortunately, all my efforts were in vain. Crystal sat at the kitchen counter and spun around as soon as my door opened.

"Good morning," I pretended everything was normal and great.

"Are you okay? I made you some tea." Crystal set the mug on the counter, then leaned back as I approached. Her face turned away. In fear? Embarrassment?

"I think I must've had food poisoning or something. I'm really sorry about yesterday."

"It seemed like more than that. You went kind of psycho."

I flinched at her words, but she continued.

"I was trying to talk to you, but it was like you didn't even hear me. You were in your own little world for hours. It was kind of scary. Did I do something wrong?"

What to say? The last thing I wanted was to go back to the day before. Especially since I felt fine. "Not at all. I just felt sick, but I feel better now. What kind of tea is this?" I picked up the mug and smelled it.

"You said ginger is good for when you're sick." She didn't look like she believed me, but I pressed on. I took a sip of the tea and smiled the brightest smile I could manage.

"This is perfect, thanks! I need to get to work a little early today, so I'm going to take off, but I'll see you tonight."

And I ran to the door.

REY SIRAKAVIT

Chapter 28

On the day of our picnic, Leon brought a canvas tote bag filled with fresh fruit, fancy cheeses, crackers, and sparkling water.

I supplied a blanket.

The weather was beautiful. Like God was smiling down on us and blowing a kiss at us through the wind.

Leon laid back on the green blanket and told me all about his childhood. His father was MIA, like mine, but his mom fell in love with and married a deacon from their church.

"It was kind of a scandal at the time," he chuckled. "But he was great. He was like a father to me. I took his last name and everything. He's actually the one who inspired me to go to law school."

"Was he a lawyer, too?"

Leon shook his head. "He grew up in the South. It was hard for a black man to get accepted into law school back then. So, he went into the Navy. He passed away when I was in college." He had a faraway look on his face, and I wondered what he was thinking.

"That must have been hard," I said, wanting to wrap my arms around him, do anything to bring his smile back. Instead, I sat in the silence with him.

Finally, he shook his head as if shaking the memories away. "I chose law because I wanted to make him proud, but I love what I do

233

and I know he's smiling down on me." He took a deep breath, then turned towards me. "What about you? What's your family like? Do you see them often?"

Ugh. The dreaded questions about family. Not talking to your family was a red flag, so I had learned to use vague pronouns and just blame it on the weather. "They're in California. They think I'm crazy for moving to the snow."

"How often do you go home?"

Responding with "Never" or "Not often" would only invite more questions. I scrunched up my face like I was doing the math, even though I knew the exact answer. Two weeks after high school graduation. That was the last time I had seen my mom. I had specifically chosen my college because they offered a summer program for incoming freshman. That program allowed me to move to campus eight weeks early. And, they offered summer housing so I wouldn't be kicked off campus at the end of each school year. Even as a senior in high school, I knew I would never feel the need to return "home", if you could even call it that. I packed my bags, got a bus ticket, and never looked back.

"Not too often," I hedged. I decided to change the subject, put him on the other end of the interrogation. "Have you ever been married?"

He shook his head no.

"Any kids?"

Another shake of the head. "How about you?"

I thought about the 17-year-old girl back at my house. Probably waiting for me to come home to have dinner. Who I had committed to allowing to live with me for the next year. Should I tell him about her? I had poured out my heart and pain to him in the hospital, but in the weeks and month since, I had not told him that Crystal was living with me. Between the light banter and occasional flirty texts, it hadn't come up.

As if reading my mind, he asked, "What about the girl, Crystal? Have you heard from her since the hospital?"

What was I supposed to say? *Yeah, the girl whose baby I thought I was going to adopt is actually living with me right now. We're kind of like roommates. And the only way it works is if I don't think about what could have been, and definitely don't give off any creepy "I-might-steal-your-baby-while-you-sleep" vibes.*

"You could say we...keep in touch." Vague was good. Had I always been this guarded? Or was it Drisk's feedback that was making me question every word I said and intonation. The truth- if it even was the truth- might hurt, but his words had wounded me, left me questioning myself. I had to let it go.

"Has that been hard?"

"I'm sorry, what?"

"Staying in touch," he repeated. "Has that been hard?"

"Actually, her mom kicked her out, so she's been staying with me since she left the hospital."

His eyebrows climbed up to his forehead.

"What are you thinking? I'm crazy, right?" I smiled, trying to deflect the coming question.

"Not crazy, but the lawyer part of me is tossing red flags all over the place. On the other hand, the Christian part of me...I don't know. If she had no place to go..."

I exhaled. Though Leon was still a virtual stranger, his opinion meant a lot to me.

"She really didn't. She's a teen, hasn't graduated yet, no family support..."

"What about the baby's father?"

235

"She won't tell anybody who the father is," I said shaking my head.

"He's probably a relative."

My head snapped up. "What do you mean?"

"Well, if she won't tell anybody, even now that she's already had the baby, it's probably not just some boy from school. A lot of times, it's an uncle, cousin, maybe even father. Some lowlife relative, though, who she doesn't want to get in trouble. It's sad. A girl is raped, and she's the one walking around feeling ashamed."

"Raped?" I whispered. I could barely say the word.

"Yeah. At the very least statutory rape. A minor can't give consent. And with all the psychological manipulation that these people use...It's rape. Simple."

"But..." My stomach started to turn and I could feel the fancy cheese start to rise in my throat. I swallowed, forcing the cheese and the memories down.

"It happens all the time, unfortunately. You're a really good person. Not a lot of people would take in a teen mom, less known one with a complicated back story." He looked like he was impressed and surprised.

"You're good people, Sierra. I'm glad I called you that day. I think it was a God-thing, because I usually don't call prospective clients. My assistant handles that."

I thought about a God who could be in a phone call, but who would allow a teen to be assaulted by a relative, or a little girl to be abandoned at a drug house. I thought about all the little girls who were traumatized by the people who were supposed to protect them. I thought about another little girl, a long time ago, who was...raped by her uncle. Before the cheese and crackers and everything else rose too far in my throat, I had to push them back down again. I tried to

236

bring myself back to the present, willing my breath to still as words that I had never uttered aloud took a hold of the edges of my mind. I swatted the thoughts and memories away.

"God works in mysterious ways," I said, letting one of the many empty platitudes that I had heard all my life fall effortlessly from my lips.

"He sure does," Leon said. I don't know if he heard the cynicism in my voice, and I did not care. All of my emotional energy was going towards not freaking out, not being consumed by memories and images that had haunted me for years. "But no matter how much evil there is in the world, I'm encouraged when I hear about people like you, people who go out of their way to live out their faith and show God's love."

"Okay, I'm no Mother Teresa," I said, allowing myself to be pulled back into the present. I smiled slightly as I accepted the compliment.

Luckily, Leon changed the subject and I gladly took the lifeline. He told me about his bad habits (chewing his fingernails) and I told him about my lifelong dream to learn to play the guitar (electric). I even demonstrated my air guitar solo. We talked until the wind started to pick up and we had to chase our bag of pita chips across the grass. We packed up and Leon walked me to my car. I was grateful when he just gave me a hug and a peck on the cheek.

And from the outside, no one would ever have guessed that a part of my soul had just been ripped open and would never be shut again.

REY SIRAKAVIT

Chapter 29

I'm barely through the door when Crystal bombards me with questions.

How was your date?

How was the food?

How was Leon?

Did you kiss?

Did you "do it"?

I alternate between nodding and shaking my head at what I hope are the appropriate times, but I'm not sure. I feel like time is tip-toeing, stretched out before me, like I'm looking at myself through a dirty window, but I look normal. Same sundress and loose cardigan. My locs are still pulled up in a fancy-looking top-knot, but one loc has slipped out. How did that happen?

My eyes find their way to my Crystal. I look at myself looking at her. But you can't tell by looking at someone, can you?

I have a thousand questions for her.

Who is Khalid's father?

Why does she never talk about him?

Who is Khalid's father?

Once again I am inspired by a teenage girl who has more faith than I do. Who was the victim of something horrendous, but chose to keep her baby, chose to keep the daily reminder of what was done to her.

When I think about sweet, beautiful baby Khalid being the result of … (I still can not bring myself to say the word), I shudder and feel the bile rise in my throat. But Crystal doesn't look like someone who was victimized. But what does a "victim" look like? We all wear masks to protect ourselves from the sharp, pointing fingers of a world that blames the victims, blames women, blames girls. Tells them to move on, grow up, get over it. If not in word, definitely in deed.

From the ubiquitous, "What were you wearing?" To its partner-in-blame, "Where were you?" The onus is always put on women to not be attacked, to not be assaulted, to not be raped, instead of on men to not attack, to not assault, to not rape. But the cultural programming has been effective, because I can barely bring myself to look at Crystal. Her eyes glistening, like my date is a fairy tale that she can't wait to hear.

But I am not strong enough to broach this conversation with her. I slink to my room, complaining of a headache and promising to tell her everything she wants to know tomorrow. Tomorrow.

Before getting in the shower, I strip my bed and vacuum my mattress, sucking up all the invisible mites that feast on dead skin cells, sucking up all the images that pop in and out of my mind that have been feasting on me.

And as I swing the vacuum hose into corners and along the baseboard, prayers that I did not even know existed bubble up and overflow out of me.

I am alive.

Three words that seem so simple, but are not to be taken for granted.

Three words that I did not want to be true about me for years.

I am alive.

And what's more, I am not forsaken.

Forsaken, a sad, religious word that just means abandoned.

I have not been abandoned. *God did not abandon me. I have not been abandoned. God did not abandon me.*

To the little girl that felt abandoned, that did not want to live, that took all the shame upon herself, you have not been abandoned, little one.

By your stripes I am healed, *I declare to the walls, to the ceilings, to the windows, to the me who is looking through the window watching this all pass by in slow motion.*

Though I walk through the valley of the shadow of death, I will fear no evil.

What happened to me was evil. And though I cannot put into words what happened to me, I can say that it was evil. And I will not fear it.

And the words of a worship song burst from my mouth. "What the enemy meant for evil, you turned it for good." I repeat these words, and it is my prayer, my petition. It is me holding on to a promise that God made. In fact, isn't that what our faith is built on? It's not just positive thinking or rainbow dreaming…It's the certainty that God can indeed make something good out of something bad. The cross was meant to kill Jesus, to end his ministry, to destroy the kingdom of God. But the enemy didn't realize that three days later Jesus would rise.

Show me the truth of these words, Lord.

Let my pain be used for a purpose.

Let the past not attack me anymore.

Let my life be a testimony that what the enemy used for evil, that you somehow, someway, will use for my good. I may not see it now. I definitely don't see it now, but I trust and believe that you can and will use it for my good.

Crystal knocks on my door. She must have heard me singing over the loud whirring of the vacuum. She asks if I am okay.

"Yes," I answer.

And I am. Or, I will be.

I want to open the door wide and pull Crystal into a long hug. I don't remember the last time I hugged her, when hugging anyone other than

241

Carmen or my godsons didn't make me feel awkward and insecure and uncomfortable in my own skin. But I don't. Not yet. I just paste my trademark smile on my face and try to not be sick all over her.

I alternated between testing out the word and avoiding it altogether. Whenever the word popped into my head, I allowed myself to feel sorry for the little girl instead of disgusted and afraid. I even pulled out a piece of paper and wrote it down. Tentatively. No subject. No predicate. Just the word. All alone.

Rape.

My breathing quickened, but taking the word from my mind to the written world emboldened me. Strengthened me. Purified me. I wrote the word again, this time in all caps, with full, dark strokes.

Leon said that the person walking around with all the shame and guilt is usually the one who is guilt-free.

So, I wrote that word, too.

Guilt. Then I crossed it out, and wrote free.

What would it be like to truly be free? What would it be like to not have memories assail you from every side? What would it be like to not have a part of your mind roped off, declared off-limits?

To be...healed?

I wrote down that word, too. Healed. And before I knew it, I was writing down lots of other words and names. As tears fell, my fingers flew across the pages of my legal pad. I wrote down everything I remembered and then like a watermark, turned the legal pad sideways and wrote RAPED on top of the words that I had already written. Raped meant that eight-year-old girl was not guilty. Raped meant someone else was responsible, someone else should be carrying the weight of the shame, not me.

But even as my mind wrapped itself around the word, it was still just a word, written on a jumbled-up piece of paper. Taking the word from the page to saying aloud was a very different thing. Even though I repeated the word over and over.

Raped.

Raped.

Raped.

I was raped.

God wasn't looking at that eight-year-old with disgust. She was raped.

God wasn't blaming her. She was raped.

God wasn't holding her responsible for something that she could not consent to. She was raped. Every time I said the word, I felt a stone removed from my heart. A weight lifted from my shoulder. I felt like I could breathe. For the first time in twenty-five years, I felt like I could breathe and it was not through a filter or mask. I laid my head on my pillow and wept.

When I dried my eyes, I knew I had to tell someone. Frances Anne Rogers. I couldn't wait until the day of my therapy. I practically burst into the room and cut through all the pleasantries and just started talking.

"I think I was molested. I mean, I have flashbacks sometimes. They seem so vivid, so real, but then there are parts that I don't really remember."

"That's normal," she reassured me. "The brain protects you from memories that are too painful for you to deal with until you're ready. What do you remember?"

"I remember my uncle rubbing my shoulder. I remember him sitting on the bed next to me. Or was I on his lap? I remember him

243

kissing me and telling me to stop crying. I remember wanting to tell him to stop because it hurt so bad, but he had his hand over my mouth. I can't remember if it was one time or many." I stopped. But just as suddenly, I started talking again. The words flowed from my mouth so quickly that I had no time to dissect them, to analyze them, to make sure I was saying everything in just the right way. Frances Anne Rogers nodded, so I kept talking

"I tried to tell my mom, but all she said was, 'Stop lying'. And it must have happened again because in different memories we're in different places. It's all a jumble, though."

"You've been repressing these memories for a long time, and now that you've opened them, you might start remembering more. Healing is a process, though. It won't happen all at once. Some days, you might feel like it's all behind you, and other days, you might feel sad and overwhelmed. Either way, it's okay. The important thing, though, is to not give in to that feeling of despair."

The feeling of fear, that I had no control over my own body, that I wasn't safe in my own skin had terrified me for so long. I'd be okay for months, and then all of a sudden, a memory would hit me like a freight train, taking me out. I'd had to take days off of work. Miss church. Cancel on my friends. I had been so close to giving in many times before, and I did not want to go back. Even though my heart was racing, my head was clear. I could breathe. I was not hiding in a corner. I almost smiled at the feeling of freedom I felt.

"So, what happened recently to make you feel ready to open up about this?"

I thought back to the conversation with Leon. But it had started even earlier, hadn't it? I couldn't pinpoint exactly when, why, or how, but I knew that God had been leading me in this direction for a while. God wanted my healing even more than I did, and I had been dragged along, kicking and screaming. Subconsciously, I had always believed that *"The cure is worse than the illness."* But for God's grace, I would never have been able to bare my soul and reveal my darkest secret. But I was realizing that it was not my secret. It was not my shame. It was not my fault. And I could feel myself coming unstuck.

"It's been a long time coming," I said.

My homework was to write down the memories as they came and my feelings. Frances Anne Rogers even encouraged me to take a few days off to take care of myself. But the very thing that I feared all these years, the very reason that I always pushed the memories down was because I thought they would overtake me, swallow me whole, and leave me destroyed. But they hadn't. I was bigger, and I didn't have to hide in my house.

In fact, I wanted to go to the rooftop of the highest building I could find and shout! I didn't know what I'd shout, but I was filled with gratitude and peace and feverish energy and wanted to share it with the world.

REY SIRAKAVIT

Chapter 30

Instead of going to the rooftop, I decided to tell the most important people in my life, starting with Carmen. How would she respond? She was my best friend, so I knew she would be supportive, a fact that for some reason had never occurred to me before. But when I went to Carmen's house for dinner, her boys were running around showing me their new ninja moves and before I knew it, we were hugging and saying good night.

I wanted to tell Leon. To thank him for helping me to see what had been right in front of me for years. But everything with him still felt so new. I didn't want to scare him off by divulging something so private.

I wanted to tell Crystal, to assure her that she was not alone and to let her know that she had inspired me. But I didn't want to force her to confront her own trauma if she wasn't ready. Instead, I hugged her for so long that eventually she pulled away and noticed my wet face.

"What was that for?" she asked.

"I just want you to know that you can always talk to me." I looked her in the eye, the same eye that I had been avoiding for days, maybe weeks, ever since I'd thrown up all over the living room and spiraled into a cleaning frenzy.

"Okay," she laughed nervously, like I'd gone crazy and she didn't know what to say to the crazy lady.

"I'm serious. You can tell me anything."

She just raised one eyebrow, then walked back to her room, Khalid attached to her hip.

So, I didn't tell anyone.

But instead of the heavy secret I had been carrying, it felt like a surprise that I had to keep to myself until the time was right. The surprise wasn't what my uncle had done to me, but what God had done for me.

And things that would normally have set me off, didn't.

At work, I had a flashback. A picture of my uncle touching me, taking his clothes off. I allowed myself to remember the memory. To remember the fear. I sat with the eight-year-old who felt alone and scared. And when the memory ended, I was okay. My cheeks were a bit damp, but I brushed them dry, turned to my computer monitor and got back to work.

At church, someone gave a testimony about being an assault survivor, and I stayed. I didn't slink out. I was calm and empathetic. It wasn't until the woman was done talking that it even occurred to me that I hadn't tuned her out as soon as she started talking.

I had always thought that I would drown if I let myself remember. That the pain, the shame, the remorse would overwhelm me. But it didn't. Tears of joy and gratitude flowed down my cheeks. The only regret I had was that I hadn't pursued healing earlier!

I kept saying *Thank you, Lord*, but I didn't feel it was enough. I wanted to prove I was okay, prove I was healed.

So I pulled out my copy of the mostly blank adoption application. A part of me was convinced God healed me so I wouldn't ruin my relationship with Leon. God used a spark and a hint to get me to confront being molested. But even if I married Leon and we had lots of babies, I would always remember being rejected because I couldn't answer a few questions. Questions that seemed so simple, now.

I looked at the first question I had skipped. "Describe your family." I quickly wrote: *It was just my mom and me growing up. My parents never married and I rarely saw my dad. But my mom had lots of siblings that all lived within blocks of us. She was the youngest of four.* Why had that been so difficult to write, to think, to say a few months earlier?

The next question was a bit harder: Have you ever been abused? My fingers hesitated for a second, then I began writing again: *I was sexually abused by my oldest uncle when I was eight years old. I told my mom, but she didn't believe me. Because of this, we do not talk and I have chosen to not have a relationship with her or the rest of my family.*

They asked the same question in lots of different ways: Have you ever been abused? Have you ever been sexually abused? Have you ever been physically abused? Have you ever been raped? Have you ever been assaulted? Then all the follow up questions. Have you ever witnessed someone being abused? Have you ever abused someone? They asked how a child's abuse might trigger me, how I would respond, how I would cope, and how I would help the child to heal from their own trauma. Whereas months ago, the words on the application page had caused so much fear, now they were just words. I had grown so much, learned so much, conquered so much.

My pen flew across the pages, as if someone had taken a hold of my hand. I wrote about family and childhood trauma and forgiveness, questions I had so resolutely skipped before. And when I ran out of space, I flipped the page over and continued on the back. After so many years of holding everything inside, I was finally letting everything out. I cried for that little girl who had spent twenty-five years blaming herself. And through the writing, I was able to forgive myself. Forgive the eight-year-old me. Forgive myself for letting the memories terrorize me all these years.

Tears fell, but they did not blind me. They did not control me. I was free. *Thank you, Lord.* I wrote until my hands were exhausted and I fell into a deep sleep.

For days I reviewed the manual from the adoption classes and read articles online. I came back to the application, read what I wrote, finished incomplete thoughts, prayed, and wrote some more. And with each page completed, I felt another level of breakthrough. Another level of healing. Another level where the pain could not reach me. I didn't have all the answers, but I had more than before. I knew myself better than before. And I was not afraid of who I was or what I saw.

Chapter 31

Once I completed the application, I scanned it and emailed it to the county. For days, I did not walk. I floated.

Mikaela asked me to help her with some code she was writing.

"Email it to me," I smiled.

Crystal asked if I would watch the baby while she went to mid-week Bible Study.

"With pleasure," I crooned. (Crystal was convinced I was in love.)

Nothing bothered me.

And when Leon called me at seven on a Saturday night, asking if I wanted to grab a late dinner, I agreed.

But it was time for the go-with-the-flow mask to come off. I needed to be honest with Leon, and myself.

"What's going on between us? I feel like we have a great time when we see each other, but we've only gone out about four or five times in just as many months. Are you seeing someone else? Or are you not as interested as I thought? Either way, I need you to be real with me."

He grabbed my hand, his eyes locking with mine. "I'm interested. Honestly, I'm just busy. I have a lot on my plate, but that's what I like about you. You're not clingy. You're doing your own thing. You're not just sitting around waiting for a man to complete your life."

I shook my head, as if he'd asked me a question. "That sounds like a compliment, but I want more. And I don't want to feel bad for wanting more. I'm not saying we have to see each other everyday. But once a month?" I shook my head again. "That doesn't work for me. If you don't have time for a relationship, I get it. But I need more than what you're giving."

A range of emotions flashed across his face, his eyebrows bouncing up and down. Surprise. Annoyance. Contrition. Resolve. He was like an open book. I wondered if he was as easy to read in court.

"I mean, I don't even know your social media handles!"

"Except for my business, I don't use social media. I'm not interested in people trying to find me."

What did he mean by that? Who would be trying to "find him"? Did he have a lot of ex-girlfriends who were collecting dust on the shelf, still waiting for him to make a move?

"Okay, you want more? How about we take a trip together?"

I rolled my eyes, dismissing his words, sure that I had misheard him.

"No, for real. Next month I'm going to a conference. Why don't you come with me?"

"Why?"

"Because I want to spend more time with you and I want you to know I'm serious."

"Won't you be busy?"

"During the day, yes, but I'll have the evenings free. We can hang out then and do whatever you want. We can even make our own Thanksgiving dinner."

"Wait, when is your conference?"

"National Adoption Day. It's the Saturday before Thanksgiving. Most counties try to finalize a lot of adoptions around that time so that foster kids can have permanency at Thanksgiving. It's mostly symbolic, but lots of judges and lawyers volunteer to work on that Saturday to make it happen."

He must have noticed my look of confusion.

"In addition to finalizing the adoptions, some counties throw these huge events to celebrate National Adoption Day."

"Do they celebrate here, too?"

"Yeah, but with the weather, it tends to be small, indoors events. In Cali, some counties are doing festivals with booths, clowns, face painting, entertainment for the kids. I'll be attending a conference and some other events in California all that week. I go to make connections, drum up some business, etcetera."

"You can join me," he continued.

"Which part of California?"

"Near LA. Wait, where are you from?"

"Lynwood. A small city near Compton and Los Angeles."

"That's not too far from where I'll be! I just booked a suite in a beautiful hotel. You'll have your own room, of course."

I couldn't focus on everything he was saying, I was so overwhelmed by it all. Had he just invited me to California with him? Leon, the guy I had barely seen a handful of times since we started dating? Not "dating", because I didn't know if this was exclusive or not. Since we had started "talking". That was a word from back when I was in school, but I had no idea what the current lingo was for being in a quasi-relationship with someone where you're dating, but not really dating, even though you really wanted to be dating.

He put his hand on top of mine.

"It'll be our first Thanksgiving."

A "first" Thanksgiving implied that there would be more. Was he saying what I thought he was saying?

"You can have Thanksgiving at your mom's, or we can order a meal...Oh! The suite has a full kitchen. We can even cook our own Thanksgiving meal if you want. I make a mean mac-n-cheese."

That made me smile. "Let me think about it. It sounds wonderful, but I haven't been home since I left for college. Like, I have not actually stepped back into the state," I confessed. "My family's not close like yours. If I go, it could get ugly. There's a lot of anger and resentment."

I paused, not wanting to get into more detail, but from his eyes, I could tell that he knew what I was saying without forcing me to say it.

"Well, don't punish the whole state just for a few folks who will never know if you came or not. But you're stronger than you think. If you decide to go see your family, I can be your emotional support animal. I promise I'll be with you for as much or as little of the day as you want."

That almost brought tears to my eyes, but I had not cried in front of Leon. Leon, who said things that only a great boyfriend would say, but who was not officially my boyfriend. I took a deep breath, hoping that the extra oxygen would help me make sense of all the emotions coursing through me.

"I don't want to ruin your trip."

"Well, I'll be alone-"

"In a fancy hotel," I interrupted.

"But *on Thanksgiving*, missing my family. You definitely won't be ruining anything for me. You'd probably make me the happiest man."

"If all the activities are on Saturday, why are you staying through Thanksgiving?"

He shrugged. "I need a vacation. If I'm home, I'll just work. But you don't have to stay the whole week. You can come whenever and stay only as long as you want. Maybe just Wednesday and Thursday, or Wednesday through Sunday…"

"Wow. A whole week? You're really serious about this vacation!" He smiled longingly at me. I wanted to jump in his arms and shout "yes", but instead I asked, "Separate rooms?"

"Of course!" His eyebrows raised in affected shock.

"I'll think about it."

And I did think about it. I thought about it for the rest of the dinner. I thought about it on the drive home. I thought about how I'd never been to his home, but here I was thinking about going on a trip with him. I thought about sharing a hotel with a man who wasn't my husband, even if we had separate rooms. I thought about spending Thanksgiving with someone who wasn't even really my boyfriend. But, spending a holiday together was a big deal. Taking a trip together was a big deal. Even though he had never said the words, maybe he did think of me as his girlfriend. And maybe the trip would finally cement it and take our relationship to the next level. Not sexually, of course, but it was a huge sign of commitment, wasn't it? I thought about how quickly he'd offered to support me. I thought about how going home could finally prove that they didn't have a hold over me anymore. But I didn't need to prove anything to anybody. I bowed my head over the steering wheel as I parked the car in the garage, but I didn't move. *Lord, what should I do?*

Go.

The response was almost immediate. So clear that I looked around the car for the source, but the voice sounded like my own, only softer and gentler. Was that God? I'd asked for an answer, but was this one word from him? So simple. So direct.

No. It couldn't be from God. It must just be my flesh. My own thinking. I couldn't go to California. With Leon. For Thanksgiving! It was all preposterous! Besides, it was going to be my first Thanksgiving with Crystal. I couldn't just abandon her and Khalid. But when I asked Crystal what she wanted to do for Thanksgiving, she said she was going to spend the day with her mom and family.

"If you don't have any plans, I'm sure you can join us," she offered, taking away my final excuse.

Maybe this was the final step in my process. I smiled at the thought. To be healed, truly healed, had seemed like such an impossible dream only months before. If I could go back home and confront my mother, I could truly say I was healed and they didn't have any power over me anymore.

Drisk had accused me of using celibacy to hide behind. Frances had said the same thing. And maybe they had been right. Maybe it had been easier to take sex completely off the table than to face my trauma head on. I hadn't even been able to complete my adoption application because I couldn't fill out a few pages that dealt with my childhood! Memories from twenty-five years ago were preventing me from moving forward and living my life. Even though I had tried to push them down for years, how many times had they prevented me from being completely free and vulnerable? Would they always be there, just below the surface, trying to ruin my chance at love?

To even consider going home would have sent me in a tailspin of cleaning and crying and recriminations. But God. God had used a random comment to articulate what I had been unable to admit to myself for years. To bring me to the point where I could actually consider it. It was truly a miracle. I bowed my head. No tears poured out, just words of praise. *Thank you, God. Thank you. You are a mighty God and a strong tower. I will follow you wherever you lead me.*

REY SIRAKAVIT

Chapter 32

The holiday season had barely dawned when Carmen needed a caffeine fix, so we met at our favorite coffee shop for some java and much needed one-on-one time. The shop was packed as always. We had a small table and had to squish our chairs close to each other. I had so much to tell her, and sitting next to her, instead of looking at her across a table, would be much easier.

"I finally finished my adoption application."

"That's awesome! Did you get the letter from the therapist?"

"Not quite. I'm still working on that, but when I initially turned it in, I left a lot of it blank. Just skipped whole sections." I laughed ruefully, remembering how shocked I had been that Ms. Wilson was less than impressed.

"And they accepted that?"

"No," I smiled. "I guess that's why the social worker threatened to reject my application if I didn't go to counseling. Apparently not being willing to answer questions was a red flag." I shook my head at myself and foolishness. What had I thought would happen? "I realized the reason I had such a hard time filling it out is because…" I swallowed, my eyes flitting across the coffee shop, trying to focus on anything except my best friend beside me. Outside of therapy, I still hadn't said it out loud. But I had been waiting for that moment for a while. I cleared my throat and pressed on. "Because I was molested when I was a child, and the application just brought up a lot of memories that I didn't want to deal with." Before I was done talking, Carmen already had her arms around my shoulders.

I took a deep breath.

I had done it. Said it out loud.

The sky didn't break. The ground didn't open up and swallow me.

I really could do this. Think about it and talk about it and not be overwhelmed by it. I continued, buoyed by my victory.

"I was eight years old, and my uncle took me into a room...I don't remember where we were or where Debra, my mom, was, I just remember him taking my panties off..." I trailed off, wanting the memory to become clearer, but also glad that the screen had faded to black in my mind.

"Did you ever tell anyone?" Carmen's voice was low, barely above the hum of machines and conversations.

"Yeah, I told my mom."

"What did she say?" Carmen's arms tightened around my shoulder. Did she already know what I was going to say?

"She didn't believe me."

"I'm so sorry. The courage it must have taken, and then the slap in the face to not be believed. No wonder you don't have a great relationship with her."

That was an understatement. But maybe things could change. I remembered the second thing I wanted to share.

"That's not all. I'm- uh- I'm not going to be able to spend Thanksgiving with you guys this year."

"Really? Why not?"

"I'm going back to California for Thanksgiving."

Carmen shifted in her seat beside me, refusing to let me avoid her eyes this time.

"What? Why?"

"I think it's time for me to confront my mom."

"Wow. Are you sure? That seems like a really big step."

"It is. It's huge. Honestly, there's a part of me that really doesn't want to. But I feel like this is something God is leading me to do. Maybe he wants me to prove that I really am healed."

Carmen's eyebrows tightened, and she shook her head. "You don't have to prove anything to anybody."

I tilted my head, looking over my shoulder at my best friend. "You're always encouraging me to do hard things. I would have thought you'd be all over this, pushing me to go."

"In all the years I've known you, you've been adamant that you would never go home. You didn't even want us to go to Disneyland last year!"

"Disneyland is overrated," I mumbled.

"Exactly!" Carmen stared into my eyes. "I feel like there's something you're not telling me."

"There is one other thing." For some reason, telling the next part seemed a lot harder than telling about being molested. What would she think? If she already thought going back to California was a bad idea, how much worse would she think about it once I told her who I was going with? Would she think I was going back only to be with Leon? Was I? When I looked into my own heart, even I didn't know what my true motivation was. They were so interconnected, I couldn't tell where one reason ended and the other began.

I cleared my throat. "I'm going with Leon."

Carmen just blinked at me.

"I know you probably think I'm crazy."

She bent her head, leaned forward until our shoulders touched. But still, she didn't say anything. I was too nervous to even pick up my chai. Instead, I just fiddled with my napkin. The silence stretched between us while the noise of the background chatter grew. I could just make out the conversation behind us. Someone was complaining about having a hangover. I guess I wasn't the only one making a morning confession to a friend.

Finally, Carmen took my hand, squeezed it, and said, "This is huge. I guess you guys have gotten a lot closer than I realized. I mean, things must be really serious between you."

That was a logical guess. Unfortunately, Carmen was wrong. It was still sporadic, with only a random text here or there. But taking a trip together was a big step. "I think he's more serious about our relationship than he comes across, that's for sure. And if you're worried about anything happening between us, you don't have to. We're getting separate rooms."

"Wow, I just can't believe you guys are going on a trip together and I haven't even met him yet! But going home, honestly, that's even more shocking. Do you really think you're ready for that?"

"No!" I laughed. "I mean, I haven't been home or seen my mom in fifteen years."

"How often do you talk to her?"

"Never. She doesn't call me and I don't call her. She just sends me a birthday card every year." Did my mother ever wonder why I never came home? Did she care? Did I care if she cared? I sighed. "But I'm not going home for some happy reunion. I feel like God wants me to go and confront the people and the place that have had a hold over me for more than half my life."

"Well, if God is leading you, I completely support you of course."

I nodded. God was leading me, right? That was his voice that I heard, right?

"This is a lot to take in, but I'm proud of you. Really proud of you. Being able to talk about what happened to you after all these years, that takes incredible courage. And your therapist must be really supportive."

I pressed my lips. I hadn't exactly talked to Frances Anne Rogers about going home. What would she say? Say I wasn't ready?

"I know you think I'm always pushing, but it's only because you're so amazing! You've been able to accomplish so much. You put yourself through college. Moved to a new state where you didn't have any family and didn't know anyone. You bought your own house as a single woman. You've maintained your virginity. And now come to find out you were molested? You're my best friend, but you're kind of my hero. No joke. So I have no doubt that you can go home and slay those dragons, too. A lot of people talk about obeying God, but you're doing it. No matter how hard, no matter how scary. You just do it. You're taking risks. You're a survivor. You just dropped three bombs on me, and I'm over here crying more than you are!"

"Maybe I should be the next sponsor/face of Nike," I joked.

"I'd buy all your gear," Carmen smiled, then her face got serious again. "If you ever want to talk about what happened, you know I'm here for you."

I brushed the tears from my cheeks and wrapped my arms around Carmen's shoulders. While being molested was not my choice, going home was. I hoped she was right and that I wasn't making a huge mistake that I would regret for the rest of my life. "Will you do me a favor?"

Carmen nodded. "Of course. Anything."

"Pray for me." And she did. Right in the middle of the crowded coffee shop, she took my hands and prayed. She bowed her head slightly, her eyes on a faraway spot over my shoulder, and whispered, "Lord, thank you for everything you're doing in Sierra's life. Thank you for healing her of the abuse she suffered. I thank you that it no longer has power over her. God, we ask for wisdom. Peace. Help Sierra to continue to trust you and follow you wherever you lead her."

As she said the almost exact same words that I had prayed earlier, I felt like a giant spotlight was illuminating the decision, revealing all the holes and gaps. Where was the Lord leading me? To the edge of a cliff? I could only hope that he would call me back before my feet went over the edge.

Chapter 33

Once again, I found myself in Frances Anne Rogers' office, a jumble of emotions, waiting for her to respond to the not-quite bombshell that I dropped on her.

"Last week you told me that for the first time in your life, you were able to acknowledge that you had been molested, something you had never been able to say aloud. This week, you're talking about going home. Do you think you might be trying to tackle too much too fast?"

Once again, someone was questioning the wisdom of me returning home. But if I were her, sitting across from me, wouldn't I have had the same reaction? Disbelief. Concern. Worry. Why would the Lord ask me to do something that made no sense to anyone else? But I was certain I had heard "Go", so I had to hold on to that, even if it made no sense to anyone else. Even if it felt like everything was moving too fast.

But twenty-five years was long enough to live in fear.

"I've never been back and hadn't planned on it either. But if I say that I'm healed, then it shouldn't be a big deal, should it? I refuse to let what my uncle did to me ruin another relationship."

"How do you think it's ruined your other relationships?"

I immediately thought about Drisk and his accusation that I had been hiding behind my virginity instead of simply obeying God.

While other friends throughout high school and college seemed to struggle with "sexual purity" and taming their raging hormones, saying no had been easy for me. Maybe too easy.

"I think I've been afraid of intimacy. Afraid of letting down my guard. Afraid of getting too close, of letting men see the real me, who allowed herself to be..." I swallowed, then started over. "It was sick what my uncle did to me, but for years I thought I was the one who was sick and dirty and I carried that shame around. I tried to hide it, but I was horrified that if someone got too close, they might find out my secret. So even though I've wanted to get married and have a family, I haven't really let anyone in for long enough or get close enough to see behind the veil that I've held up."

"Do you think confronting your mom will help you be more vulnerable?" Frances Anne Rogers leaned in as if pulled by an invisible cord, as anxious to know my answer as I was.

"I hope so. Regardless of how she responds, I don't want to be afraid of the truth anymore."

"What about your uncle?"

I stopped her. "I don't think I'm ready for that, yet. Maybe I'll never be."

"That's okay."

I smiled, but she held up a finger as if something of great import had just occurred to her.

"You smile to cover up your pain. That's part of the veil. There's this perception that Black women, in particular, have to be super strong, superwomen, show no pain, no fear. Do you feel like that's true for you?"

Was this white woman asking me about how societal expectations of Black women affected me? I nodded, my throat too thick to speak.

"Well, you don't have to wear your 'happy face' in here."

I nodded, unsure what to say or how to respond, but glad that my first impression of Frances had been so wrong.

"What about Leon? Does he understand what's at stake for you?"

I shook my head. I had barely talked to Leon, less known told him why going home might be so difficult.

"I guess I don't want to ruin our relationship," I said, "if you can even call it that."

"Why do you think it might ruin your relationship?" When I didn't answer, she followed up with, "Do you feel pressured to go?"

"No, it's not that."

Frances gave me space to go on, but when I didn't expand upon my answer, she pivoted.

Her delivery was calm and patient, but insistent.

"Where are you going to see your mother? A neutral location is always best so you can control how to get in and get out. Do you want Leon to be there with you? If you do, how much will you tell him? Will he know how to support you? Do *you* know how you'll need to be supported?"

No. Nope. Not even.

She fired off the next round of questions. Her delivery was calm and patient, but insistent. "Even if you're not confronting your abuser, confronting their enabler can be just as difficult. Your mother was supposed to protect you, but she didn't. What do you want to say to her? How do you think she might respond? What if she still doesn't believe you? What if your uncle is there? Do you have an exit plan? And what do you hope to gain from this?"

One question after another I had no answer to, but I had to say something. After all, I was a mature adult making a life-changing decision. I had to at least appear like I had thought through the ramifications.

"You know, I might not even see her. Just going back to the state is a moral victory. If I overthink it, I'll chicken out. I'll just see how it goes."

But that was a lie. I would not "just see how it goes". Sierra Harris, the eternal planner and list maker, was not going to just wing it.

Until then, all I had been concerned with was to go or not to go.

I smiled, even though I knew I didn't have to, to cover up the fact that I hadn't considered any of her questions.

I smiled to assure her that I would think about all she had said.

I smiled even though I was leaving with a different weight than the one I had entered with.

When I got home, I pulled out my yellow legal pad and wrote "Confronting Debra" across the top. Below it, I jotted down every possible response and worst-case scenario, based on books I had read and movies I had seen. Based on my fears. I made a list of the who's and the what's and the how's. Everything was thought through. Contingencies mapped out. I had a plan A, a plan B, and a plan C. I was ready. I could do it. And I felt better. More calm and in control. I wished I could go back to Frances' office and show her my list and answer every question like the intelligent, prepared adult I was. I had accounted for everything.

Except for Leon.

Leon was the wild card. While half of my plans depended on being able to completely avoid my uncle, the other half depended on Leon being there for emotional support. I was fairly confident that if I chose the right time (the day before Thanksgiving in the late afternoon when my uncle would still be at work, but my mother would be home) and place (my mother's house), I could do it. But I couldn't drag Leon all the way to my mother's house without sharing the full story with him. And telling my therapist was one thing, a very important one thing, but telling Leon...I knew I wasn't ready for that. We weren't ready for that.

Even though we were going halfway across the country together, even though I thought he could maybe possibly be "the one", we had only been on a few dates. I couldn't trust him just because he had a great smile and seemed insightful. I would go, but Leon didn't need to meet Debra. I would do that on my own. And the rest of the trip would be spent figuring out if Leon really was the one.

Chapter 34

I pulled my legal pad out of my purse and scanned the list on top to be sure I had everything. Each box was checked and my ride share was scheduled to arrive at any moment. I yawned, stuffed the list back into my purse and wheeled my bag to the front door. It was too early for breakfast. I would have to grab something at the airport once I cleared security. I said a little prayer for Crystal and Khalid. Crystal would be alone- in my home- for three days. Once again, I considered calling Carmen and asking her to take Crystal. Or maybe I just shouldn't go. Leon was already in California, speaking at a seminar for adoption professionals. He didn't need me. But Crystal did. Khalid did. She'd said she would be okay and Lavondra would pick her up for Thanksgiving dinner, so I had nothing to worry about. But what about my house? Did I really trust Crystal to be alone in my home for three days?

I pulled out my cell phone, hovering between Carmen's name and Leon's, unsure who to text.

"Leon- Can't make it after all"?

Or, "Carmen, come get Crystal!"

I shoved the phone back in my pocket. I was not going to cancel and I was not going to kick Crystal out, not even for three days. Really, just three days and two nights. I'd be back Friday night. It wasn't like

I thought she would steal anything. After all, she'd been in my home alone every day for months while I went to work. And even if she did, the most expensive thing I owned was the baby crib that Khalid was at that moment sleeping in. I took a deep breath.

No, the pit in my stomach had nothing to do with Crystal. I flipped to another page in the pad, past the "Questions for Leon" and to the "Confronting Debra" page.

Within hours, I'd be at my mother's house. Even though I had a well-thought-out list, which was almost like a script, I knew that things may not go the way I planned. People weren't actors in the movie I had created. No one would be obligated to say the lines I had prepared. I was not guaranteed a happy ending or a satisfying conclusion. So, what was the point in going?

I reminded myself of all the reasons I had told Frances and Carmen and Leon. But the only reason that mattered was the one I was certain I had heard from the Lord: Go. For some reason that I could not explain, the God of the universe wanted me to go on this trip. And as desperately as I wanted it to be about growing my relationship with Leon, I knew that it must also have something to do with Debra. Maybe she had changed. That was Plan B. She had changed and felt sorry and wanted to make amends for not believing me all those years ago and had been wanting to reach out but was too ashamed to.

It would be a miracle. A *Thanksgiving* Miracle.

And, of course, I would tell Leon the whole story while we walked hand in hand along the pier, and he would wrap me in his arms, and for the first time in forever I would feel safe in a man's embrace, not nervous or embarrassed. And sharing such an intense and intimate experience would cement our love.

The sound of tires on gravel pulled me from my reverie. I said one final prayer, then headed to the car.

Except that was not my final prayer. Neither the driver nor I were in the mood for talking, so I prayed throughout the entire car ride. *I can do it.* I prayed in the ridiculously long predawn line that snaked around the airport. *I can do it.* I prayed as we crossed the snow-covered Rockies and descended to sea level. *I can do it.*

No fancy language, no calling fire down from heaven. Just four simple words that reverberated from the deepest part of my soul to the highest part of heaven. A statement, a plea, a reminder of the truth. *I can do it.*

When the plane taxied down, I wanted to jump up and shout, "I did it!" I was officially back in California, back in the state that I had fled from so many years before. We'd barely landed, but the sun already shone brightly through the airplane windows. The pilot announced it was 78 degrees. I looked out my window, reminding myself that it was the same sun that shone in Denver. Still, I shivered. Around me, everyone else was taking off their winter coats, smiling at being in a warmer locale, ready to enjoy vacations, family, and the ocean.

Not me. My plan was to pick up the rental car I had already reserved, then head straight to Debra's. I looked at my watch, the cheerful pink hearts seeming to mock me, yet also reminding me of my strength. It was just after lunch time. I should have had plenty of time.

But we sat on the tarmac, waiting for a gate to open. And the longer we waited, the more I felt I had forgotten how to breathe. In, then out? Or out, then in? I closed my eyes. What would happen if we ran out of oxygen? Would I pass out? Would I vomit? I had not accounted for this, but I could already start to feel the bile rise in my throat. With every inhalation, it moved further up. I leaned down and grabbed the travel size package of cleansing wipes from my bag. I pulled a handful free and began wiping off the tray in front of me. Then the screen. Then the entire seatback. The armrests. The overhead buttons. Windows. Pockets. Seatbelt. Chair.

"Wow, normally people clean before the flight," the man sitting next to me said with a smile. He slid over then stood. I looked around me. The seatbelt light was off. People were standing in the aisle. I let out a breath and smiled. I had remembered how to smile.

I followed the crowd off the airplane and landed in a sea of people, all headed in the same direction. Rental cars. The line extended through the door and around the corner. I sent Leon a quick text letting him know I had made it. I wasn't surprised there was no response. The conference must still be in session. I clicked through my phone, trying to ignore the glowing number letting me know that my perfect window of opportunity was rapidly closing. By the time I had my rental and was driving through southern California traffic, it was late afternoon. Plan A was already coming apart, and I had barely made it out of the airport. I had no time for lunch, which I probably wouldn't have been able to swallow anyway. I just zipped in and out of lanes, heading toward the home that had felt like a prison, so I could finally be free.

REY SIRAKAVIT

Chapter 35

I sat in the rental car in front of the ranch-style house I had lived in most of my life. It hadn't changed much. I had driven to it almost as if on autopilot. So much looked different, but so much looked the same.

You can do it, Sierra. You can face it. It doesn't hold any power over you anymore. I pulled the latch of the short wrought-iron fence and walked up the driveway. A part of me had been hoping Debra would not be there, that she'd be out doing last minute Thanksgiving shopping, but there was a car in the driveway. I didn't recognize it, but I also hadn't kept up with what she was driving over the years. I didn't know much about Debra outside of the generic Christmas cards she sent every year. I didn't know if she still worked at the same job. I didn't know if she was seeing someone or even if she had gotten married! How would she feel about me just showing up after all these years? Would she be excited? Would she be angry? I took a deep breath. There was only one way to know.

I pushed the doorbell, hoping that maybe the car in the driveway wasn't hers. Or maybe one of her sisters had picked her up and they were off running errands together. That way, I could say I had come but she wasn't there, and I could be proud that I had faced the fear and could move on with my life.

I pushed the doorbell again, preparing to leave, just about to give myself the W, when Debra opened the door.

You don't have to stay, I reminded myself. "Hi."

"Sierra? I thought you were a delivery person. What are you doing here?"

Not exactly the reaction I had hoped for, but at least she hadn't slammed the door in my face.

"I was in town and wanted to see you."

"What a surprise! I knew you'd come home one day! Look at you! You were always such a beautiful girl. And your hair."

She reached out to touch one of my locs, but I instinctively pulled back. She dropped her hand to her side, but kept talking. "Your aunt Gayle has locs, too. I never liked them, but they look good on her. They look good on you, too. Where are you staying? I changed your room to a workout room, but I can probably move some things around if you need."

"That's okay. I have a hotel."

"Good. Good. So, what brings you?" She finally slowed down and stopped talking. I had forgotten how much she could fill the space with her nonstop chatter.

"A friend of mine is visiting, so I decided to tag along."

"Awesome, awesome. Are you still in Denver?" She leaned against the door jam, her body leaned halfway and halfway out.

"Yep."

"You ever think about moving back?"

"Nope. I'm pretty happy out there." Debra was just as I remembered her. Except for a few more sunspots by her eyes, she looked just the same. She didn't try to hug me, and I didn't hug her. We were like mere acquaintances that had crossed paths in the grocery store. But we weren't. And the things I needed to say probably shouldn't be said in front of the house for all the neighbors to see and hear. "Can I come in?"

"Of course!" Debra laughed, and I half expected her to say *"Where are my manners?"* as if we were in some southern comedy / drama. She opened the door wide and as I stepped into the house, it was as if I was being pulled into a time portal full of memories. I felt my skin catch fire, like a thousand mosquito bites had suddenly appeared up and down my arms and neck. It was a nervous reaction that I hadn't had since I was a kid. Since I had been home, probably. Now that I was in the house, I didn't know where to look. I examined the flecks in the carpet, longing for a vacuum to suck up all the pain and memories, but instead settling for my fingernails that were busily trying to scratch them away.

"How's the weather out there? It's so cold. I don't know how you stand it." I finally looked up at the banality of the question.

"We haven't seen each other in fifteen years, and you're asking me about the weather?"

"I don't know much about what's going on in your life, Sierra. You don't exactly keep in touch."

Was that the problem? That I didn't " keep in touch"? I almost laughed as I scratched. Just like I couldn't control the nervous reaction, so much about this visit was out of my control. And even though I couldn't control how Debra would respond, I knew this would be no prodigal reunion with singing and celebration and slaughtering of the fatted calf.

She was barely curious about the daughter she hadn't seen for fifteen years. She was more interested in the Rocky Mountain weather than in what I was doing and who I had become. And as soon as I started talking, any curiosity she may have had would certainly burn off like the early morning haze in LA.

Or would it? What did I really need to say? Just coming home was victory enough. Except for a little nervous itching, I was okay. I had conquered my fear.

But that was not entirely true. While she may not have been very curious about me, there were some things *I* was curious about.

"Do you think it's weird that you don't know anything about my life? You've never been out to see me in Colorado. You didn't even come out for my graduation!"

"I had to work."

"I didn't invite you."

Debra hmphed and spun on her heels. She walked toward the kitchen, leaving me to either follow her or turn and get back in my rental car. I followed her. The house hadn't changed much. The couch was probably different, but I didn't take the time to do a physical inventory. She stopped at the kitchen counter, picked up a knife and half-peeled apple. There were bowls and cutting boards scattered all over. She must have already started preparing for Thanksgiving.

"You have always been so hateful." The vitriol in her voice shocked me. With each word a piece of skin from the apple flew onto the counter. "You walked around this house with an attitude. Like you were too good for us. I wasn't surprised when you went off to college and didn't look back." She shook her head as if trying to shake off the bad memories. As if *I* had wronged *her*. As if I had something to feel bad about. And the words, the emotions, the resentment, that I didn't even know were there, spilled over and out. I stopped scratching.

"I'm sorry if I was shell-shocked from having to be around my abuser all the time."

"What are you talking about?" Debra looked up from her apple, eyebrows pinched in confusion. It was my turn to humph.

280

"Uncle Miller. Your brother. He molested me when I was a kid and you did nothing about it. Nothing." There. I had said it. A weight that I didn't even realize I had been carrying fell off my shoulders. I felt cool and light and free. Like I might just float away. But I was not done. I looked her in the eye, waiting for her response. Would she throw her arms around me in sorrow and repentance? Beg for my forgiveness? Would she cry? I had never seen my mother cry. Not at sad movies or break-ups, not at my grandmother's funeral. She did not cry when I summoned up the courage to tell her what my favorite uncle had done to me. I don't remember what she said. Just the look on her face. A look that dismissed me and everything I said. The same look on her face at that moment in her kitchen.

"What? You used to run to his arms when he came over. Always spending the weekend at his house. You loved him. He was like a father to you."

"Yes, I loved him. Yes, he was my favorite uncle. Did that give him the right to…do what he did?"

"Of course not. I'm just saying maybe it didn't happen like you remember it."

"So, you think I made all this up? Made up all the memories of him touching me?" She went back to peeling. I plunged on. Now that I had come so far, I had to make her understand. Make her see. "Of him taking my clothes off? Of him taking my underwear off?"

"Stop!" She slammed the apple and knife down, sending apple peel flying across the counter. "I don't want to hear this! Did you just come home to cause drama?" She turned back to the stove. God forbid anything as important as the daughter she hadn't seen in over a decade declaring that she had been abused delay her pre-Thanksgiving preparations.

"Didn't you hear what I said? Don't you care?"

She shrugged. "It was so long ago, who knows what really happened. If he...touched you, you should've said something at the time."

"I did tell you! I told you he hurt me."

"How was I supposed to know that's what you meant? You were just a kid and you know how big your uncle is. He rough houses sometimes, but he doesn't mean any harm." Did she realize the irony of her words, of how much pain I endured then to be penetrated by a man who, by her very own words, was "so big"?

I could feel the anger rising in me, but I grabbed hold of the only prayer I could think of: *Lord, give me strength.*

"It happened. And I thought it was my fault. For twenty-five years, I have tried to forget. For twenty-five years, it has haunted me, terrorized me. "

"Stop." This time her voice was low. So low I barely heard her.

"So now that you know, what are you going to do?"

Debra shook her head, shaking off any emotion that she might have been feeling. The moment had passed. And honestly, I was glad. Regardless of how she responded, I was really healed. The memories didn't have any power over me anymore. Even a detached mother couldn't change that. All the anger and fire I felt only moments before melted away. My healing wasn't contingent on Debra affirming me, reassuring me, or even believing me.

You see the truth, Lord. Help me to walk in your truth and light.

"What am I supposed to do? Miller's my brother. And that was a long time ago." Her voice sounded hoarse. But not from emotion and empathy. Hoarse, like filled with resolve that comes during a bitter fight. I didn't want to be the one Debra was fighting against. Let her fight against herself.

So that was it. Discussion closed.

"We're having Thanksgiving dinner at Miller's house tomorrow. Are you going?"

I practically choked on disbelief. Was she crazy? After all I had said, did she really expect me to go to his house and eat turkey like nothing had happened? "No. I'm not going."

"Everybody will be there. All your aunts and cousins." I pictured myself blowing up in front of all my family, and all their kids. Baring my pain and wounds for them all to see. Trying desperately to get them to believe me. Even though I was healed, I was not a masochist. I shook my head.

"Are you going to stay for dinner tonight?"

What would be the point? "No, I think I'd better leave." There was nothing more to say.

I picked up my jacket and purse. I couldn't believe I had come all this way, had divulged so much, just for her to continue to defend herself and her brother. What about me? Her daughter? I looked back over my shoulder to where she stood, frozen at the counter. "You know, this is why I left home and never came back, why I haven't been back in years. Instead of comforting me, all you've ever done is protect him."

"Look, sometimes things happen and you just have to move on. Don't think about it anymore." She picked up a soapy sponge and wiped the counter of apple bits leaving a layer of bubbles all over the green tile. She rinsed out the sponge, then wiped the counter off again, catching some, but leaving many more bubbles behind. She repeated the process, wiping and rinsing, again and again and again, while I just watched. Waiting for her to say something. Anything. Stop me from leaving. Finally acknowledge my pain. But she didn't. She just kept wiping. Like she was locked in a six-second time loop. What was she thinking? What was she trying to forget? Would she even notice that I was gone?

As I reached out for the doorknob, ready to put this day behind me, the door swung open in front of me.

Chapter 36

The sun was shining right through the door. I couldn't see who it was. For a second, I imagined it was Miller. His large body blocking the doorway, demanding that I recant and apologize, calling me a liar. My heart stopped and I took a quick step back. Surely God would not expect so much of me.

"Sierra, this is your cousin Felicia." Debra smiled at the girl in the doorway, the girl who, once the sun was no longer shining in my eyes, was certainly not Miller. The girl was about fifteen or sixteen, with long hair that shaped her face. The back was pulled into a spiral bun. Debra reached around me, wrapping the girl in a hug, ignoring the palpable tension between us, welcoming the girl into the room as if she belonged and I was the outsider. Which I was.

"Hey Aunt Debra, here's the cinnamon you asked my momma for."

How many times had I been the errand girl for my mom and aunts when I was her age? A flood of other memories came back, memories of playing in the cul-de-sac with cousins, riding our bikes up and down the streets. Playing jump rope and tag and eavesdropping on the grown folks gossiping. Not all the memories were bad. But for years, all I had associated with Lynwood was my uncle's abuse and my mother letting me down. She didn't feed me to the wolf, but she sure didn't step in when the wolf was devouring me. So, I had put aunties and cousins and mother and uncle in the same box in my mind, labeled DO NOT OPEN. And here was this cousin, whom I had not thought about or seen for years, pushing against the lid, saying *"Open, open, open."*

Felicia held out the small plastic bottle. I tried to place her, but for the life of me, I couldn't. Out of my mom's three older sisters and brother, I couldn't remember any teen girls named Felicia. When I had moved away, I didn't stay in touch with anyone, and no one stayed in touch with me. Fifteen years was a long time. What else had I missed?

"It's good to meet you," I said, surprised at how clear and strong my voice sounded. Then it hit me. She would have only been a toddler when I left for school. And now she was looking very grown-up. Even though she was just wearing a t-shirt and jeans, she looked like me. Or how I imagined myself at her age. Clean. Neat. Serious. Focused. There was an intensity about her.

I tried to think which of my aunts would be her mom, but I was too embarrassed to ask. And if I just listened long enough, Debra would slip it in somewhere as she bragged about Felicia's grades and school activities as if she were her own daughter. I smarted, but reminded myself that I didn't care. I had disowned my family in deed, if not in word, so I couldn't be jealous if my mother was fawning over her niece.

"Felicia even went to a Coding Camp in Oakland last summer. That your uncle Miller *paid for*," Debra said. Was she trying to convince me that Miller was a good guy just because he paid for his niece to go to camp? Was that supposed to wipe the slate clean? Remove all memories?

"I.T. is a good field to go into," I said, as if by rote, my mind still spinning and trying to take in all the details that Debra was throwing out except for the one that I wanted.

Felicia spun towards me and grabbed my arm. "That's right, you were a computer science major, weren't you?? I love coding! OMG, I have so many questions!"

Her bubbly personality and optimism shone. At her age, I was depressed and just biding my time until graduation. My high school years were a blur. Covered in mist and gray fog. I spent all my free time studying and trying to avoid Miller. I would never want to see anyone dull her shine. Anyone. Especially not the person who had dulled mine and who was paying for summer camps and trying to look like the perfect uncle, above suspicion.

Above suspicion.

Was I just being paranoid? Bitter? I didn't know anything. But that wasn't true. What I did know was that if he'd molested me, what would stop him from doing the same to her? My mind went through a hundred different scenarios. Calling the police. Strangling him. Telling my aunt. Telling my mom. But with no evidence, who would care. Who protects Black girls?

There are no allies here. In my home. Among my people.

Tell her.

My throat tightened. No, Lord, I begged. It was one thing to tell Debra, who regardless of what she said, already knew. Had already heard. But it was a wildly different thing to tell Felicia, the cousin I hadn't even known I had.

No. I would get back in my car and drive back to the hotel and spend Thanksgiving with Leon. I would put all these people and supposed-family out of my mind.

But if I had done so much for Crystal, who was not related to me, how much more should I want to help Felicia?

One tear, then two pushed their way out and down my cheek. I quickly brushed them away. I shouldn't have come. What was I trying to prove? I should've called first. But as quickly as the thoughts came, I brushed them away, just as I had the tears. I was done feeling guilty and taking the blame. Miller should be scared and ashamed. Miller, not me.

"Why don't I walk her back home? That way you can finish your Thanksgiving prepping in peace."

Debra nodded and smiled, gave Felicia a hug and kiss on the cheek. "Be careful," she said to Felicia, proving that she did want to protect those she loves. Why not me?

Help me to forgive her, Lord.

She waved at me, like I was just on my way up the street and would be back any minute. But I was not coming back. No, "Good to see you," no hug. Just a wave. I waved and let the door close behind me. What more did I expect? I could not even be sad about it.

"Lead the way," I said to Felicia, clueless as to which direction she lived. Then it occurred to me, "You don't live with Miller, do you?" I hesitated for a quick second, not ready to see him.

Felicia laughed. "No, but he said I could come stay with him if I wanted. I'd have my own room and a quiet place to study. I'm thinking about it." She shrugged.

Give me wisdom, Lord, I whispered.

I pray I'm not too late.

I pray his pecker falls off.

I pray for your justice, your perfect justice.

"There are a lot of good schools in California, but I'm thinking of going out of state for college. Was it hard to leave? Were you homesick?" She asked.

No," I said honestly. "You know how in the morning sometimes it looks really cloudy, but then it burns off and it turns into a hot, sunny day? Well it's not really 'burning off'. All the dirt and smog are

289

still there. Still in the air. Just because we don't see them, doesn't mean we're not breathing it in. For a lot of years, I was breathing in the toxicity of living at home and I'm finally in a place where the air is clean and I can breathe clearly. I wouldn't trade that for anything."

"What was so toxic?"

And here it was. My opportunity to speak or be silent. Silence doesn't only protect the abuser. It also protects the abused. From being accused. Questioned. Shamed. Blamed. But for the victim, silence is a double-edged sword. I would not be silenced anymore.

"When I was a little girl," I said, my voice cracking. I started again. "When I was a little girl, 'Uncle Miller' was my favorite." I curled my fingers around the words "Uncle Miller", and laughed sarcastically. "I would have done anything he asked, 'cause I knew my Uncle Miller was the best and would never hurt me. Well, he did hurt me. When I was eight years old, he molested me."

I pried the words free. That's why I came. To be free. But maybe it wasn't only my own freedom that I had come for. I locked my eyes onto Felicia's. I ignored the noise of my pounding heart, the noise of cars whizzing by, of kids playing in the street. "When I got old enough, I left and swore I'd never come back."

"Where did you go?"

"College in Colorado. I stayed on campus during the summers. Went with friends during the holidays. But moving away wasn't enough, because for all these years, I actually blamed myself." I paused. "And for some reason that I can't explain, I feel like I should tell you. Has anything like that ever happened to you? I know you don't know me, but if it has, you don't have to be afraid to tell me." I kept walking, glad that though she had slowed, she kept walking, too.

"Did you tell Aunt Debra?"

"I did. After the first time it happened." And suddenly, I was no longer on the street next to Felicia, I was in a bedroom. I was laying under a green and blue quilt. But I was still shivering. I rubbed my feet together to get warm. Could he feel how cold I was? He rubbed his hands up and down my arms, which made me shiver even more. He stroked hair. His thumb caressed my forehead. A tiny sputter caught in my throat. Why wouldn't he stop? And later, I hid the soiled underwear in the bottom of my trash can. When Debra saw me crying, I tried to tell her. *Uncle Miller hurt me. He did it to me.* Her lips moved but I couldn't understand any of the words she said, any of the excuses she made. All I understood was that what happened must have been my fault and I shouldn't have said anything.

I looked at Felicia who was biting her lip and had fallen silent. "Wait, you think he…? Uncle Miller would never do anything like that. Not to me." And there it was. That implication that it was my fault. I had asked for it. Wanted it. Didn't stop it.

"He plays around…but I don't think he…I mean sometimes he brushes up against me, but just by accident. You know how guys are."

"Yeah, guys. But not your uncle."

"Honestly, he would never do anything like that!"

"I'm glad."

I sighed. In relief. Because what would I have done if she said he had? What could I have done? How could I protect her when no one had protected me? How could I protect her when I hadn't been able to protect myself?

Felicia stopped outside a house that looked just like Debra's. Same wrought iron fence. Same paved driveway. Same brown stucco. Same mentality: protect Miller. Who knew how many generations of Harris women had been protecting Harris men?

"Are you gonna come in and say hi to my mom?" Unfortunately, I still couldn't remember which aunt Felicia belonged to, and I was emotionally drained.

"Maybe next time," I said. Felicia looked as relieved as I felt, but we still exchanged social media handles. "Message me if you ever need help writing a program," I added.

"That would be awesome," she said, trying to sound normal like I hadn't just told her that the uncle she trusted was a child molester. "Some of these online communities can be hard to break into."

I nodded, ready to turn and to walk away, but something held me back. I had to try one last time. "Let me just say one more thing. I know you said nothing's happened and I'm relieved to hear that. I really am. But, if he ever tries something, I want you to know that it's not your fault. And you can tell someone. Even if they don't believe you, keep talking until you find someone to listen. A teacher. Your school nurse. Me."

I didn't know if I should hug her or not, so I just waved and watched her turn inside, praying that I was wrong, praying that her mom wouldn't let anything happen to her. But I also knew that sometimes the people who were supposed to protect us, didn't. Maybe it happened to them, too, and no one had believed them. I sighed as I walked away. When would the cycle end?

Chapter 37

When I got back to the hotel, Leon wasn't there. Before getting in the shower, I clicked the deadbolt, so even if someone had a key, they couldn't get in. I felt dirty and helpless, and hoped that the hot water would wash away all the fear, anger, and sadness.

Lord, I did what you wanted, but what was the point? It made absolutely no difference. Debra didn't believe me then, and she still doesn't. You told me to tell Felicia, but she says nothing's happened. I don't understand, Lord. I wished the Lord would speak, would tell me that I had done the right thing. I hadn't expected it to be easy. I hadn't expected a parade, a rainbow in the sky, or even applause. But was a thank you or even just a hug too much to ask for? Anything to let me know I was on the right track.

I replayed the conversations in my mind, thought about what I should've said, or could've done differently.

I thought about Debra telling me to just "let it go", but Debra didn't just want me to "let it go", she wanted me to pretend it never happened.

I had two choices, though. I could either let all the what-ifs consume me, or I could... not. I looked at myself in the mirror. *You did it, Sierra,* I told myself with pride. I squeezed the water from my locs, repeating the truth of those words until I felt a measure of peace and calm. Then I pulled out my Bible and spread out on the big hotel bed.

I opened up to Psalms, right in the middle of the Bible, prayers of David and other heroes of the faith. Prayers of adoration, prayers of lament, prayers of confession, prayers of curses upon one's enemies. One verse jumped out at me, beckoned me to sit still and listen and claim the words for myself: *Even if my father and mother abandon me, the Lord will hold me close.* (Psalm 27:10, NLT).

I wasn't the first person, nor would I be the last, who had been abandoned by their parents. But the Lord would hold me close. The Lord *had* been holding me close. Preserving me and preparing me for the next stage in my life.

Marriage.

Because I couldn't take all the baggage from being molested into the future. What if I had gotten married without ever having addressed it, and wound up ruining my marriage? I didn't want to be a statistic. So as hard as it had been, I praised God. I was finally free and ready for the life that God had in store for me. A life with Leon.

I rolled off the bed, glancing at my watch. It was after nine o'clock. I unbolted the door and pulled it open to view the kitchen and living area that our rooms shared. Leon was sitting on the couch, laptop open. He looked up as he heard me.

"Hey, beautiful. When did you get back?"

His smile alone was almost enough to erase all my disappointment from the day.

"A while ago. How was the conference?" I stood in the doorway between my room and the living area.

"Can't complain." He stretched his arms up over his head. He looked as tired as I felt. "I'm hungry. Did you eat at your mom's?"

"No. It wasn't a great visit."

I looked at him, wanting to tell him everything. Wanting to celebrate my victory with him. Yet I was proud that even though he

295

had promised to be my "emotional support animal", I hadn't needed him after all.

"I'm sorry," he said, his eyebrows dropping. "Do you want to grab dinner? We can eat in the hotel restaurant, or, since you're a local, we can go to one of your favorites."

I thought about finding a restaurant along the pier.

We drove to Redondo Beach, a popular area not too far from the hotel, and found a table for two at a Mexican seafood restaurant, *Los Siete Mariscos*, the Seven Seas. After dinner, we held hands and walked along the pier, just as I had imagined. He told me all about work and the conferences he'd attended. I wanted to tell him about Debra. But what was there to say? "Don't bother inviting her to the wedding"? And I wasn't ready to tell him about being molested. So, I told a partial truth: my suspicions about Felicia.

"Ever since I took all those adoption classes on abuse, I've been hyper-aware of signs and what to look for. But she denies it. And I didn't actually see them together or anything. Maybe I'm just being paranoid."

He stopped, then turned to stand in front of me. "If there's one thing I know, it's to trust your gut. My mom calls it women's intuition. My sister calls it her spidey-sense."

Leon laughed, then continued. "Whatever you call it, though, you're probably not wrong. You're not a crazy person who just makes things up out of thin air. Whatever happens, you did your best."

I squeezed his hand. "Thank you." I *had* done my best. Whatever happened was out of my hands. Or was it? But how did you rescue someone who insisted they didn't need rescuing? My head pounded and my palm itched. I craved the feeling of a soapy wet rag in my hand. I thought back to Debra. Maybe we were more alike than I wanted to believe.

"I'm sorry I wasn't there."

Leon stopped walking, then brushed his thumb across my cheek. My spidey-senses were at high alert. This was it. The moment he would say he wanted to be exclusive. Or told me he loved me. My eyes landed on his lips. Or kissed me passionately?

But he dropped his hand and resumed his pace.

"So, should we make our own Thanksgiving dinner tomorrow?"

Dry turkey and canned cranberry sauce were the furthest things from my mind. But I cleared my throat, swallowing the disappointment, pretending I was perfectly content to just walk and talk. Or, walk and not-talk. At least, not talk about anything that I really wanted to talk about.

"Do you mean *we* or *me*?" I asked, trying to make my voice sound as normal as possible.

"We. I'll make the mac-n-cheese."

I raised my eyebrows slightly.

"I told you that's my specialty."

"I don't know," I said letting my voice drip with disbelief. "There's a lot of ways to mess up mac-n-cheese. It can be too wet. Or too eggy. Or too cheesy."

He threw up his hands, pretending to be shocked. "What? There's no such thing as too cheesy. It's in the name."

His shoulder bumped playfully into mine, we laughed, and continued walking. And even though I wanted more than homemade mac-n-cheese from Leon, I could feel the stress of the day dissipate. I was grateful to have someone to laugh with, who could so easily help me forget all my worries. And I felt no pressure from him about sex. He was a gift, exactly what I had wanted in a man.

"Well, as good as that sounds, making a traditional Thanksgiving turkey dinner -in a hotel kitchen- doesn't sound all that fun. It's been an exhausting day. Let's just go out."

Leon suggested American, but I knew no soul food restaurants would be open on Thanksgiving.

I thought for a second. "How about we just do something completely different? Like sushi?"

"That sounds perfect!" he said with a nod, and promised to find the perfect restaurant. By the time we returned to the hotel, my feet hurt from all the walking, and my face hurt from all the forced smiling. I couldn't wait till my head hit the pillow. I bowed my head to pray, but as soon as my eyes were closed, sleep took over.

* * *

The next morning, as soon as I opened my eyes, memories of the day before flooded me. Debra showing more care for the counters she scrubbed than she did for me. Felicia looking at me with a mixture of disbelief and pity. Leon walking beside me on the pier, saying so much, yet nothing at all. I lay in bed, remembering and praying. Eventually, Leon knocked on my door.

"Happy Thanksgiving," I said, smiling.

"You ready for breakfast?" he asked.

When I nodded, he took my hand and I followed him out of the room and to the hotel restaurant.

"Are you a big post-Thanksgiving shopper?" he asked.

I shook my head, grateful for the small talk. "I went out a few times, but after hearing so many news stories about people getting mauled over a $50 TV, I decided to sleep in. No doorbuster is worth your life!" We laughed.

"So, what do you want to do today?"

"I'm thinking I'd like to go back to the beach. Even though I grew up so close to the ocean, we rarely went. Debra, my mom, complained that it was too much work and it would stress her out. Even in high school, it wasn't something that my friends were interested in."

"We could do that. Do you mind if we go a little later, though? I have a few emails to send."

His smile was irresistible. Just the right mix of confidence and wistfulness.

"If you're busy, I can go by myself."

"Would you mind? I would hate for you to have to sit around waiting for me."

So, I drove back to the same pier we had walked along the night before and found a cluster of rocks to sit on. I stared out at the ocean, trying to figure out where it ended, but of course it was impossible. The vastness was almost overwhelming. I inhaled the sharp scent of the sea water, watching the push and pull of the waves. Watching the waves rush towards the shore like an excited child, then retreat. As the water lapped up the sand, it had to release what it had already captured. Let go. Everything that had seemed so important before, receded and faded into the background.

When I returned to the hotel, hours later, Leon was on the couch, laptop beside him. He finally pulled himself away from his computer for dinner. Even though it was Thanksgiving, the restaurant was packed. It reminded me of my first Thanksgiving in college, a Thanksgiving I had spent alone. Almost everything was closed, including the college dining hall, and I was lucky to find a fast-food restaurant off-campus. I spent my first Thanksgiving as an adult away from home, eating a cheap burger off the dollar menu. And it was the happiest day of my life. I considered sharing the story with Leon. But decided against it.

We ate our sushi, and once again, I waited for Leon to make a move. To declare his intentions or his affection. But he didn't. I fell asleep that night remembering the peace and longing I'd felt at the ocean.

On Friday morning, it was time to leave. Leon walked me to my rental car, and as I dropped my bag into the passenger seat, he surprised me by wrapping his arms around me. Then his lips were on mine, coaxing them apart, gentle yet insistent. I felt butterflies in my stomach and didn't want the sensation to end. Finally, we pulled apart, breathing heavily. I smiled up at him.

"You didn't kiss me once the whole trip." It was a statement, but also a question.

"You can guess why. I don't know if I would have been able to control myself with you just a couple doors away."

I nodded, relieved that my fears were unfounded. "So, when am I going to be able to see you again?"

He rubbed the back of his neck. "The holidays are rough. A lot of custody hearings. But I'll call you. And I'll be thinking about you." He kissed me on the forehead, and I felt myself leaning forward, into the kiss, wishing it were more.

"You seem so different," he said, pulling away.

"Really? In what way?

"I don't know. But I think going home was really good for you."

I nodded. There was so much I wanted to tell him, so much left unsaid. So much that would have to wait until next time, whenever that might be.

Nothing had gone the way I hoped. On one hand, the trip had been great, but I felt just as uncertain about the state of our relationship as I had before we left. There had been no proclamations, no grand gestures. Just a couple breakfasts and dinners and a kiss that lit a fire in me. But did I know Leon deeper than before? Did he know me? Except for the little about Felicia, I hadn't told him anything about Debra, Miller, or the reason I hadn't been back to California for so long. What kind of relationship was that?

The flight back to Denver was over before I knew it, and I still didn't have any answers. The traffic moved as slowly as my relationship with Leon, further cementing my foul mood. By the time I pulled into my driveway, there was about an inch of snow. I debated shoveling it, but decided to wait to see if it would just melt off. I grabbed my carry-on bag from the back seat and dragged it up the walkway behind me. I couldn't wait to get in the house and take a shower and sleep in my own bed. I pushed open the door. There beside the door were two suitcases and an overflowing diaper bag. My heart stopped.

REY SIRAKAVIT

Chapter 38

"Welcome home!" Crystal said. She sat on the couch, TV flickering in front of her. Khalid lay on a colorful baby play mat, waving his chubby arms in the air and kicking his chubby little feet at the toys hanging over him. A wave of emotion washed over me. I hadn't realized how much I had missed him. Ignoring the two suitcases already by the door, I kicked off my shoes and went to pick Khalid up.

"How are you guys doing?"

"Good. How was your trip? You and Leon didn't do anything you shouldn't have, did you?" Crystal asked playfully.

I laughed at the irony. "No, we were on our best behavior, *Mom*."

"Do you think he's the one?"

I thought about that. He seemed so perfect. He checked off every box I could think of. He had truly been worth all the years of waiting. But something was definitely missing. So all I said was, "We'll see."

I looked around the room. The kitchen was clean. There was a pile of Khalid's toys and the things that Carmen had donated stacked in the corner. And, of course, the bags by the door.

"What's going on?" My heart beat fast, my mind raced, hoping that Crystal wasn't going to say what I thought she was. Were they moving back home to stay with Lavondra, Crystal's mom? Had their Thanksgiving reunion gone better than mine, each forgiving the other for the past and committing to support each other moving forward?

While that thought made me happy for them, I selfishly wondered what that would mean for me. And Khalid. This was the only home Khalid knew. My arms tightened around him, even as I prepared myself for the inevitable.

"You know Sister Johnson, from Bible Study?"

Of course I knew Sister Johnson. I was the one who had taken Crystal to church. To my church. What was going on?

"Well, she slipped on some ice and broke her ankle."

"Oh no!" I said, truly sorry for Sister Johnson, but unsure what any of that had to do with the packed bags by the door. And how did she know this before I did? There hadn't been any news of that in the church newsletter that was emailed once a week.

"Yeah, it was really bad. At Bible Study on Wednesday, she said she has to be in a cast for about three months, and she really needs help getting around, getting food. And I know I'm wearing out my welcome over here, so I thought…I could help her out."

Crystal, whose idea of cooking was microwaving a hot dog, was going to go help Sister Johnson? The idea was laughable.

"I told her my idea and she loved it. She said I was being a good Saritan."

I raised my eyebrows. "You mean Good Samaritan?"

"Yeah, Good Samaritan," Crystal repeated.

"What about Khalid?"

Crystal held out her hands for the boy. "He can help, too. Can't you boy?" She cooed to the baby. "And I think God wants me to help someone like you helped me. You know, pay it forward."

While Crystal smiled with pride at her scripture reference and spiritual growth, instead of being proud, I brewed. This couldn't be happening. Not like this.

"I thought you were going to stay with me for the school year?" I knew I was being selfish, but the thought of Crystal and Khalid moving out, possibly for good, hit me hard.

"Don't worry, since my classes are all online, I'll still be able to finish up on time." It seemed like she had all the answers and had thought everything through. Except she was wrong. She and Khalid hadn't worn out their welcome. I loved having them there, sharing life with them. But maybe that was why she was leaving. Did she feel uncomfortable with how much I loved Khalid? Was I coming on too strong, being too possessive of the child that I had wanted to adopt, but hadn't been able to? My mind raced with questions for Sister Johnson, arguments for Crystal, and defenses for myself. But I reminded myself to pray. Not just for myself and what I wanted, but for Crystal and Sister Johnson. What did they want? What did they need?

All I had wanted to do was wash the airport off me, lie in my own bed, and enjoy the makeshift family the Lord had blessed me with. But even that was going to be taken away. I sighed, forcing a smile that I didn't feel. But maybe this was for the best. Maybe without the distraction of Khalid and Crystal, I could really focus on my relationship with Leon.

"So, do you need a ride?"

* * *

I swiveled in my chair at work, thinking about Crystal and Khalid, then Leon, then Felicia. I'd gone from an empty house, to a full house, back to an empty house. Again, I tried to see how God might be using this for my good.

Mikaela popped over. "Guess what! We finally set a date! Not this summer, because that would be way too soon, but the next summer. I'm so excited!"

I stopped swiveling in my chair, but kept swiveling in my mind, like I was on a merry-go-round of emotions. Depending on what I looked at, I could be happy, excited and proud. But change the view, and all of a sudden, I was nervous, anxious, and downcast. While the door with my own family was closed for good, I had peace about it and knew I had done my best. And while I hadn't been able to adopt, I still got to be a part of Crystal and Khalid's life. But now they were moving. And while Leon wasn't exactly the perfect boyfriend, he could very well be "the one". With so much uncertainty in my own life, the last thing I wanted was to talk about Mikaela's wedding. But I shoved all my problems to the background and focused on her and her newest wedding topic for discussion: the revolving door of wedding dates. From late spring to early fall, she and her fiancée had played with different dates and times of the year and kinds of venues. I couldn't tell if he was just stringing her along or if they were just that indecisive.

When Mikaela finally headed back to her desk, reassured they had made the right decision in choosing to wait a whole year, I typed in my password, bringing my computer back to life. Ready to get to work and lose myself in the beautiful complexity of the latest program I was working on. To not have to think about personal problems. But my cell phone rang, ending all hopes of that. I did not recognize the number, but I picked it up anyway, as if by instinct.

The caller introduced herself as a home study worker for the county.

"I believe you had been working with Ms. Wilson before? Well, your file got transferred to me and I see you started your home study way back in…" I heard the ruffling of paper, as she finally found what she was looking for. "April? I am so sorry it's taken us so long! We've been so backed up, but if you're available, I can come out this week."

"Sure," I said without even thinking.

"Great! Thank you so much for your patience with us. I know it can be incredibly nerve-racking."

As the social worker, whose name I hadn't even caught, prattled on, I immediately wanted to kick myself. Why had I said yes? That was not the plan. Leon was the plan. Getting married and starting a family with him. The only reason I had even finished the application was just to prove to myself that I could and to close the door on that chapter of my life for good.

"Great, then I'll see you on Thursday at 3."

"Oh, what about Ms. Wilson?"

"I'm sorry, I don't think she's with the county anymore, so I was assigned your file. Is that okay? Did you have a connection with her?"

A "connection"? If you could call the animosity between us a connection, then yes, we had had a connection. A very negative one.

"No, that's fine. I was just curious." I wondered where Ms. Wilson would have gone, and who would have hired someone so stressed and bitter.

Forgive me, Lord. Even though she was mean and unprofessional to me, she had also given me the kick in the pants I needed to go to counseling, which had turned out to be exactly what I needed.

"Okay, great, well then I'll see you in a few days."

As I re-typed my password into my computer, I replayed the conversation in my head. Why didn't I just hang up? Or just say no? No would have been the easiest thing to say.

I texted Leon.

TO LEON BAKER:

Can I get your opinion on something?

If things between us kept progressing, he really should be part of my decision, too. But what decision? To meet a social worker and tell her I wasn't interested anymore? I thought about all the hours I had spent in classes and completing the application and how I could just be done with it. Finish the home study. Even if I never used it, never needed it, it would be done. All I had to do was answer some questions and show her around my house. Things were still baby-proofed from the first home study...which had come in handy for Khalid. And it wasn't like I was so busy. There was no one else to cook or clean for since Crystal had moved out. I tapped my fingers on the edge of my desk.

But what would I do with it since I had no intentions of adopting? Would I take my home study to Leon and tell him, "My heart is ready. My home is ready. Are you ready?" And like nothing short of a romantic drama, he would pick me up in his arms and twirl me around and we would start our family.

I laughed at the silly fantasy, shaking my head.

And, really, was meeting one more social worker that big of a deal?

Still, I would tell Leon. Just in case.

I glanced at my phone. No response yet.

After work, I drove home. As soon as I pulled into the driveway, I peeked at the phone screen. Nothing. After I made dinner for one, my phone finally beeped. I grabbed it, scrolling to the new messages screen, but it was just a text from Crystal asking how to use a pressure cooker. Then a text from Carmen asking about the trip to California. Still nothing from Leon. Maybe he was busy playing catch-up from being out of the office for a week. Surely he would call, or at the very least, text back tomorrow. I picked up my phone over a hundred times, and over a hundred times saw no new notifications or missed calls from Leon. The days passed and before I knew it, I was opening the door to another social worker.

It felt like déjà vu. From the tea and snacks that I put out to the outfit I was wearing. But this time, I didn't feel pressure to be perfect. It was a courtesy visit, as if I owed the county for all they had invested in me thus far, and couldn't say no.

As the social worker talked about the process, it occurred to me that I had never received an "ALL CLEAR" letter from my therapist. Should I mention it? Or since I didn't have the letter, would that look bad? I decided to ask anyway. What was the worst that could happen, she would leave once she realized I didn't have it?

"Yeah, that was an inappropriate request," the social worker's eyebrows scrunched. "She can't mandate something like that. You're either approved or not. She must have really seen something in you to want to give you more time, though." She smiled and continued on with her spiel. This was nothing like the previous home study meeting that had been so full of tension. She asked the same exact questions, and I gave basically the same answers. But instead of frowns and grunts, this worker smiled and nodded as she made notes. She wanted to know about my career, my parenting style, and my family background.

"Are you seeing anyone?"

Months ago, the questions about my childhood and abuse had been the reason that I couldn't complete the interview, now the question that was hardest was if I was in a relationship! How to answer?

Technically, we'd never talked about being exclusive. For all I knew, he was seeing half the women in Denver. Which would make sense for how infrequently I saw him.

But we had taken a trip together. Didn't that count as being serious?

But he also didn't know what I was doing at that very moment. Even though I had tried to talk to him in advance, he never responded. He didn't know about the important things that were going on in my life.

"Nothing too serious," I began, "but maybe one day it will grow. I guess it's too soon to tell."

And that was the end of that.

Soon I was showing her around the house. We started in the guest room, aka Crystal's room, aka the kid's room. The crib was still set up next to the bed.

"The crib can be converted to a full," I said. I walked around the room, where only a week before Khalid had been playing on the floor. "There's so much space in here. It really is a shame that it's empty." We walked down the hall toward my office. "And one day this'll be turned into a kid's room, too," I said, looking at the half-empty room and mismatched furniture. After answering so many questions about kids and having a family, I could easily envision the room being a children's space. Or even a teen's room. I pictured a miniature Leon sitting at the desk, studying for the SATs. Same infectious smile, but calling me "mom". I sighed, pushing the longing back down.

"And that's really it."

After looking in every drawer, in every closet, and behind every door, the worker was finally done. It was past nine o'clock, but I wasn't drained. In fact, I felt hopeful. Energized. After sharing my hopes and dreams for a family, I didn't feel discouraged. I felt like I was speaking my hopes and dreams into reality. Not in some quasi-spiritual, "name it and claim it" philosophy. I just sensed the truth that God knew my heart and my desires, and that he had given them to me for a reason.

REY SIRAKAVIT

Chapter 39

The home study worker assured me that after our three-hour visit, she had seen enough.

"What with the holidays, I won't have this complete until the new year, though. Thanks so much for your patience! I know it can feel like things move so slowly with the county."

I nodded, grateful to be truly done. But at the same time, my desire to be a mother kicked into overdrive.

Every picture, illustration, commercial of a baby set my stomach clenching.

"You're only 33. You have plenty of time," Carmen consoled me. We were sitting on my couch in my empty living room. I wanted to believe her, but did I? My birthday was coming and then I'd be 34. Considered a "high-risk" pregnancy. And while lots of women gave birth all the way through their forties, I also wanted to be young enough to be able to enjoy it. And all things being equal, I wanted to be married and get pregnant and have a baby. And I wanted that with Leon.

"Do you love him?" Carmen asked.

What was there not to love? He was handsome, charming, a faithful Christian. And deep. He really studied people and understood their motivations. I could talk to him for hours. At least, I imagined I could. He was always so busy, always distracted by some task for work that pulled his attention away. Even during the trip to California, I'd only had half of his attention. While the trip was supposed to deepen our relationship and take us to the next level, we ended up right where we began. I didn't know him any more deeply than I had before we left. And did he know me anymore?

But I didn't say any of that to Carmen.

"What are you doing for your birthday?"

"Nothing big. Just dinner at my house?"

I loved that my birthday was a week before Christmas. You couldn't forget it. Even if you were an absentee boyfriend.

"Will we finally get to meet Leon?"

"Probably not," I said, erasing all hint of disappointment or embarrassment from my voice. She was probably beginning to think I'd made him up. Sometimes I felt that way, too. The phantom boyfriend.

"I'm thinking I'll just invite a few of my lady friends over for dinner. Low key."

I didn't want to put all my hope for my birthday on Leon. I wanted to see him, but that didn't seem likely.

So, I invited a few friends from church and work, plus Carmen, Crystal, Mikaela, and the ladies from the adoption classes, Jessica and Yvette. And even though they all worked and had families or relationships, they all came. They made me a priority. I felt loved and touched. What I did not love so much was answering question after question about Leon.

"Where's Leon?"

"Are we going to meet the infamous Leon tonight?"

"Is Leon coming?"

"How are things going with Leon?"

"Are things getting serious?"

314

Finally, someone asked a question that had nothing to do with Leon.

"What's been the highlight of your year?" Mikaela asked. And although I didn't have a fancy ring like her, my answer was immediate.

"Meeting Crystal," I answered immediately. "Getting to be a part of what God has been doing in her life...I'm really proud of you," I said, looking directly at her and putting my arm around her shoulder.

"This is supposed to be about you," she said, her eyes glassy.

"Well, our friendship has changed my life." I hadn't planned on making a speech or saying anything fancy, but I felt a sudden urge to share with my friends, my sisters, some of what I had learned over the year. "Because of Crystal, I realized how important prayer is. I mean, I've been a Christian for over twenty years, so I've always known that prayer is important. But for the past few years..." I shook my head, saddened at the pathetic state of my prayer life, or lack thereof. "I really only prayed to bless my food or during church. But when I met Crystal, let's just say I realized there was something missing from my life, and only God could give me what I needed."

"I've talked to you all about how I'm not close to my family. Well, each of you has been like family to me, and I'm so grateful for you all. I'm grateful for the encouraging texts," I looked at Yvette and Jessica. "I'm grateful to have someone to laugh and blow steam off with at work," I smiled at Mikaela, hoping she wasn't too freaked out by how spiritual the evening had turned. "I'm grateful for a friend who always tells me the truth, even when I don't want to hear it," I said turning to Carmen. "You all have blessed and touched me in so many ways! Happy Birthday to me!"

Carmen leaned over and hugged me, then they sang a soulful rendition of Happy Birthday. Mikaela and the other women from work left soon after. Then, the rest of the women gathered around and prayed a special birthday blessing over me.

Prayers for wisdom and courage. Prayers that my new year would be filled with love.

Chapter 40

The Sunday after my birthday, I pulled out a big box of ornaments and my artificial tree, and lit some pine scented candles around the living room.

Even though I still hadn't seen Leon since Thanksgiving, nothing could ruin my mood. Christmas music played in the background and I did what I had told the ladies that I had been doing: I prayed. I continued to pray for Felicia, wanting to be wrong but asking God to put a hedge of protection around her. I prayed that God would grow Crystal into the mother he desired her to be. I prayed for healing for Sister Johnson's ankle. I prayed for my godsons, that they would grow into godly men who feared the Lord. And I prayed for Leon. Or, more accurately, my relationship with Leon.

Give me wisdom, Lord.

Wisdom and clarity. I didn't want to be wasting my time with someone who didn't feel about me the way I felt about him.

Before I knew it, it was time for church.

I sat in the row behind Carmen and her family. I waved to Crystal who was sitting next to Sister Johnson and wanted to go grab Khalid out of her hands, but I contained myself.

After the service ended and everyone was milling around, my godsons clambered over the pew, planting sticky, wet kisses on my cheeks, but I didn't care. I hugged them hard for as long as they would allow before they wrenched themselves free and ran off. Carmen and Travis walked around the old-fashioned way. As we stood in the aisle, making small talk, Mr. Vegan walked up to Travis and clapped him on the shoulder.

"Hey, thanks for the invite. We'll see you later." They gave each other the man-hug/back clap, and then he was gone.

"Yeah, we should be going, too. We don't want to be late." Travis smiled and gave me another hug. He picked up his coat, calling after the boys.

"What are you guys up to today?"

Carmen's eyes flitted around the sanctuary, as if she was suddenly nervous to make eye contact with me. She picked up her coat, brushing away invisible flecks of dust.

"Umm, Travis's parents are having a little party at their house. We were going to invite you, but I didn't think it was a good idea."

My eyebrows lifted. "Yes, because you know how I hate parties," I rolled my eyes good-naturedly, curious as to why Carmen was acting so weird. "Is it a Christmas party?"

"Not really." Carmen let out a breath, like she was divulging a secret that she had been sworn to keep. "Remember how I told you that they always wanted to adopt? Well, they're adopting a little girl and are having a small get-together for her today after church."

"What? Are you kidding?"

"Yeah, it was kind of a surprise to us, too. But I told you how they've always had a heart for adoption and they're still pretty young. Anyways, of course you're invited but with everything going on in your life right now...I didn't know if you'd want to go or not."

Why wouldn't I want to go? Just because my life was on a merry-go-round with no certainty, didn't mean I didn't want to celebrate with Travis' parents. Over the years, I'd spent much time with Mr. and Mrs. Evans during the holidays and at the boys' birthday parties. They were kind, generous, and wise. I was so happy for them. And so happy for the child they were bringing home.

"Of course I want to go!" But if I was honest with myself, there was a tinge of jealousy there, just below the surface. Would I ever have what Mr. and Mrs. Evans had? A wonderful marriage? A family? Children?

"If you're going to come, why don't you invite Leon? We still haven't met him."

I nodded. That was a great idea. In theory.

In the parking lot alone, I called him. I knew he'd be busy with church, so I didn't expect him to answer. But he did.

"I miss you! I can't believe it's been so long since I've seen you."

"I miss you, too. I was hoping you could come with me to a-"

"I'm sorry, I really can't. I'll be here for another hour or two, then I have to prepare for court tomorrow."

"You're working on a Sunday?"

"Yeah, I can't help it."

"I don't know how much longer I'm going to put up with these fake excuses."

"What? You called me at the last minute…"

"Even if I had called you earlier, you would have had some excuse. If it's not one thing, it's another. I'm not even surprised. Why did I even bother? I'll talk to you later."

I hung up the phone, tired of playing cat and mouse with Leon. Tired of playing cat and mouse with my future.

As much as I wanted it to be otherwise, Leon was not showing any signs that he was serious. That he wanted to be in a relationship. Maybe I was wasting my time. Maybe I really was supposed to adopt. Maybe that's why I had finally been able to finish my home study.

Carmen texted saying not to bring a gift, but I didn't want to show up empty-handed, so I dropped by a toy store on the way home. Instead of a toy, though, I was drawn to the book aisle. On prominent display was a little girl with afro puffs, proclaiming "I love my hair!" I picked it up, grabbed a gift bag and tissue paper, and was back on the road.

Throughout the drive, I prayed.

Lord, clean my heart.

Renew a right spirit within.

Carmen's in-laws lived in a beautiful old neighborhood of Denver. You could tell there were a lot of retired people because the lawns were all perfectly manicured and the gardens were elaborate.

At the party, Mr. and Mrs. Evans introduced their daughter, 11-year-old Amari. They took pictures with their adult biological children and Amari. Then they took pictures with the kids and their spouses and grandchildren. I hadn't noticed before, but they were all wearing purple.

Amari wasn't much older than the oldest grandchild, but Mr. and Mrs. Evans looked younger and happier than I had ever seen them.

"Amari," I called, but the girl ignored me. I took a few steps toward her and tapped her gently on the shoulder. Finally, the girl looked at me.

"Oh, sorry! I'm not used to that name yet."

"Did you change your name when you got adopted?"

"Kind of," her eyes sparked. "Nobody calls me by my real name, and my nickname was even worse, so Mr. and Mrs. Evans said I could

321

change my name when I got adopted. But it's still hard to remember sometimes."

"I'm sure! What was your name?"

"Bird. 'Cause I guess I have skinny chicken legs." We both looked down at her legs instinctively. They were indeed skinny. She giggled happily and did a little chicken dance, making me giggle.

"Well, Amari is a beautiful name."

"It means love."

I nodded my head, smiling at *her* infectious smile. God only knew what this girl had been through, but she smiled and danced and giggled like she didn't have a care in the world. I handed her the gift bag. "I know you're a big girl, but I thought this was a message that all Black girls need to hear."

As she opened the book, she smiled. "That's me!" she cried with big eyes. "I always wear my hair in afro puffs!" Suddenly, she threw her arms around me. "Thank you, I love it."

Mrs. Evans appeared. "What's that?" she asked smiling. Everyone was smiling. The pure joy just emanated throughout the house.

"Just a little book I got for Amari." Mrs. Evans looked at the cover of the book. "This is wonderful, thank you Sierra." Without another word, Amari ran off, book in hand. Mrs. Evans put her arm around me.

"I hear you're thinking about adopting, too."

"I was," I said. "But a lot has changed since I began the process."

"Well, we'll be praying for you. There are so many children in the system."

I nodded, trying to sound hopeful, but Mrs. Evans must have seen through it.

"Don't give up. God's got you," she said with a squeeze.

"Can I ask you a question?"

"Sure, that's what the party is for. Let everybody ask their nosy questions all at once then we can move on with our lives." The way she said "nosy", I knew she must have gotten some doozies.

"Well, when I took all my adoption classes, they said they really don't recommend changing older children's names." I let the unspoken question linger in the air for a moment before adding, "I know it's none of my business."

"No, that's a good question. Actually, it was Amari's decision. She hated her name. And she had decided long before she met us that if she got adopted, she would change her name. But truth be told, I'm glad she did. This child's name was 'Loveyouforever'. Can you imagine?"

My heart stopped. Loveyouforever? *My* Loveyouforever? How many "Loveyouforever"'s could there be in Denver? How many Loveyouforever's could there be in the *world*?

"Yeah," Mrs. Evans continued. "She hated her name. Never used it. They called her Bird. Not much better if you ask me. Sometimes I wonder about people. Trying to come up with the most creative names. Anyway. She decided she wanted to change her name to Amari. Amari means love…. You okay?" Mrs. Evans asked. I nodded, knowing that the look on my face must have been crazy.

"Sorry, I just need to," I began, then stumbled away. If there had been any part of me that still thought I might adopt, that closed the door forever. Slammed shut.

REY SIRAKAVIT

Chapter 41

I was happy for the Evans. I really was. And, of course, I was happy for Loveyouforever.

She was adorable. And she looked so happy. Isn't that what I had prayed for, day and night? I had prayed for a family for her. Prayed that she wouldn't be another statistic, spending years in foster care, never adopted. So why was I so upset?

No, I wasn't just upset. I was angry. It seemed like God was just giving out happy endings to everyone except me. But I refused to wallow. I would enjoy every moment of my Christmas, even if I was single. And childless. And snowed in.

It had started to snow early on Christmas Eve, ensuring we would have a white Christmas. But the snow kept coming. All day long. By Christmas morning, I could barely open my front door. I considered going out right away, but I hated to shovel in the snow. If I waited until it stopped snowing, though, the snow might very well be too high for me to shovel by myself. Maybe I should invest in a snow blower, I thought, blowing on my hot chocolate that was piled high with white powder, just like my driveway. Otherwise, one winter day I might wind up snowed in for weeks, my body discovered by a neighbor once the stench from my house became unbearable. I pulled out my remote control and cued up my favorite Christmas movies, desperate for something to improve the funky mood I was in. If I was

325

ever able to get out of my house, I might go to Carmen's for dinner. But if not, I was determined to be content and cozy.

After a while the sound of metal sliding against concrete interrupted my movie. Some brave neighbor had already started shoveling. Good for them. I decided to stick to my plan. Wait and see. I hit the up arrow on the remote, drowning out the responsible neighbor. I just wanted to escape, but the sound grew closer. What were they doing? Sharpening their shovel on the edge of my driveway? When I couldn't take it anymore, I walked to the window. A figure in a fur-lined trapper hat was plowing their way through the knee-deep snow burying my driveway.

Leon.

I smiled as butterflies filled my stomach.

Leon was shoveling my driveway.

I walked over to the kitchen and refilled the tea kettle. While it heated, I stood by the window, watching him work. He cleared a path from the street to the garage, but the snow was obviously high and heavy. As soon as the tea kettle started to whistle, I filled a mug with hot chocolate and pulled on my winter coat and boots.

I stepped slowly through the snow that was up to my shins, then silently held the covered mug out to him.

"Wanna come in?"

"Nah, I'm just getting started." He took a sip from the mug then handed it back to me.

I took the mug from him, then reached up and kissed him on the lips. His lips were cold, covered in snowflakes.

"It's cold. I'll be in soon."

I went back in, but didn't turn the TV back on. Leon just kept me guessing. First the trip. Now this. I couldn't remember the last time a man had performed such a romantic gesture. It was the stuff of movies, wasn't it?

After about an hour, there was a knock at the door. He stomped his feet and then pulled his boots off.

"This is my first time seeing the inside of your house."

"I know."

He looked around, examining it. "It's nice."

We stood by the door. Feeling awkward. He finally looked back at me.

"We had our first fight."

"I know."

"I don't like fighting with you." He pulled me into his arms, giving me plenty of time and space to resist if I wanted. I didn't. I leaned into the hug, and rested my head on his shoulder.

"I know I work a lot. And once my practice really takes off and I can bring on more staff, it'll be different."

I nodded, not knowing what else to say. Not wanting to break the moment.

After a while, he pulled away and put a box in my hand.

"Merry Christmas."

"What is this?"

"Well, I'm tired of seeing you wear something that some other guy bought you." He handed the box to me, and I looked at it confused.

"What are you talking about?"

"Just open it."

I pulled the red ribbon, my brain racing. The box was too big to be a ring.

And it was too soon.

Right?

Right. Too soon.

"Something classy. Like you," he said.

My hand stalled over the open box. To call the glittering band of diamonds a watch would have been an understatement. I was not brand-conscious, but I didn't live under a rock, either. The watch was obviously expensive. Unlike my own, this watch had a diamond to mark each hour. More stones circled the pink face. Even the dial was a ring of small diamonds. It was radiant.

"This is gorgeous," I breathed, unable to take my eyes off of it.

The whole band sparkled in the light.

I pulled off the heart watch and tossed it onto the couch. I considered telling him that I had bought it myself during a post-Valentine's Day sale, but I shook the thought away. If Leon was trying to make amends, I wouldn't ruin it for him. I looked up at him with a big smile. He gently slipped the new watch onto my wrist. It was officially the most expensive thing I owned.

"So, is this your way of saying you're sorry?"

"No. Shoveling your snow was 'I'm sorry'. This is your Christmas gift."

"Well, thank you and I forgive you."

I kissed him gently on the cheek, then stood up.

"Well, my gift for you isn't nearly so grand." I pulled the gift bag from the side of the couch, glad I had been ready with Leon's gift. He smiled as he took the bag, his hands already pulling the tissue paper out.

"You're like a big kid," I laughed.

"I love gifts," he replied. "It's one of my favorite things about Christmas." Opening the bag, he pulled out a book about the true story of a civil rights lawyer.

"This is awesome! I've heard good things about this book," he said.

"Well, next year we're going to have to set a spending limit," I said without thinking, almost immediately wishing I could take the words back. But Leon just smiled.

"What, you don't like the watch? I can take it back." He motioned towards my wrist, but I pulled back, giggling like a child.

"No, I love it!" I leaned against him, staring at the watch, and running my finger over the band. Was it possible to be in love with a piece of metal?

"Do you want to stay for a movie?" I asked, scanning my brain for an appropriate Christmas movie that also had a bit of romance thrown in.

"I don't watch TV, but you can watch something while I start on this book you got me," he smiled and leaned forward, kissing me on the forehead.

I sighed, blithely unaware of the bombshell that was coming. I shouldn't have been surprised at what the watch would cost me.

REY SIRAKAVIT

Chapter 42

I sat at my desk, thinking about Leon. As always, he'd been a perfect gentleman on Christmas, leaving before it got too cold outside, or too hot inside.

He hadn't mentioned anything about New Year's, though, so I hadn't either. I looked down at my wrist. I had wanted a grand gesture, and had finally received it. But it didn't make our relationship any clearer. In fact, it made it a lot grayer. Who bought someone such an expensive gift without being in a committed relationship with them? But at the same time, who accepted such an expensive gift without knowing the status of the relationship? The trill of the phone grabbed my attention. Maybe it was Leon.

The screen read UNKNOWN CALLER. I hesitated for a second before pressing the green button.

"Hello, Sierra!" The caller identified herself as a social worker with the county. Before I could politely hang up excuse myself, she continued. "I have good news. I think we've found a fit."

A fit? What did she mean, a fit?

"This would be a permanent placement, with the goal of adoption. The children's foster family is moving out of state, and we'd like to minimize the number of moves for them, if possible. I know your home study was just completed, so everything should be good. Can I tell you a little about the children?"

Children? As in, more than one?

"It's a sibling set of three," the social worker continued. "Two girls and a boy. The girls are Brandy, aged 13 and Chardonnay aged 12, and the boy is Cisco, aged 6. If you're interested, I can send you their profile."

"Umm, what made you think I would be a good fit for three kids?"

"Well, you're very organized and structured, and the kids will need lots of routine. You also talked about wanting to travel and not allowing fear to hold you back. It's something that the oldest girl, Brandy, has said that really stuck with me. In the end, though, making a match is a bit of an art and a science. Would you like me to send you their profile?"

She emailed me the picture and short paragraph profile, and in an instant I was looking at the picture as she talked. I stared at the children. My heart thumped so loudly in my chest, I was certain she could hear it through the phone.

The three kids were standing in front of a tree. The two girls were almost the same height, but one, presumably Brandy, was about half an inch taller. She stood with her arm protectively around Cisco. Her thick curly hair was pulled into 3 sections, an afro puff in front, and two ponytails in back. The little boy was wearing a striped green tee. But it was Chardonnay who I couldn't take my eyes off of. She wore a black and white tee that read "love stinks" with a picture of a skunk below the words.

A skunk.

I spun around in my chair, picturing the onesie that had been hanging over my computer for months, then had been put in a drawer. The onesie that I had prayed over, near, and with…The red skunk onesie that had come to epitomize all my hopes and dreams for being a mother.

It was a random coincidence.

Or, was it a sign?

Just moments earlier I had been thinking about Leon, and where things stood with him. Now, my mind was going full steam ahead considering all the possibilities of what it would mean to go from zero to three in the blink of an eye.

Lord, do you want me to adopt these children? I rubbed my hands together, as if the answer were written on my palms.

* * *

I wiped the countertops down, pushed the Keep Warm button on the oven, then looked around the kitchen and living room. Everything was clean. Immaculate.

Tea!

I pushed the button on the hot water kettle. I wanted everything to be perfect when Leon came. Even though he didn't have time for dinner, he promised to drop by after work once I told him I had something important to talk to him about. I was hoping to sweeten up with the pecan pie in the oven and some relaxing chamomile tea. The perfect one-two-punch.

Or so I hoped.

The doorbell rang and I dropped the dishcloth into the sink, rushing to the door.

You've got this, Sierra, I told myself.

After giving him a quick hug and letting him take his shoes off, I offered him the pecan pie. It wasn't homemade, but it was delicious and gooey, and one of his favorites.

"I'm good," he said, waving away the pie. "I've had too much sugar today."

I turned towards the whistling kettle. "How about some tea?"
He shook his head again. "No thanks. It's too relaxing and I still have some work to do tonight." I looked around the kitchen, at a loss.

What to do?

He sat on the stool and grabbed my hands. "What's up? What was so important you had to talk about tonight?"

I let out the breath I hadn't even realized I'd been holding, letting a wide grin out as well. "Leon, you're never going to believe this, but the county matched me!"

He laughed. "Yeah, I'm not surprised."

"What do you mean you're not surprised?"

"You're an amazing woman."

Since he didn't know about me not completing, then completing, my home study, he couldn't appreciate how important this was. How monumental.

"You should contact your caseworker, though," he continued, "and let her know you're no longer interested. Otherwise, they'll keep floating your file around and matching you with all kinds of kids."

I hesitated for a moment. Then spoke slowly, enunciating each word one at a time.

"What if I am interested?"

"Why would you be interested?" His brows furrowed, a look of confusion spreading across his face.

"I've always wanted to be a mom. You know that."

"I thought that after everything that happened with Crystal, you decided against adopting."

"I did," I nodded, "But then this social worker called..."

"Just because someone offers you something, doesn't mean you have to accept it."

I tilted my head and shot a look at Leon. Obviously, I didn't have to accept the match. But what was he offering me? I ran my fingers over the watch on my wrist.

"Listen, let me just tell you a little about the kids." I read the profile aloud to Leon, holding the wrinkled printout in my lap.

"Brandy (age 13), Chardonnay (age 12), and Cisco's (age 6) mother was an alcoholic. The children were put in foster care when their mother was driving drunk and ran into a wall. The children were not injured, but their mother was arrested for reckless endangerment. Shortly after she was released, she was driving drunk again and was killed on impact.

"Brandy and Chardonnay have the same father. He lives on the east coast, and hasn't seen the girls in years. At his request, parental rights have been terminated.

"Cisco has fetal alcohol syndrome. Father unknown.

"Brandy is the oldest. She hopes to be a flight attendant and travel the world.

"Chardonnay, goes by Ché. She has struggled the most with her mother's death and has been caught stealing from the mall. She is currently on probation.

"The county is looking for an adoptive home for all three children."

I took a deep breath, then looked at him, waiting for his response.

"Wow. Those names."

"That's your first reaction? About their names?

"They're all named after alcoholic beverages. It's sad. What kind of job is little Cisco gonna get?"

"Okay, forget about their names for just one minute. What about their story? Doesn't it move you?"

"Of course it does! How could it not? And it moved you, too. That's one of the things that attracted me to you. You're so compassionate."

"It's not just compassion," I said, and this time my brow furrowed.

"Good, because whoever adopts them is in for a lot of work. If he's got FAS, that could mean lifelong learning disabilities, physical disabilities, behavioral and emotional issues."

Was he trying to scare me or just wanting me to be realistic?

"Look, I respect you for even considering this, but I'm not trying to be the father for some dr-"

"Stop," I said, cutting him off. "Don't even say it." Secretly, I had the same fear, but the mother bear in me was stronger than the fear. "You're making so many assumptions, and you're being really mean." Was that how he was in court? Go for the jugular, win at any cost? And if he was that way in court, was that how he was in real life?

"It's not like they're yours, or anything. You would've had better sense than to name your kids after your favorite alcohol." He laughed mockingly.

"That's not fair. They're good kids. They can't be held responsible for the bad choices of their mother." His eyebrows raised at "good." But I stuck by my choice of words. They were good kids regardless of what Chardonnay did. You didn't have to be in foster care to steal from the mall. Lots of perfectly good, successful people went through that phase. I didn't waste my time telling that to Leon, though.

"If we were all judged by the worst things we've done, we'd be in serious trouble. Can you just think about it?"

He nodded and I tried to relax, leaning back into the sofa.

"So, do you need to get going?"

He looked at his watch. "I can hang out for a bit."

As we sat on the sofa, Leon with his laptop on his lap and me staring at the TV, I thought about all the things I still didn't know about him. He said he never watched TV. But did he even have one? What was his house like? What was his sofa like?

After so many months of quasi-dating, I definitely didn't know him as well as I would have liked. And I definitely would never have guessed he could be so mean or cold.

All weekend I did the only thing I knew to do. I prayed. I hoped that Leon would call at any moment and say he had changed his mind, he supported me adopting the kids.

But he didn't.

At church on Sunday, I was the first one to jump out of my seat and run/walk to the altar at prayer time. Sister Johnson, plus two other women from the prayer team and Mr. Vegan, stood at the front, arms out and waiting for someone to ask them for prayer. Instinctively, I headed toward Sister Johnson. But maybe a married man's perspective would be helpful. I made my way to Mr. Vegan and leaned forward, so that only he could hear me.

"How can I pray for you?" he asked.

I took a deep breath, then dived in. "I've been wanting to adopt for a while and I was recently matched with three siblings. My," I paused for a second, unsure what to call Leon, then decided to keep it simple, "my boyfriend isn't supportive. I just need to know what the Lord wants me to do."

Mr. Vegan nodded as I whispered. I felt a little bad calling him that since he was praying for me, but I didn't know what his real name was. I reminded myself to ask Carmen or Travis. He- *Mr. Prayer Team Member Who Was A Vegan*- nodded again, then started praying.

"Lord, Your word says that if anyone lacks wisdom, they should ask you. Master, grant your daughter wisdom. Help her to know her worth and that she is valuable in your sight. Show her that these children have been matched with her for a reason. You care for the orphan. Give her courage to do what is right. In Jesus' name."

We both said, "Amen." But as I walked away, instead of feeling better, I felt a heavy weight on my neck. I lifted my hand to the back of my neck, rubbing the muscles, the metal around my wrist cold on my skin. I knew what I needed to do, but didn't want to do it.

Chapter 43

As soon as I heard Leon's car pull into the driveway, I was out of my seat and at the front door. Nervous energy filled me.

He kicked his shoes off as I held the door open for him. I loved that about him. So thoughtful. Even with the little things. Surely he had changed his mind. I kissed his cheek and gave him a hug.

"How was work?" Even though I was nervous, I could imagine this was our life.

"Brutal. I've been in negotiations for weeks with this couple that's getting a divorce. They can't even decide on who gets the silverware."

"Does seeing so many marriages end up in divorce ever make you not want to get married?"

He collapsed onto the couch. "No," he said with a shake of his head. "Divorce brings out the worst in people, for sure, but most of the time they'll tell you that they saw red flags early on and ignored them."

I nodded.

"And some people just want to get married, but not necessarily be married. They like the idea of it more than they like the actual person."

I nodded again.

He took my hands in his. I waited. Like waiting for my sentence. Solitary confinement or life with Leon.

"Look, I thought about it. I really did. But I just can't do it, and I don't understand why you want to so badly, either. This is not the only way for you to become a mother."

I fell back into the couch. I wasn't surprised, but the surety of knowing Leon's choice caught my breath. I tried to pull my hands back, but he gently held on. *We are not at battle, this is not a war*, his fingers said.

"It's not just about wanting to be a mother. Or even a wife. It's about being able to wrap your arms around someone who feels alone."

"So, you want to be needed?"

"No, I want to *be* love." The sermon from so many months ago came back to me. 'Be love,' the pastor had said. There was definitely a part of me that wanted to be loved, but I know God was calling me to something more. To BE love. To embody God's love. "These kids deserve to be loved. And I'm going to do my best to make sure they are. And for whatever reason, someone thinks I may be a good mother for them."

"You're not their savior, Sierra."

"I know that. But if I have something they need, should I turn my back on them? Can you imagine if the good Samaritan had said 'Sorry, I don't want anybody thinking I'm a savior, so I'm just going to leave you here. Good luck.' That would be crazy."

From the look on his face, I could tell Leon did not like the analogy. So, I pulled out the big guns.

"And God tells us to care for the orphans."

"I'll sponsor a child. Heck, I'll sponsor a whole orphanage if I have to."

Unfortunately, the big guns had fired blanks.

"So, you really never want to adopt? Is it just these particular children with their specific background, or do you not want to adopt at all?"

Instead of answering, he turned the question around on me. "Don't you want to have kids of your own?"

"Sure," I swallowed. I wanted to be a mother so badly I could taste it. "But these kids need a family now."

"I want to have a family, too- with you. Our own kids. Not clean up somebody else's mistake."

The words were unfiltered and harsh, but wasn't that the very same thing I had thought about adoption?

Leon was offering me everything I thought I always wanted. But for some reason, it didn't feel right.

"Are you saying you want to get married?"

"Yeah, of course. I mean, not right now. It's really busy at work right now, but," he rubbed my hand, "one day. Don't you? Sierra, tell me you haven't thought about you and me walking down the aisle together?" He tugged on my hand, pulling my whole body closer to him. He kissed the side of my face, below my ear.

"Leon, you've never even said I love you. And we hardly ever see each other. You're asking me to turn my back on these kids just for the offhand chance that you and I might one day get married. That is, if you ever find enough time in your busy schedule to actually see me more than once a month and get to know me and fall in love with me." I hated how breathless and petulant I sounded, but I was tired of tiptoeing around the problem.

"I don't want to rush into anything, but I care very deeply for you. I see us going the distance. Don't you?"

Did I? Up until a couple weeks ago, everything that Leon was saying would have made me the happiest woman in the world. But I wasn't so sure anymore.

Every time I had thought God was leading me in one direction, I was wrong. Every time I had thought I understood why things were happening, I was wrong.

The heart is deceptively wicked above all things. My heart had deceived me. Played tricks on me. Led me astray. As much as I wanted to, I couldn't make this decision based on my heart or feelings. My heart told me to run towards Leon. But the theme of this year had been "be love". Not, be *loved. Be* love. *Show* love.

And, for some reason, I couldn't put the skunk tee out of my mind, even if it didn't make sense to anyone else. What would Leon think? If he wasn't moved by their background story, or the biblical mandate to care for orphans, he wouldn't be moved by the completely insignificant coincidence of a girl wearing a skunk tee shirt. And maybe I shouldn't either. Maybe it was only a sign because I was desperate to see one.

But maybe it was more.

I tried again.

"Leon, you're an adoption specialist."

"No, I practice family law. Not just adoptions. Just like I help people get divorced, I help other people adopt, but that doesn't mean I want to adopt."

His voice sounded cold. Colder than I had ever heard him sound before.

"And after you've seen the kind of things I have....Adoption is hard. Not everybody is cut out for it."

He shrugged, like it was so simple.

"Well, I guess that's that."

"You don't think you'll change your mind?"

"Do you think you'll change yours?"

At that, he stood. "I guess I should go." He walked over to the door and pulled his boots back on. The snow hadn't even completely melted off them yet. As he bent over, I grabbed his coat off the hook beside the door. I silently pulled the watch off my wrist and slid it into his coat pocket. I held the coat up for him.

"You know, when I first met you, there was Crystal and her son. Now as soon as she's moved out, there are these kids. You accuse me of being too busy, but I don't think you have room for a man in your life."

I shook my head silently. Neither my life, nor my heart, felt too full. All I felt was the bitter sting of loss. Of being so close to something I wanted so badly, and having it snatched away.

If I don't choose Leon, and the future he's offering me, I'll be all alone, Lord. I could be single for the rest of my life.

The sound of the deadbolt clicking into place echoed through the empty room, the room where I had lamented so many disappointments. Would I fall on the couch, or even the floor, overwhelmed with loss and sadness? But I wasn't sad. Not really. Because Leon was right. My life was full. Ever since I started praying and trusting God and focusing on others, my life had been full. And if Mr. and Mrs. Evans could adopt in their sixties, and Sarah and Abraham could have a child in their old age, I would choose to trust that God was not limited by my sense of time. I wouldn't let fear rule me.

I pulled an ornament off the tree, then another and another. I got an empty box and began to fill it with the colorful balls that now seemed so out of place. Next, the tree came down. Then I vacuumed up all the little pieces of shavings from the artificial tree. But I didn't clean like a maniacal woman or someone possessed. I cleaned with purpose.

I texted Carmen about the breakup, then powered my phone off. I turned on some worship music and prayed.

I prayed for Leon, that he would find the right woman and that he would be the right man.

I prayed for the children each by name. For Brandy, the oldest, to not feel the burden and responsibility of being a mother to her siblings. For Chardonnay, the girl in the skunk tee, that God would give her positive outlets for the pain and loss she was experiencing. I prayed against negative influences and peers. I called on the power of God to heal in her everything that was broken. And I prayed for Cisco. In the picture he looked mischievous. He had bright eyes and a half-grin, like he was concocting a plan in his mind. It reminded me exactly of my godsons.

I prayed and cleaned.

Prayed and organized.

Prayed and decorated.

And as I prayed, the loss didn't seem so huge. Maybe I had loved the idea of Leon more than the reality of him. Or maybe all the praying I had been doing had given me the strength I needed.

I took apart the crib and converted it into a full-sized bed. The conversion was almost complete.

REY SIRAKAVIT

Chapter 44

I leaned over the bed, tucking the last sheet into the last corner.

For weeks, I had tackled my to-do list with a laser-like focus. I shopped, read blogs, prayed. And even though I had until the end of February to pull everything together, I still felt stressed and anxious. So, I took a day off, hoping that the sooner the kids' rooms were done, the sooner I'd be able to calm down.

The guest room that Crystal and Khalid had once slept in became a retreat for two pre-teen girls. And even though I frequently reminded myself of the social worker's words, "Just the necessities. Keep it simple," I couldn't help but go a bit overboard, with frilly curtains and hanging stars from the sky. Matching purple and blue dream-themed comforters on parallel full beds. (It was impossible to tell that one had been a crib just a few months earlier!) For the final touch, I hung a coordinating memory board in the narrow space between the beds. I considered once again if I should have given Cisco the full bed and bought matching twins for the girls. Would they prefer bigger beds or more space? Was it too late to pack everything back up and start over? My heart raced. If I couldn't even settle on a mattress size, how was I going to handle the thousands of decisions that moms are bombarded with on a daily basis?

Moms.

I was going to be a mom!

A motherhood birthed in tragedy and trauma.

Did the size of the mattress really matter?

I sat on the edge of the freshly made bed, overcome with emotion.

I'd heeded the social worker's words, but there still had been so much to do in so little time. Especially when your emotions were a roller coaster. One minute I was feeling fine about Leon, the next I was singing Toni Braxton's "Unbreak My Heart"! Especially once I looked at the calendar and realized I'd be single on Valentine's Day. Again.

For the seventh year in a row.

I was beginning to think I was cursed, doomed to spend every Valentine's Day alone. And no matter how much my friends assured me Valentine's Day was a made-up holiday created to sell chocolate, bears, and jewelry, it still stung. I wanted someone to hold and love me on that one day.

I also couldn't shake the feeling that maybe Leon-and Ms. Wilson-had been right, maybe I wasn't cut out to adopt. I was damaged and traumatized. What kind of mother would I be?

The phone rang, cutting into my pity party. It was the social worker.

"Hi Sierra, I'm sorry but the foster family has had a change of plans." My heart dropped and I sank onto the bed.

It's not about you, Sierra, I reminded myself, pushing the disappointment down.

The social worker continued. "They actually need the kids out by tomorrow instead. I know this is last minute, but is there any way-"

"Yes!" I interrupted. "Of course!" I looked around the finished room. God had known.

"Great! I'll drop the kids off at your house after school tomorrow."

"What have you told them? About me."

"They know that this is an adoption placement. That you're single. And that I'll still be around once a month to monitor how things are going. See you tomorrow!"

Tomorrow.

As soon as I heard the sound of tires on ice, I popped up from my place on the couch. I had been trying to pray, but my mind was all over the place.

Before I could even get the door open, a little body pushed his way in.

Cisco. He had a pink smear across his cheek and a small cellophane bag with printed hearts filled with candy between his fists.

"Where's my room?"

He pushed past me and into the house.

The social worker was only a few steps behind.

"Sorry about that. They had Valentine's Day parties at school and he is pumped up on sugar." She pushed past me, calling out, "Cisco, where are you? Come back here!"

Brandy was next. She held out her hand. "Hi, how are you?"

"I'm good, how are you?" I responded, taking her hand in mine.

"I'm good. How are you?" She repeated, and I laughed.

"Still good. Why don't you come on in?"

"Um, Ché is getting our stuff."

"Okay, well maybe I'll go out and help her."

"She doesn't need help," Brandy said. She cut her eyes at me, sizing me up. I wished I could tell what she was thinking. But by the look on her face, maybe I didn't.

"So, what should we call you?"

"You can just call me Sierra."

Chardonnay trudged up the driveway dragging two big duffle bags, then dropped them on the doorstep. She stared at her sister. Then she looked at me. "Who are you?"

"I'm Sierra. Who are you?" I reached down to pick up one of the bags, but she pulled it out of my reach.

"We got it. I'm Chardonnay." She rolled the syllables off her lips, enunciating each syllable like it was a prize.

"Nice to meet you."

"Do I have to call you Mom?"

I shrugged. "Sierra, Mom, Ms. Harris. Which do you prefer?"

Cisco popped his head out. "Why is everybody out here? Are we having a snow fight? I wanna have a snow fight!" Before the social worker could grab him, he shot out the door and into the bank of snow on the grass. They'd only been there for five minutes and already I was exhausted.

"What are we doing for Valentine's Day? Can we have a party?" He practically bounced.

"I don't know about a party, but we can bake cookies."

"With frosting?

I nodded.

"Yay! A cookie party!" Cisco threw his arms around my legs and I felt the spark. And I knew.

My life wasn't going to be perfect. There would be no fairy tale ending, but I knew that God had answered my prayers. Spectacularly. Uniquely. For me and for them. For their good and for mine.

I had gone years with just occasional prayer, impromptu, unguarded, as needed. But as I looked at the three anxious faces staring up at me, I knew that wouldn't be enough anymore. Even though I never would have said it, I had lived my life like I didn't need God. I had health insurance, car insurance, flood insurance, three weeks of paid vacation, and a 30-year fixed mortgage. I was completely self-sufficient. But my relationship with God had become a religious routine. It took being single and childless in my mid-30s, for me to realize how much I needed God. Even though I went to church (almost) every Sunday, that hadn't been enough to force me to confront the trauma from my past and really start praying.

But because I finally had started praying, I could see how much God had done. It was truly a miracle. And just like God had done for me, I wanted to see God bring healing to these kids, too. My kids.

Lord, teach me how to pray for these children that you have entrusted to me. I need to experience you in a way that I never have before. I need your power. I need your love, your mercy, your grace. I need you!

Keep praying. The voice was as clear as day. And this time, I did not question whose voice it was or where the voice came from. Not just occasional prayers. Not a prayer method. Not a prayer strategy. Just connecting with God. Daily. Not out of duty or obligation, but because I realized I needed God to help me see my life through His eyes.

And so that is what I did. No matter what happened, I knew I would be still praying.

Made in United States
North Haven, CT
10 February 2023

32359706R00209